Oliver O. Howard

Nez Perce Joseph

Oliver O. Howard

Nez Perce Joseph

ISBN/EAN: 9783337422660

Printed in Europe, USA, Canada, Australia, Japan

Cover: Foto ©Andreas Hilbeck / pixelio.de

More available books at **www.hansebooks.com**

NEZ PERCE JOSEPH

AN ACCOUNT OF

HIS ANCESTORS, HIS LANDS, HIS CONFEDERATES,
HIS ENEMIES, HIS MURDERS, HIS WAR,
HIS PURSUIT AND CAPTURE

By O. O. HOWARD

BRIG. GEN. U. S. A.

BOSTON

LEE AND SHEPARD PUBLISHERS

NEW YORK CHARLES T. DILLINGHAM

1881

DEDICATION.

TO

EDWIN GREBLE, Esq.,

OF PHILADELPHIA,

A TRUE FRIEND OF EVERY PATRIOTIC CAUSE, AND WHOSE
BELOVED SON,

COL. J. T. GREBLE,

WAS THE FIRST REGULAR OFFICER WHO FELL
IN THE LATE CIVIL WAR,

IN GRATEFUL ACKNOWLEDGMENT OF HIS GENEROUS
HOSPITALITY AND ENDEARING
AFFECTION.

O. O. HOWARD.

PREFACE.

It occurred to me that some account of an Indian tribe, at peace and in war, might be interesting and useful, especially to readers in the Eastern States. The people of the east consider the Indian problem more dispassionately, but are likely to receive colored or false impressions, on account of their distance from actual Indians, and from the scenes of conflict.

There are few Indians in America superior to the Nez Perces. Among them the contrast between heathen and Christian teaching is most marked. Even a little unselfish work, both by Catholic and Protestant teachers, has produced wonderful fruit, illustrated by those who remained on the reservation during the war, and kept the peace; while the unhappy effects of superstition and ignorance appear among the renegades and " non-treaties." The results to these have been murder, loss of country, and almost extermination.

While endeavoring to relieve the account of the campaign from the stiffness of military reports, and desiring to make it as pictorial as possible for common reading, yet I have hoped that the military student might find it profitable to study the battles and marches herein de-

. iii

scribed. They afford an exhibit of this peculiar service, the Indian campaigning of our day.

If I have dealt too familiarly with the names and doings of my brother officers, they will forgive me when they plainly see that my object is only to portray, though I confess inadequately, their meritorious labors.

The Indian service now devolving upon our army is necessarily arduous and unpopular. It involves a work that our peace-loving people think might be avoided. But fair-minded Americans cannot ignore, or fail to commend, the ability, industry, and perpetual sacrifices of their soldiers.

O. O. H.

Vancouver Barracks, August 7, 1879.

CONTENTS.

CHAPTER VII.

CHAPTER VIII.

CHAPTER IX.

CHAPTER .X.

CHAPTER XI.

CHAPTER XII.

CHAPTER XIII.

CHAPTER XIV.

CHAPTER XV.

CHAPTER XVI.

CHAPTER XVII.

NEZ PERCE JOSEPH.

CHAPTER I.

JOSEPH THE NEZ PERCE CHIEFTAIN AND HIS PEOPLE. — WHERE LOCATED. — THEIR LANDS AND HUNTING-GROUNDS.

NEAR the confluence of two mountain-torrents, which unite and flow into the Snake River, some twenty-five miles above the present town of Lewiston, Idaho, is a rough valley, which bears the euphonious name of Imnaha. This valley, small and narrow as it is, and environed by the rugged hills of the Snake country, was formerly the home of a branch of the Nez Perces, — that tribe of Indians which is now so well known in America, — a tribe remarkable for presenting some of the best and some of the worst features of Indian life and character.

The old chief, who figures in the early times of Oregon, and in the accounts of the celebrated Hudson Bay Company, was called Joseph, and later "Old Joseph." Indeed, Joseph appears to have been the name of a dynasty rather than of an individual. Here in Imnaha, in a nook sheltered from the storms of winter, old Joseph set up his lodge. He was acknowledged to be the hereditary chief of the remnant of the "Lower" Nez Perces. He

1

was a sturdy old Indian, strongly knit in frame, and with a face usually mild, but exhibiting the signs of an iron will, which made him at once noticeable in the Indian or Americo-Indian councils that so frequently disturbed the peace, when our people first began to jostle the then quiet holders of the soil in this region of the far West.

The old chief, as well as certain of his tribe, entered into some agreements with Governor Stevens, of Washington Territory; but to the white man's improvements and encroachments he usually maintained a sour and persistent opposition. He married a wife among the fierce and treacherous Cayuses. These are the people who thirty years ago figured largely in the history of Eastern Oregon, and who used to embroil with themselves, and with each other, the voyageurs of the great Fur Company, and later, the Catholic and Protestant missionaries, and who finally capped the climax of their diabolism by the "Whitman Massacre."

Two boys were the fruit of the old chief's marriage.

They were nearly of the same age. Some neighboring white men regarded them as twins.

The one who took the name of the old chief was called "Joseph," "Little Joseph," or "Young Joseph;" the other, "Ollicut."

When I first saw them they were already young men. Their father had died a year before, in 1873.

Though "Young Joseph" succeeded to the chieftainship, Ollicut generally participated in all affairs of government. The former was noticeable for the peculiar expression of his face. It appeared to partake of the mild obstinacy of his father, and the treacherous slyness of his mother's people. He was about six feet in height, and finely formed. His brother's countenance was in complete contrast. He was considerably taller, lithe, and active; he appeared frank, open-hearted, and generous. Joseph wore a sombre look, and seldom smiled. Ollicut was full of fun and laughter. . . .

Before proceeding with the narrative in which these Indian youths bear a prominent part it may be interesting to recount some facts concerning the tribe to which they belong.

In these times of hurried work and hasty reading not one man in ten will stop to look up the data of geography; yet the tenth man may be curious enough to do so. The ordinary atlas gives only the most general notion. Even a tract of a hundred miles, which it takes four days of the fastest foot-marching to get over, and which contains hills, mountains, valleys, and streams of every variety of aspect, is represented by a bit of blank space as clean and objectless as were the unknown parts of Africa on the maps of our early days. The newspaper editors would be more patient with Indian chasers if they could be made to realize how deceptive the small-scale atlases are.

I notice that Irving, in *Bonneville's Adventures*, refers to the Nez Percés, for the first time, as not far from his camp on the " upper waters of the Salmon River." This is a little indefinite, for there are numerous branches of the "upper waters of the Salmon;" but as he speaks also of the Horse Prairie as being in that vicinity, — " a plain to the north of his cantonment," — this fixes the locality pretty well. Find Bannock City on the map of Montana,

let your eye pass a little to the south, and you will see
"Horse Prairie," in very fine print even on the largest
maps; close by is the Rocky Mountain divide.   From
Horse Prairie cross this divide by either of the rough
trails and you soon strike the head waters of the Salmon.
Here was probably Captain Bonneville's camp in the
winter of 1832–1833.   By the route our troops lately pursued, from Lewiston, Idaho, to Horse Prairie, the distance
is in the neighborhood of three hundred and twenty miles;
and to cross the "mountain divide" to Bonneville's cantonment would be about twenty or twenty-five miles
further.

It was there where the hunters came galloping back,
making signals to the camp, and crying, "Indians! Indians!" Captain Bonneville immediately struck into a
skirt of wood, and prepared for action.   The savages
were seen trooping forward in great numbers.   One of
them left the main body and came forward simply making
signals of peace.   He announced them as a band of Nez
Perces, or pierced-nose Indians, friendly to the whites;
whereupon an invitation was returned by Captain Bonneville for them to come and encamp with him.   After array-
ing their persons and horses, painting their faces, &c.,
"they arranged themselves in martial style, the chiefs
leading the van, the braves following in a long line,
painted and decorated, and topped off with fluttering
plumes.   In this way they advanced, shouting and singing, firing off their fusees, and clashing their shields.
The two parties encamped hard by each other.   The Nez
Perces were on a hunting expedition, but had been almost
famished on their march."

This indicates the region over which the Nez Perces roamed and hunted game. The Salmon River and its tributaries furnished an immense territory for them. The paths made by them in their expeditions after Buffalo, antelope, and other game, are even now clear and well defined, — five or six, and sometimes as many as ten or twelve, distinct horse trails, parallel and as near to each other as horses can walk with ease. These trails constitute some of the peculiar signs of these Indian tribes. They often make a side hill look as if terraced, and are as graceful in their windings as if made by a skilful engineer. These, sometimes called " The great Nez Perces trails," extend, as we have seen, for hundreds of miles : for the more permanent home of the Nez Perces was then, as now, nearer where the Salmon, the Clearwater, and the Grande Ronde, flow into that almost endless and peculiar river, so well named, " The Snake."

Captain Bonneville, after his winter cantonment in Horse Prairie, in the spring of 1833, made his way toward the Pacific by Powder-River Valley, where Baker City, in eastern Oregon, now is ; by Grande Ronde, now a magnificent basin, filled with pretty villages and fine farms ; thence over the mountain ridge northward to Imnaha and Wallowa, at that time called " Immaha " and " Way-lee-way." From this locality they were guided by the Indians through the beautiful region lying between Dayton, the Blue Ridge, and Wallula, which we now commonly name " The Walla-Walla Country." One may, to-day, stand in midsummer on a spur of the Blue Mountains and behold at a glance fifty square miles of rounded hills and graceful valleys, covered with waving grain. It is this country — a strip fifty miles broad, following the windings of the Snake from the Powder River to the Columbia Valley — that was occupied in early times by the Nez Perces; or, more accurately, by that portion of them usually designated as "the lower Nez Perces." It was mainly the controversy concerning this rough region that caused the recent outbreak.

In early years the lower Nez Perces were much more numerous than now. They lived along the Snake River, above and below the mouth of the Grande Ronde, a stream of curious windings from the noisy waterfall in the Blue Ridge to the grand circular flow that embraces the villages and cultivated fields of eastern Oregon, and on to the immense foaming torrent that rolls through the rough valleys of Wallowa and pitches down the terminating canyon into the larger Snake.

When Mr. Spalding, a remarkable Protestant missionary, whose name is to-day a household word with the Christians of the tribe, came, in 1836, to the Nez Perces, Old Joseph and his band were induced to cross over to the mouth of the Snake, and settle for a time near the Lapwai, to cultivate a small farm there, and send their children to Mrs. Spalding's school. The sudden massacre of Dr. Whitman and his family, by the Cayuses, in 1847, caused the Spaldings to leave the country in haste.

At that time a rival chief, "Big Thunder," succeeded in displacing Old Joseph's band by the usual cry, "This is not your country. Go back to Imnaha and Wallowa, where you belong." Thereupon the old man, doubtless chagrined by the selfish conduct of the other bands, and disappointed by the sudden departure of the white people whom he had trusted, returned to the Wallowa region. Thenceforth his band seems to have resumed with a will all the old superstitions of the tribe, and added new ones. The counsel he gave his children was, "Be at peace if you can, but never trust the white men nor their red friends. Raise ponies, eat things that grow of themselves, and go and come as you please."

The main tribe, "the Upper Nez Perces," occupied the Lapwai, from which we have seen that Old Joseph was driven in 1847. With these the government has had most to do in times past. With these Governor Stevens made his celebrated treaty of 1855, to which Old Joseph gave his assent; and well he might assent to this the first treaty, for it embraced in its established boundaries all his lands, and allowed him and his people to live in the same place, and in the same manner, as the Lower Nez Perces had lived for generations. Therefore we are not surprised to find his name appended to an instrument which in itself was not inequitable, but which was preliminary to the usual course of dispossessing the Indians of the property and rights which they claimed.

CHAPTER II.

JOSEPH'S YOUTH. — HIS EARLY ADVANTAGES. — THE CHAR-
ACTER OF HIS PEOPLE. — HOW THEY LOOKED AND WHAT
THEY DID IN THE DECADE FROM 1836.

THE missionary, Mr. Spalding, was a brave man, and
his excellent wife was the embodiment of Christian
sweetness, self-sacrifice, and 'devotion.

He planted his mission among the Nez Perces on the
Lapwai in 1836, and he remained there, more than a
hundred miles from the nearest settlements, cut off from
all association with white men, for eleven years.

The Indians trusted him, loved him, and even now the
old men never tire of talking of his instruction, and of
the messages he sent them just before his death.

At one of my visits to Lapwai an old Indian, short
and dumpy, dim-eyed and shrivelled in appearance, sat
on a box in the back office of the agent, and through the
interpreter talked to me for an hour of these early times,
and of the Spalding family. He was the father-in-law of
Young Joseph. He said in substance : " I was a wild boy,
like the boys of the Dreamers. My father hunted the
buffalo far away. The squaws planted the little patches,
the boys fished for salmon in the rivers, and rode the
ponies ; we were all just like the other wild Indians.
Sometimes we were fighting the Blackfeet and the Snakes.
Mr. Spalding came. He made the men work. We said :

'You make squaws of us!'" He kept on. "A few Indians used the hoe — then more and more. His klootch-man (Mrs. Spalding) had a big school — many, many tilicums (grown people) went. It was not a little school like that one there (pointing to the school building). There were many children. Old Joseph's band was here then. His children went to the school."

"But Young Joseph and Ollicut would be too young!" I suggested.

"Yes, they were little, but they went to the school."

Allowing Young Joseph to have been thirty-seven at the time of the war he would have been seven years of age at the time of Old Joseph's return to Immaha from Lapwai. From this it will appear that the boys learned very little from books. Neither spoke more than a few words of English when I met them, though I believe they understood English much better than they pretended.

The missionary's letters give us a few openings through which we may obtain glimpses, — the shadows of the faithful workers in this beautiful Lapwai valley, toiling on, planting much, and seeing little fruit from the seeds of knowledge which they scattered in this untoward soil. He says: "I was located at this place on the Clearwater or Koos-koos-ky River." The Lapwai is a small stream that flows westward and empties into the Clearwater. In 1839, besides this station, where was the school of Mrs. Spalding, there was another, about sixty-five miles distant, among the Nez Perces at Kamiah.

In 1844 he writes: "The assembly on the Sabbath, at Lapwai, varies at different seasons of the year, and must continue to do so until the people find a substitute in the

fruits of the earth and herds; for their roots, game,
and fish necessarily require much wandering. I am
happy to say that they are very generally turning their
attention, with apparent eagerness, to cultivating the soil
and raising hogs and cattle, and find a much more abundant and agreeable source of subsistence in the hoe than
in their bows, and sticks for digging roots."

In another place an exhibit is given of their nomadic
ways.

"For a few weeks in the fall, after the people return
from their buffalo hunts, and then again in the spring,
the congregation numbers from one to two thousand.
Through the winter it numbers from two to eight hundred. From July to the first of October it varies from
two to five hundred."

This gathering, as well as the school, increased every
winter, as the quantity of provisions raised in this vicinity increased.

How true is the following sentiment of this grand old
pioneer of civilization! and how long it has taken the
conductors of Indian affairs to learn the lesson! He
says: "My earliest attention was turned toward schools,
as promising the most permanent good to the nation."

"Besides eating my own bread, produced by the sweat
of my brow," (quite different from some modern laborers
in the Indian vineyard,) "there were the wandering children, of a necessarily wandering people, to collect and
bring permanently within the reach of the school. Over
this department of labor hung the darkest cloud, as the
Indian is noted for despising manual labor; but I would
acknowledge with humble gratitude the interposition of that

Hand which holds the hearts of all men. The hoe soon brought light, hope, and satisfaction, the fruits of which are yearly becoming much more than a substitute for their former precarious game and roots, and are much preferred by the people who are coming in from the mountains and plains, calling for hoes, ploughs, and seeds, much faster than they can be supplied, and collecting around the station in increasing numbers, to cultivate their little farms; so furnishing a permanent school and congregation on the Sabbath from four to eight months, and, as the farms are enlarged, giving food and employment for the year. . . . That the men of the nation (the chiefs not excepted) rose up to labor when a few hoes and seeds were offered them, I can attribute to nothing but the unseen hand of the God of missions. That their habits are really changed is acknowledged by themselves. The men say that whereas they once did not labor with their hands, now they do; and often tell me, in jesting, that I have converted them into a nation of women."

Not long after this the school plans were put into execution, and we get another glimpse of progress: " It [the school] now numbers two hundred and twenty-five in daily attendance, half of whom are adults. Nearly all the principal men and chiefs in this vicinity, with one chief from a neighboring tribe, are members of the school. . . . They are as industrious in school as they are on their farms. Their improvement is astonishing, considering their crowded condition, and only Mrs. Spalding, with her delicate constitution, and her family cares, for their teacher. About one hundred are printing their own books with a pen. This keeps up a deep interest, as they daily have new lessons to print, and what they print must be committed to memory as soon as possible. A good number are now so far advanced in reading and printing as to render much assistance in teaching. Their books are taken home at night, and every lodge becomes a school-room." And the farming was not behind the school.

"Last season about one hundred and forty cultivated from one-fourth of an acre to four or five acres each. . . One chief raised one hundred and seventy-six bushels of peas, one hundred of corn, and four hundred of potatoes. Another, one hundred and fifty of peas, one hundred and sixty of corn, a large quantity of potatoes, vegetables, &c. Ellis, I believe, raised more than either of the above mentioned. Some forty other individuals raised from twenty to one hundred bushels of grain. Eight individuals are furnished with ploughs. Thirty-two head of cattle are possessed by thirteen individuals; ten sheep by four."

These are facts and figures which speak for themselves, and reinforce what our noble Bishop Whipple says of Indian missions; viz., that they are the most remunerative, where there is faithful labor, of any missions among heathen people. I will venture another extract from this remarkable letter — remarkable, indeed, for the writer was thought to be in the very centre of Egyptian darkness; at any rate, far remote from a sign of civilization, except what he and a few other devoted souls were then planting. The extract concerns the moral character of the Nez Perces, as it then appeared to him. He says:

"On this point there is a great diversity of opinion. One writer styles them more a nation of saints than of savages; and if their refusing to move camp for game, at his suggestion, on a certain day, reminded him that the Sabbath extended as far west as the Rocky Mountains, he might well consider them such. Another styles them supremely selfish, which is nearer the truth, for, without doubt, they are the descendants of Adam." Thus Mr. Spalding finds a "dark side," but he remarks kindly:

"I must, however, confess that when I attempt to name it, and hold it up as a marked exception to a nation in similar circumstances, without the restraint of wholesome laws, and strangers to the heaven-born privileges of enlightened and well-regulated society, I am not able to do it. Faults they have, and very grave ones; yet few of them seem disposed to break the Sabbath by travelling and other secular business."

The Apaches said to me, "Apache no Domingo;" *i. e.*, the Apache has no Sabbath. The Nez Perces were better taught. "A very few indulge in something like profane swearing. Very few are superstitiously attached to their medicine-men, who are, without doubt, sorcerers. . . . Lying is very common, thieving comparatively rare; much gambling among the young men; quarrelling and fighting quite rare; habit of taking back property after it has been sold is a practice quite common, and very evil in its tendency."

This is quite a favorable showing to human nature. I fear some villages of white men, say in Italy or Mexico, or even in Canada, would hardly exceed this standard.

I love to contemplate these wonderful beginnings, and to trace the abundant and happy results which have flowed from them.

In spite of the non-fulfilment of our treaty obligations
to give the Nez Perces land that they could rely upon as
their own, and to protect them in their occupation and
title; in spite of the hurricane brought upon them by the
Cayuse and other wars, and the withdrawal of aid and
instruction for years; in spite of the plunderings of men,
who, among other knaveries, drew five thousand dollars
from the government to build them a school-house, and
built them one worth less than three hundred; in spite
of our shrewd Yankee ability, which has found mines of
gold and silver within their boundaries, and has cut down
their territory to one-sixth of the generous limits marked
out by Governor Stevens; in spite of all this hardship,
and of this wrong-doing to a people just beginning to
bear the ignominy (to them) of manual labor, — still they
have kept on in the path in which they were started by
the worthy, self-sacrificing missionary. I mean, of course,
the Christian, friendly Nez Perces, comprising two-thirds
and more of these Indians, now and all these years
remaining contentedly on their present reserve.

It was amid these influences that Joseph and Ollicut
spent the first few years of their lives. They also made
frequent visits to Lapwai afterwards; and in later years
sometimes they helped their father-in-law on his farm: so
that, though they had imbibed the spirit of their mother,
and were, doubtless, much affected by the recital of the
wrongs of their father, and subsequently had been deeply
influenced by Indian dreamings and superstition, still it
is evident that the remarkable knowledge they afterwards
displayed had here its abundant source.

In following the subsequent career of these young men,

wicked and disastrous as it was, one cannot help ruminating upon the old problem, which suggests itself of every failing genius, *i. e.*, "what might have been," the grand possibilities in these superior natures. But the rule is as fixed as the stars, that the sins of the fathers shall be visited upon the children unto the third and fourth generations of the men who hate God.

Smart as these youths were, their tendency to evil, like that of Lochiel and Glengarry, was undoubtedly inherited. While we abhor their crimes, and shudder at the horrid outrages which their people, as bad as the barbarous Celts, have committed, we nevertheless admire their wild courage, and cannot help wondering at their native ability. With them, as with the Highland leaders when the madness was on them, it meant war. It was hate and destruction in every form. The refinements of war they had never learned. Perhaps, with General Sherman, Joseph might say, "War is cruel, and it is difficult to refine it." Certainly the Indians' attempts to do so were very few.

CHAPTER III.

JOSEPH'S CONFEDERATES. — HOW THEY LOOKED IN EARLIER TIMES. — THE "TREATY" AND "NON-TREATY" INDIANS.

IT is difficult to explain the almost uniform injustice which the American people have practised toward the Indians. I do not believe that we are worse than the French, the Spanish, or than our English neighbors in British Columbia, though surely we can nearly match the massacre of St. Bartholomew, the cruelties of the Inquisition, or the ferocity of London rioters, in our dealings with the red men. I am inclined to believe the jar to be in our unadjustable system, which, like a machine built upon a springy soil, is perpetually out of gear. Our fathers, finding the Indians here, and being disposed to peace, first recognized in them the right of occupancy of the lands. This recognized right the Indians have always misunderstood. They have believed it to mean much more than simple occupancy.

As our new settlements have rapidly extended we have entered into, and recorded, solemn treaties, by which we have made of the numerous small tribes so many nations.

Soon the national and local laws, which are constantly in conflict with the laws of these independent nations, go into active, and often antagonistic, operation. For example: the settler, in carrying out the homestead law, plants his stakes on the Indian's farm. A petty contest results. An Indian or a white man is killed. Close upon this follows a horrid Indian war — a war so outrageous that *bona fide* forgiveness, anywhere in the neighborhood of the remembered crimes, seldom, if ever, succeeds.

This is substantially the history of a portion of the Nez Perces.

Governor Stevens came to them in 1855, and settled the grand and liberal treaty which bears his name, and which was confirmed by the United States Senate. It prescribed for them limits, but limits so ample that even "Old Joseph," who was always tenacious of "Indian rights," agreed to the stipulations. It included all the country that they occupied when Captain Bonneville found them, in 1833, embracing the Lapwai, the Imnaha, the Wallowa, and the Grande Ronde country. Was it possible to preserve these extended limits in face of the constant flood of immigration? Certainly it was not done. In 1863 the negotiation of another treaty had to be attempted. The new treaty finally agreed upon excluded the Wallowa, and vast regions besides. It did much more than simply reduce the limits of the reserve. It made a breach in the tribe, that was never to be closed. It divided the Indians who had sent delegates across the continent to visit our fathers and to solicit an increase of knowledge, into two great and hostile factions. One party agreed to all the terms of the instrument, and stayed within the boundaries fixed, and have always called themselves "treaty Indians." The other persistently refused to accept the new limits, and were denominated the "non-treaties." All the dissenting bands,

2

except that of the sub-chief Looking-glass, have pitched their lodges outside of the present Lapwai reservation.

We have already noticed the home of Old Joseph and his band, south of the Snake. It is now important to fix in mind the other bands of "non-treaties" who became the confederates of Joseph's band, in peace and in war, to resist efforts of the white man to displace them, or change their mode of life.

The principal "non-treaty" chief, who often disputed with Joseph the command of the united forces, was White Bird. He and his band roamed over that rough, mountainous territory, along the Salmon River, and its tributaries. They had no permanent abiding-place. One deep valley, now well-known from the terrible battle fought there, is named the White-Bird Canyon. The small stream that flows through it, and empties into the foaming Salmon, is also named White Bird.

There was, also, a band which roamed between the Salmon and the Snake, over that wild country that became Joseph's hiding-place during the war. It is a fastness resembling those of the Scottish Highlands, where the mountain clans held out so often against all efforts of English troops to dislodge them. The chief of this band, since my acquaintance with it, was Too-hul-hul-Sote. He was a cross-grained growler, — a sort of sub-chief to White Bird, and a "Dreamer drummer," called by the Indians a *Too-at*.

Again, south of the Snake, not far above the mouth of the Grande Ronde, is the Ashotin creek. Here, too, was a small band, which always acted in concert with Joseph's people.

The remaining bands of malcontents were situated to the westward, on the opposite side of the reservation, and hunted through the region south of Lewiston. They acknowledged Hush-hush-cute as leader, — a wily chieftain, about the age of Young Joseph. It could be said of him, in the words of Scripture, his heart was deceitful above all things and desperately wicked.

Now, there were, on the present reservation, a large number of the friendly Nez Perces, the most of whom remained true throughout all changes, and some of whom helped us during the conflict; namely, the present head-chief, James Lawyer, and his people, mainly located at Kamiah, on the Clearwater, seventy miles from Lewiston; the sub-chief, Jonah; James Reuben, the son of the late head-chief, and their people, located on the Lapwai, and near the Nez Perces Agency; also Catholic Indians, situated eight miles from the agency, on the Little Mission Creek, who dwell, habitually, in their small log-village, near their church. The whole number of these friendly Indians has been rated from two to three thousand. A recent census lessens the number. But the count, which was attempted by a half-breed during the war, could hardly be reliable. The Indians, at times, were much afraid that Joseph and his warriors would suddenly return and exterminate them; therefore they indulged their wandering propensities. Some went away among the Cœur D'Alènes, the Spokanes, Cayuses, and other neighboring tribes, and many doubtless took up new camping-grounds, where they thought they would be safe from distrustful white men, and from the hostile bands who *might* beat the troops, and suddenly return to do them mischief. Probably there are in existence at least two thousand friendly Nez Perces.

The "non-treaties," after they were finally separated from the others, and arrayed against us as enemies, were, as I estimate them, about seven hundred, men, women, and children. Perhaps more. There were at least three hundred and twenty-five warriors at the battle of the Clearwater.*

During the campaign many well-sketched pictures of scenes connected with these Indians were sent to illustrated papers, but, as published, the appearance of the Indians themselves was misrepresented. They were depicted with hair flying in all directions, in the ordinary wild Indian style, with meagre attire, and with long lances poised above their heads. They do not so appear in fact. They carry rifles, not lances. The friendly Nez Perces now for the most part are dressed as white men; the hair, especially of those at Kamiah, is cut short. This gives them much the appearance of the Mexican ranchers who live along our southern border. The women invariably wear long skirts, and usually crop their straight, jetty hair by a square cut at the neck. The shawl is habitually drawn up over the head, so that one has to be in front to see a woman's face. This, too, is like the Mexicans. I have noticed, on church, council, and gala days, that bright handkerchiefs often took the place of bonnets, shawls, or hats as head-gear. The

---

* The unusual proportion of men over women and children is accounted for by the numerous renegades from other tribes, who joined Joseph without their families to engage in a plundering warfare.

children are dressed much as among the whites; and though often in some fanciful attire they are for the most part plainly clad.

An old account, (Francher's,) mentioning the "Pierced Noses" and "Flat Heads" as early as 1811, says, "They do not go naked, but both sexes wear habits made of dressed deer skin, which they take care to rub with chalk to keep them clean and white."

The Nez Perces of to-day take pains with their personal attire, as they did forty years ago. The Christian portion at Lapwai and Kamiah, as they gather inside and outside their church buildings on Sundays, present a fine appearance.

The men average in height five feet eight, are strongly built, and always show grace in their movements. They are so constantly on horseback that they seem to be almost part of the animal. You can tell them at great distances by the ease and grace of the arms, as, in Indian style, they carry the whip up and down. This is quite in contrast with the angular, jerky motions of our white couriers and hardy frontiersmen.

Their women are usually short of stature, but have bright, intelligent faces, and a healthy, not uncomely, appearance. They ride as well as the men, but are generally perched at the top of a load, and, usually, each has a child in arms, or one clinging behind.

CHAPTER IV.

THE CAUSES OF WAR WITH THE NON-TREATIES. — THE ATTITUDE OF GOVERNOR GROVER AND THE CITIZENS.

IT is sometimes amusing, and sometimes extremely vexatious, to find statements which have been many times refuted reappearing in important publications.

Alexander Hamilton said, " Lies, often detected and refuted, are still revived and repeated, in the hope that the refutation may have been forgotten, or that the frequency and boldness of accusations may supply the place of truth and proof."

With regard to the Nez Perces, there are two parties who are responsible for untruthful statement, the enemies and the would-be friends. The enemies of the Nez Perces who are, *per se*, the enemies of all Indians, desired greatly to make it appear that the " Treaty " and the " Non-treaty," the Protestant, the Catholic, and the Dreamers, were all alike bad. They argued that all should be treated as hostile ; that the worst treachery lurked behind the friendliest looks. The cogent reason given for this opinion was, that *Indians* are *Indians!*

The would-be friends, with a view of defending a people who have always been reputed as friendly, have striven to represent all these Indians — friends and foes, the farmers of Lapwai, and the murderers of Camas Prairie — as aggressors, whose conduct justified a general war. So it is constantly asked, "How is it possible that Indians, always so well disposed as the Nez Perces, could go to war?" Or, the statement is made, "When WE visited the Nez Perces, a few years ago, they were far advanced in civilization. It must have required great provocation to induce them to go to war." May I ask the reader, then, to bear in mind the facts? The Christian Nez Perces, including all treaty Indians, both Catholic and Protestant, constituting a large majority of the entire people, have always been, are now, and probably will continue to be, friends of the government. The "non-treaty Indians" — Joseph, with his band and his confederates, whom I have already described — regarded the Nez Perce people proper as their bitter foes.

A year after the death of Old Joseph the war with the Modoc Indians, and the treacherous massacre of General Canby by them, took place. As is always the case in Indian wars, all Indians, far and near, were agitated by this outbreak. The "non-treaties," now led by the ambitious young chief, Joseph, became suspiciously restless. In the summer of 1874 a delegation of citizens came from a hundred miles distant to Lapwai, to meet General Davis, the then department commander, who had just closed the Modoc campaign. The delegation alleged "That the Indians, including the 'non-treaties,' had assembled in large numbers in Paradise and Hog-Heaven valleys, ostensibly for the purpose of digging roots, hunting, and fishing, and that they were talking very saucily to the settlers, and had committed various trespasses upon the farmers of the country." The troops were sent thither. This, for a time, put an end to the troubles, and probably prevented bloodshed.

General Davis thought the moving cause of the restlessness and sauciness was that these beautiful and fertile valleys were being rapidly occupied by an industrious and thrifty class of white farmers and stock-raisers. In his investigations he could discover no other cause.

About this time, several "non-treaty" Nez Perces had assumed an attitude of insolence toward the Indian agent at Lapwai, Mr. John Monteith, and toward the other employees of the government, which foreboded evil, if not actual hostilities.

A large gathering of Indians was soon to take place, about the fourth of July, at the Wee-ipe, situated east of Kamiah. It is a small grassy prairie, surrounded by forests of huge firs, whose sombre shadows are often deepened by contrast with successive sunny glades.

Here had been an annual assemblage of the non-treaties. Many other Indians came to participate in horse-races, or to win or lose in gambling horses, furs, and other Indian property.

This year the notice circulated was for a "talk," and the agent was curious and wished to be present, but he thought the Indians would prevent him, unless defended by troops. Therefore the troops, Colonel David Perry and his company, marched some two hundred miles from Fort Walla-Walla, and were there with the agent for a few days. He reasoned that if the Indians met for pastime and enjoyment, the troops in the vicinity would not hinder, but if for evil purposes, they would serve as the ounce of prevention.

Colonel Perry and agent Monteith found the Indians assembled as anticipated at the Wee-ipe. The "talk" took place, but like the old congress at Philadelphia it was annoyed and constrained by the presence of armed men. It proved but a brief council. General dissatisfaction seemed to prevail among the non-treaty Nez Perces. This was particularly the case with Joseph's band, the claimants of Wallowa Valley.

There was evidently, thus early, some mischief hatching in the neighborhood of Joseph's lodge. The young man was yet hardly in the saddle as chief. The sentiment of his followers and of his neighbors was divided, The wary, cautious malcontents of the tribe thought they would lose by a war. They counselled a persistent but peaceful opposition to the van of the army of settlers now approaching, no longer from the East but from the West — from the Pacific. The young men, with Ollicut at their head, were for war. During the same year, in the fall of 1874, Colonel John Green, an officer of prudence and experience in Indian matters, was sent to Wallowa, with two cavalry companies, to keep the peace. The troops did keep the peace as long as these Indians were roaming in that valley, and then were withdrawn to their posts.

A summary of the views of the Governor of Oregon, the Hon. L. F. Grover, expressed in a letter to the United States government, written in July, 1873, gives the opinion and the temper of the majority of intelligent citizens of this state.

I. He opposes the withdrawal of citizens from Wallowa for the purpose of securing the same to Joseph's band.

II. He recites the stipulations of Governor Stevens' treaty of 1855, which includes Wallowa, to which Old Joseph assented.

III. He quotes the supplementary treaty of 1863, to which the majority of the Nez Perces assent, but which the minority of bands refuse to sign. The new treaty gives Wallowa back to the United States. Old Joseph and all the " non-treaties " protest against this action.

After Old Joseph's death, his sons, Joseph and Ollicut, lay claim to the same Wallowa, saying that the Nez Perce bands are independent, and not bound by a majority of other bands. The governor argues that they must be so bound, according to all law and precedents.

IV. He cites the Act of Congress of May 28, 1867, by which the lands of Wallowa went to Oregon, and were open for settlement. Eleven townships were thus formed. Eighty-seven farms are entered or occupied already. The government ought now to consider the Indian title extinct. If the government yields to the claim of Joseph, it will be obliged to yield to a score more of just such claims in this neighborhood.

V. The governor begs for the uniform policy of the United States, namely, " of removing as expeditiously as circumstances would permit, ALL INDIANS from the confines of the new states."

The country to which Wallowa Valley is the key, is greater in area than Massachusetts. Its restoration to the aboriginal character would give a serious check to frontier civilization.

VI. Again he says: There is room enough for the malcontents on the Lapwai reserve. Joseph himself is reported as not averse to this, but those about him want to roam, and will not give up their nomadic ways.

Further, Joseph's band have already refused Wallowa, as a reservation, for a permanent home. They simply want the possession to gratify a wild, roaming disposition.

VII. The governor, in behalf of the settlers and of the state of Oregon, urgently presses his views, and asks that the preliminary steps, just taken by the government in the interest of the Indians, for the white settlers to vacate the Wallowa country, be rescinded.

So much for our ideas of justice. First, we acknowledge and confirm by treaty to Indians a sort of title to vast regions. Afterward, we continue, in a strictly legal manner, to do away with both the substance and the shadow of title. Wiser heads than Joseph's have been puzzled by this manner of balancing the scales.

CHAPTER V.

THE FIRST INTERVIEW WITH JOSEPH.—CAUSES OF TROUBLE.
—INDEPENDENCY.—IMMIGRATION.—AN INDIAN KILLED.—
THE WASHINGTON COMMISSION.—ITS REPORT.

MY first personal interview with the young chieftain was in 1875. I had, the previous September, succeeded to the command of the Geographical Department which included within its limits the Nez Perces.

To better acquaint myself with my command, I soon visited the military posts, and the different Indian agencies. On arriving at the Umatilla agency, in Eastern Oregon, and while sitting and conversing with the sprightly Frenchman in charge of the office, a Cayuse Indian, accompanied by the stout interpreter McBean, came in. The latter said:

"Here is a messenger from Joseph. He and ten of his Indians are at Young Chief's camp. Joseph and his tilicums want to have a talk with the agent, and with the new commander."

I had already heard of this band, so, with the agent, I expressed a desire for the interview. The messenger then left.

In the course of half an hour the eleven strangers made their appearance. They were all quite carefully dressed in Indian costume. They were noticeably tall and stout for Indians. At the time, I was out of doors with the agent, looking at his buildings. The Indians first approached in single file, Young Joseph ahead. One after another took the agent's hand, and then mine, in the most solemn manner. Joseph put his large black eyes on my face, and maintained a fixed look for some time. It did not appear to me as an audacious stare; but I thought he was trying to open the windows of his heart to me, and at the same time endeavoring to read my disposition and character.

An Indian is usually a shrewd physiognomist. I think Joseph and I became then quite good friends. There was at the time little appearance of that distrust and deceit which some time afterward very strongly marked his face, especially while listening to white men in council. He said through the interpreter:

"I heard that Washington had some message for me. I came to visit my friends among the Cayuses. Young Chief told me to speak to the agent. That is all."

We answered: "There is no word from Washington. We are glad to see you and shake you by the hand."

The Nez Perces then formally took their leave and retired in company with other Indians of the Umatilla reservation.

After becoming more familiar with the situation of affairs with the Nez Perces, I appreciated the drift of this visit, and of the question concerning news from Washington. For already, General Davis had reported his belief that there would be trouble with Joseph; that there was restlessness; that his dissatisfaction, and that of others, arose because these beautiful valleys were filling up by industrious settlers.

The governor of Oregon had, moreover, succeeded in getting his petition heard, and by the President's order the disputed grounds had once more ceased to be a reserve for Joseph. Joseph and his band, and his " non-treaty " confederates, were then still clinging to the old habits and haunts, and pasturing their numerous ponies and herds on the plains of Wallowa, and along the ridges of the tributaries to the Salmon, while the white men were crowding into the Wallowa and Salmon valleys, and erecting their white cottages, and stretching out their crooked fences in plain sight of the wandering Indian herders.

Now, admitting the injustice of the United States and of Oregon towards this band, when contrasted with the rights and privileges extended to citizens, still I do not think the real cause of the Indian war with the " non-treaties " came from the reduction of the reserve, nor from the immediate contact with immigrants, and the quarrels that sprung therefrom. These, without doubt, aggravated the difficulty.

The main cause lies back of ideas of rightful ownership, back of savage habits and instincts; it lies in the natural and persistent resistance of independent nations to the authority of other nations. Indian Joseph and his malcontents denied the jurisdiction of the United States over them. They were offered everything they wanted, if they would simply submit to the authority and government of the United States agents. "No! no! no! We will go where we please, and when we please, and do as we please! Who gave Washington rule over me?" asked the growler of growlers, old Too-hul-hul-sote, Joseph's most influential confederate.

My first report was made in 1875. On this subject of "inherited causes" of trouble are the following paragraphs :

"Early in July the Indian agent at Lapwai reported the receipt of an executive order, opening Wallowa Valley, in north-eastern Oregon, to settlement by whites, and expressed fear of trouble between the whites and Indians, — Joseph's band of the Nez Perces, claimants of this valley, — especially in their annual visit to the valley for the purposes of fishing, and grazing their ponies, of which they have large herds, wherein consists their principal wealth.

"Two cavalry companies were accordingly sent for the mutual protection of the citizens and Indians in the valley, and for the preservation of the peace. These returned as soon as their need there ceased.

"The troubles at Lapwai, and at Wallowa Valley, have not thus far resulted in bloodshed; but it has been prevented by great carefulness on the part of government agents. The courts will have to settle the former, [they have done so since this reference,] and congress the latter, trouble. I think it a great mistake to take from Joseph and his band of Nez Perces Indians that valley ; . . . and possibly congress can be induced to let these really peaceable Indians have this poor valley for their own."

Now we can see how much expense in blood and treasure would most probably have been saved if this course had been pursued, — for this was before an Indian had been killed, — yet, with the idea of absolute independence in their brains I now doubt if Wallowa would have satisfied them. It certainly would have contributed nothing whatever to quieting White Bird, Looking-glass, Hush-hush-cute, and other malcontents outside of Joseph's people.

In my report, in 1876, concerning Joseph's people I said: "An Indian was killed by a white man in a dispute concerning some stock;" and these solicitous words were used: "And I renew my recommendation of a commission to hear and settle the whole matter before war is even thought of." The commission was at last ordered; but it was not till after blood had been shed, nor till after the Indians had stood up in battle array against armed citizens in Wallowa, and only stopped resistance at the intervention of troops. The commission came, and held its memorable sessions at Lapwai, in November, 1876, and labored long and earnestly to get the consent of Joseph and Ollicut, and of other disaffected non-treaty Indians, to some measures of adjustment.

At one time during their meetings Joseph was almost persuaded to yield, and Ollicut appeared to catch the spirit of peace; but the old Dreamers, the *too-ats*, talked to them earnestly, and prevailed against the commission.

The commission state the matter clearly and plainly.

The Dreamers, among other pernicious doctrines, teach that the earth, being created by God complete, should not be disturbed by man, and that any cultivation of the soil, or other improvements, to interfere with its natural productions, — any improvements in the way of schools, churches, &c., — are crimes from which they shrink.

This fanataicism is kept alive by the superstition of these "dreamers," who industriously teach, that, if they continue steadfast in their present belief, a leader will be raised up in the east, who will restore all the dead Indians to life, who will unite with them in expelling the whites from their country, when they will again enter upon and repossess the lands of their ancestors.

Influenced by such a belief Joseph and his band firmly declined to enter into any negotiations, or make any arrangements, that looked to a final settlement of the questions pending between him and the government. While the commission give all due respect to the precedents and authorities in the government dealing with Indians, and to the decisions of the Supreme Court of the United States, which recognizes an undefined right of occupancy by Indians to large sections of the country, yet in view of the fact that these Indians do not claim simply this, but set up an *absolute title to the lands*, an *absolute* and *independent sovereignty*, and refuse even to be limited in their claim and control, necessity, humanity, and good sense constrain the government to set metes and bounds, and give regulations to these "non-treaty" Indians. . . . And if the principle usually applied by the government, of holding that the Indians with whom they have treaties are bound by the majority, is here applied, Joseph should be required to live within the limits of the present reservation. . . .

If these Indians overrun lands belonging to the whites, and commit depredations on their property, disturb the peace by threats or otherwise, or commit any other overt acts of hostility, we recommend the employment of sufficient force to bring them into subjection, and to place them upon the Nez Perces reservation.

The Indian agent at Lapwai should be fully instructed to carry into execution these suggestions, relying at all times upon the department commander for aid when necessary.

The doings of the commission, approved at Washington, resulted in all the preliminary acts of the government that preceded the outbreak. Every possible effort of the agent was exerted to carry out the recommendations of the commission without provoking hostilities. But as a time comes when an ulcer will break, so the time came when the Indian sore had to come to the surface.

CHAPTER VI.

JOSEPH'S OWN BAND. — AGENT MONTEITH SENT TO JOSEPH.
— THE TALK AT UMATILLA. — OLLICUT, OR YOUNG JOSEPH,
DESCRIBED. — CAPTAIN BOYLE'S MISTAKE. — WALLA-WALLA
TALK. — INCIDENTS OF JOURNEY UP THE COLUMBIA. —
STEAMBOAT ACCIDENT. — A PROPHETIC EVENT.

THE Department of the Interior, at Washington, issued
its ominous instructions to carry out the recommendations of the November Commission to its agent at Lapwai, early in January, 1877. Copies of these instructions
were sent, with directions to me, from my own department,
to occupy Wallowa Valley, as had really been done for
three years, "in the interests of peace," and to co-operate
with, and aid, the Indian agent. The agent was Mr.
J. B. Monteith. He was a tall, well-built young man,
apparently about thirty-five years of age. His health
had not been good, yet he had been unsparing of himself
in his journeys over his reservation, and beyond, sometimes having ridden his horse, half American and half
Cayuse, for sixty or seventy miles in a day.

Monteith sent friendly Indians to Joseph and the non-
treaty Indians, and did all in his power to induce them
to do what they told the commission they would not do ;
i. e., come on the Lapwai reservation. These Indians
were already on the alert. They, in preparation for war,
were sending small delegations to other tribes.

Some time in March Mr. Cornoyer, the Indian agent of

the Umatillas, was in Portland, Oregon, and paid me a visit. He said Joseph had sent him word through his, Cornoyer's, head chief, that he and a few of his principal men wanted to come down to the Umatilla and have a talk. He, Joseph, did not think the interpreters at Lapwai had told the commission truly what he had said and wished. I replied: "Mr. Cornoyer, encourage them to come; and I will send my aide-de-camp, Lieutenant Boyle, who is a judicious officer, and has had long experience with Indians, to represent me there, and to hear and report what they have to say."

Lieutenant Boyle accordingly accompanied Cornoyer on his return to the agency, met the Indians, several from Joseph's band having come one hundred and twenty miles to Umatilla. Joseph himself did not come, but was represented by his brother Ollicut, who was frequently called "Young Joseph." This Ollicut was over six feet tall, and perfectly formed. He had small hands and feet, was very intelligent, and had, an unusual feat for an Indian, made quite good maps of the country about Wallowa, was very quick and graceful in his motions, and when he spoke in council his brother always made his speech or promise his own. I think that in private Ollicut always urged Joseph to war measures, and took the side of the reckless young men, who would rather than not have a fight with the white men. The prospective excitement of the battle over-topping any fears of remote consequences.

At his first interview with Ollicut, Lieutenant Boyle mistook this fine-looking, warlike, impulsive Indian representative for the chief, and telegraphed me accordingly to Portland. After the lieutenant had made his way from this meeting to Fort Walla-Walla, April 11th, these words came over the wires, " It is Joseph's understanding that General Howard was to have another interview with him this spring. He will be at Walla-Walla with his people on the 20th inst." To this promise I assented, and made all my arrangements to go to Walla-Walla and meet this appointment, hoping that, as the Indians had sought the interview, some permanent and satisfactory settlement of the grievous troubles could then and there be effected.

Now comes a preliminary campaign. Lieutenant Wilkinson accompanied me. The journal gives this brief notice: " Left Portland, Oregon, Monday morning, April 16th, 1877, for settlement of Indian Joseph's difficulties. Remained over night at the Dalles." It does not say anything of the waking at four o'clock in the morning; the prompt departure at five; the filling out lost sleep on the long cabin seat, to the music of the tread of the walkers and the talkers, the monotonous sounds from the engine, and the dripping drive-wheel always rolling and splashing, half in and half out or water. Then there was the breakfast, after passing Fort Vancouver. Good coffee, good salmon, always good steak and potatoes, and unfailing good company, when Captain Wolf, with manly manners and voice, sits by you. How can any one go from western Oregon to the Dalles without thinking of the unsurpassed scenery ; the grand woods, valleys, hills ; the mountains of two thousand feet ; the wild cascades ; then the five-mile railway over rough scenes, beside torrents and falls ; then a

cheery, light-painted steamboat, the table set with white
cloth, at the head of which sits a captain full of goodness
and humor! Forty miles past Wind Mountain, that
looks like a pictorial wild Indian's head in battle; past
Hood-River settlement, through diminishing mountains
and hills to the Dalles, where the high-water mark on the
hotel is five feet above your head, where the Columbia,
tired of a montonous boiling, undertook to rise, and mer-
cilessly toppled over all the poor, small shops on Water
Street!

"Over night at the Dalles." It reminds one of the dark
morning of steady knocks, from door to door, along the
upper passage-way of the Umatilla House, before break of
day, while clear sonorous tones, following each knock, were
saying, "Four o'clock! Four o'clock!" We were off at
five in the morning, among as cheerless and silent a set of
passengers as are West Point cadets on the way to and from
reveille. The first fifteen miles were by railway. Sit,
without fail, upon the left side of the car, as you are on the
south bank of the great river, going east. If this be your
first trip you will see, close at hand, the Columbia, which
is more than a mile wide at Vancouver, here, near the
Dalles, so set up on edge that you can throw a stone
across it, pressing along with the quietude and stillness
of great depth; you will notice the banks of sand in the
river bends, that have all the shape of drifting snow-banks
of the east. Graceful lines and curves are formed, and
ever forming, ever changing, in the restless breezes that
sweep up and down, or over the hills to give new
touches to the pliable heaps. Then you pass under
frowning precipices, so high above you that it requires

a trip to the rear platform to take in their lofty heads.

The steamboat "Almota," built for business, waits at Celilo. When about fifty miles below Umatilla a cylinder-head to one of the engines blew out, which delayed the steamer from about noon until midnight. Captain Baughman returned with a boat's crew to Celilo for another steamer, with which he arrived about dark, when baggage and freight were transferred to the steamer Tenino.

A clap of thunder in a clear sky; an earthquake at midnight, that makes all the doors and blinds swing and creak, and bring down the top bricks from the chimneys; the sudden and awful collision of two sleeper trains in the darkness; these and similar shocks startle human beings, but when two friends took me with them through the breaking, double cabin doors, when the rumbling, crash, and crush of the explosion beneath our feet occurred, I can testify that this cylinder explosion was more sudden and terror-inspiring. I cannot but think that somehow " coming events were casting their shadows before." For there was soon to be the crash and shock of the then unexpected war; the surprises, the delays, and the disappointments, that always go along with this dire calamity.

Having enjoyed the exhilaration and excitement of ascending the several rapids of the Columbia, rapids like those of the St. Lawrence, which demand of the pilot a quick eye and steady nerves at the wheel, at last, on the 18th of April, we arrived at Wallula.

Wallula is situated where the old fort Walla-Walla, built by the Hudson's Bay Company, was located. Its

crumbling walls are still there, surrounded by the houses
and sheds of the present hamlet.

Wallula is a sweet name, that one loves to speak. Its
sweetness, however, stops with its name. Pebbles, sand,
a constant wind, and a few old buildings in one row, with
straggling suburbs, and withered grass or flowers. Such
is Wallula, forlorn indeed! Still it is an important place.
being at the head of navigation, and the river terminus of
the railway which runs to the town of Walla-Walla. Indian Smohallie, who has grouped around him a band of
renegades, who is the high priest of Dreamer-drummers,
is on the opposite side of the Columbia. He sends his
messenger, who encounters us as we step ashore. "Smohallie wants to have a talk with General Howard."

He is answered, "All right. General Howard has no
communication for him from Washington. He must obey
his Indian agent, and go upon some reservation."

Afterwards I left an appointment for a meeting with
him and his Indians, to take place at Wallula on my return from Walla-Walla, the 24th of April.

I have been particular to mention this man because of
his history. His followers have been embraced in a score
of tribes, and his deleterious influence has been sadly pro-
ductive of suffering. He is a large-headed, hump-shoul-
dered, odd little wizard of an Indian, and exhibits a
strange mixture of timidity and daring, of superstition
and intelligence.

There is another small band of natives who are fast disappearing by disease and destitution. They are usually
located about a mile above the hamlet, and appear to enjoy their flinty beds among the millions of small stones

which the overflow of the Columbia has strewn upon the hereditary sand, rather than the fertile lands of the Umatilla, where other Indians dispute their title, and the Catholic agent insists upon the sufficiency of one wife for their fat chieftain. This chieftain, old Homily, lately found even Washington city inferior to the wastes around Wallula. "Oh!" he said, on his return home, as he shook his fat sides with laughter. "You, General Howard, may think more of Washington, but I wasn't happy there. The gravel stones and sand of Wallula make me happy. My tilicums are there."

Homily, too, begged for a talk. An odd little train of cars has been waiting while I have interviewed the messengers, and thus inspected the town. With a shrill whistle, that sets ponies to dancing, and numerous dogs to barking, we are off, at a rate that, as yet, even old Homily, on his white Cayuse, can rival.

CHAPTER VII.

JOSEPH'S OWN BAND. — OLLICUT COMES TO THE INTERVIEW.
— JOSEPH ABSENT FROM SICKNESS. — WHAT CUTE SPIES
THEY ARE. — THE GATLING GUN. — WAIT-LA-PU AND THE
COUNTRY ROUND ABOUT. — THE WHITMAN MASSACRE. — A
CHARACTERISTIC FRONTIER FAMILY. — SMOHOLLIE. — HOMI-
LY AND OTHER INDIANS WHO ARE DEEPLY INTERESTED
IN JOSEPH'S MOVEMENTS. — THE WALLULA TALK. — THESE
INDIANS REALLY JOSEPH'S ALLIES. — THE JOURNEY TO
LEWISTON, AND SEVERAL SYMPTOMS OF WAR.

IT was dark when we reached Fort Walla-Walla. A welcome spring wagon took us to the quarters of the commanding officer. How pleasant, after a tiresome journey, is a cordial welcome, a warm fire, a hot cup of tea, and a cheerful, restful chamber for the night. It is good, it is God-given, this genuine hospitality.

Ollicut put in an appearance about six P. M. (April 19.) Young chief and several other prominent Indians, among them the medicine-man, an old Indian who, seven months later, surrendered to us north of the Missouri, with a wounded, broken, almost putrid right arm, accompanied him. These Indians came to the western gate of the fort, and Ollicut gave in an excuse in the most gentlemanly manner for not having been at the fort sooner, and stated that the chief, his brother Joseph, was not at that time well; otherwise he would have been there himself to meet me. The next day was fixed upon for a talk, and the Indians sought a place to encamp for the night.

Colonel Grover arranged the band-room for our purpose on the morrow.

Talk commenced about 10 A. M. We gathered in the long, low room, having a large table, Indians on benches on one side, officers, citizens, and a few ladies opposite, on straight benches and chairs, or peeping in curiously at the doors.

The council talk amounts to little. The Indians are very polite, as a few at a five-company post would be likely to be. The wishes of the government are explained to them, but they are only delegates, and can make no "binding promises," but beg for another interview with me for the whole band, and for the Salmon River non-treaty Indians, in fact for the various companies of malcontents. I grant the petition, and agree to meet Joseph and the others at Lapwai in twelve days. The old medicine man looks happy, and Ollicut believes we shall have no trouble, and Young Chief, the Umatilla friend and advocate, wishes some new lands in Wallowa that will hold them all (Cayuses, Walla-Wallas, Umatillas, and non-treaty Nez Perces) in fellowship. Really matters did not look much like war, except perhaps the sly and thorough observation of the Indians of the strength, or rather weakness, of this post, whose companies were so reduced in numbers as to appear more like corporals' drill-squads than like captains' proper commands.

At this visit I took a good look at the gatling guns. We tried them at two hundred, three hundred, five hundred, and eight hundred yards. The rapidity of fire, — at least two discharges per second, — and the wonderful accuracy of aim, made one think that warfare was coming to its best and quickest results. But, alas! how many conditions are not thought of on trial occasions, such as wide intervening rivers, wooded buttes, and precipitous ravines, conditions of which Indians take advantage against even the best gatlings.

When I came to this "Geographical Department," three years before, there was no public conveyance except a stage coach or army spring-wagon provided for the occasion, to take me from Wallula to Walla-Walla. Enterprising citizens, not content with the desert lands on the Columbia for the establishment of new homes, had gone straight inland to Dr. Whitman's ground of Wait-la-pu and farther along the valley of the little Walla-Walla, to the vicinity of the magnificent rolling wheat country, now covered with busy and prosperous workers, to the neighborhood of the foot-hills of the Blue Ridge. Here there was for them plenty of wood, water, sunshine, grass, and fertile soil.

But oh! what a stage or "spring-wagon" road! You ate, drank, and breathed *in*, but not *out*, the finest and most abundant of dry alkaline dirt,—and you bumped up and down on the roughest and most uneven of road-beds, which lies beneath the ten inches of deceitful dust. So you may judge of the delight with which we now, with plenty of good company, and only a moderate amount of alkali, pass over the same thirty miles of country in two and a half hours by rail. But this time the enjoyment of quick communication, good society, and the modicum of disagreeables was foregone in order to visit Wait-la-pu, where the Whitman mission had been planted, and where, by the treacherous Cayuses, with their aiders and abettors, the Whitmans were massacred. . . . We reached Wallula, on the Columbia, at 6 P. M., on the 23d of April.

How can a public house at a small hamlet which is a carrying-place, or junction of water-steam with land-steam, compete with city hotels which are daily thronged with passengers at four and five dollars per head? Our host and my lady of the Wallula House were very industrious and hospitable, and made the stay of my friends and myself just as pleasant as they could. They have toiled on the frontiers from Kansas to the Touchet, and finally have set themselves down at Wallula, replete in personal experience, and primed with the overland stories of remarkable character, incidents of danger, of exposure, of plenty, and of want. Here we spent the night, and will remember the occasion longer than the last visit to the Ebbitt House, of Washington, notwithstanding its rich table, restful elevators, and other contrasts of comfort.

The work of this day was the beginning of a series of measures that kept the "Columbia River renegades" from joining the non-treaty Nez Perces of Joseph.

In accordance with his promise, a message was sent by General Howard to Smohollie (the leader of the Indian spiritists), who is in camp across and up the Columbia. . . . . Smohollie, through a messenger, requests General Howard to come to his camp, and is informed by the general that he came to Wallula to meet him by an appointment of his own seeking, and he (General Howard) is not anxious to see him. If Smohollie has anything to say to General Howard he must come to Wallula to say it. And after Smohollie's remonstrance, by a second messenger, he is again informed that General Howard has nothing to communicate to Smohollie, and does not really care whether he sees him or not. This was rather ungracious, but I suspected treachery. There was no excuse for the shrewd Dreamer's attempt to draw me across the river. All of our party regarded it then as meaning mischief. A little after noon Smohollie, having given up his first designs, crossed the river just above the village, and mustered all his people, including women and children. They were bedecked with much paint and feathers, and with all the pomp and circumstance possible came into town "to meet the General, who, by previous arrangement and promise, had with him Indian Agent Cornoyer." The talk was held in a large storehouse. . . . . Some two hundred and fifty Indian men, and about fifty women and children, gathered in and about this building. The regular interpreter (McBean) was taken ill *en route*, and could not reach us at Wallula. Having, therefore, no interpreter, except a few bystanders who had made a feeble attempt at translating, — after some preliminary and unsatisfactory efforts of these and the Indians in the Chinook jargon, the council adjourned until the arrival of Mr. Pambrun. He had been sent for, and was soon expected. He was a singularly good interpreter. He spoke the Walla-Walla tongue, now the language common to the Cayuses, Umatillas, and Walla-Wallas.

At half past seven Mr. Pambrun arrived. He was twenty miles away when our mounted messenger found him. A little school-room had been prepared. Upon notification Smohollie, with some of his principal men, Young Chief, Homily, and Thomas, reassembled. . . . . Talk ceased between ten and eleven.

These Indians had the same statements to make as the non-treaty Nez Perces. They want peace, but they wish to roam at large whenever and wherever they please. They really belong on various reservations, and the word "renegades" describes them well. I think they were meditating resistance at that time, and were only waiting and parleying to ascertain first what the "non-treaty" Nez Perces would do. Should they then, and alone, precipitate war, they knew well enough they would soon be swallowed up. The wishes of the government were carefully explained to them by Mr. Cornoyer, and they were earnestly exhorted by him to run to the shelter of the reservations. I explained to them the wishes of the government, as contained in the instructions from Washington, and endorsed the statements of Mr. Cornoyer. With apparent good feeling, except on the part of old Thomas, who lived on the Snake, near some of the non-treaty Nez Perces, and who was tremblingly fierce to know why we were sending troops to Wallowa, the Indians shook our hands, and left the town before midnight. After the adjournment, old Thomas' people rushed northward for a hundred miles, beating the steamboat, and crossing their hands, and stating that we were going to put them into the "Skookum-house" (meaning the military prison or guard-house). Father Wilbur, as the agent at Yakima is called, had previously brought us an insubordinate Indian, and we had confined him at Fort Vancouver. Thomas' Indians, although two hundred miles further inland, had heard of this, and had pleaded with me for the imprisoned Indian's release. Thus connected are the renegades in common feeling and sympathy against all white men, even where they quarrel and fight with one another.

April the 25th and 26th we spent in ascending the Columbia and the Snake Rivers from Wallula to Lewiston, Idaho.

At 6 P. M. we arrived at Lewiston. This town, of a few hundred inhabitants, three hundred miles east of Portland, Oregon, was to be the main depot, the starting-point of my operations in the upper country after war began. It well represents the world in miniature; has an enterprising newspaper, and many fair merchants, but yet thus far enjoys but few of the comforts and luxuries of existence. At this time I met by appointment Colonel Perry, commanding officer at Fort Lapwai, and Indian Agent Monteith. To them I read carefully my full instructions from the Honorable Secretary of War, General Sherman, and the commanding general, Military Division of the Pacific, especially in relation to the part the military was to have in placing the Indians upon the reservations.

The particular object of this visit was to avoid a long correspondence, and to concert measures of co-operation. The interview which Joseph and Ollicut had solicited with the non-treaty Nez Perces was arranged for, and fixed for the third of the ensuing month. Then I returned by the steamboat, the next day, to Wallula, where I could have the telegraph to conduct the affairs of my department. I wish also particularly to meet officers coming to me from Portland, and to provide for the withdrawal of our troops from the territory of Alaska. This recall of these troops had just been determined upon by the War Department, and was indeed a fortunate circumstance, as it enabled me to catch these forces on the wing, and turn them quickly towards Lewiston, as soon as the terrible storm of Indian outrages had begun.

4

CHAPTER VIII.

JOSEPH'S OWN BAND. — THE JOURNEY TO THE COUNCIL AT
LAPWAI. — GRAND PRELIMINARY CEREMONIES. — ACCOUNT
OF CHARACTERS, AND OF THE FIRST DAY'S PROCEEDINGS.

IT seemed to Eastern people, a few years ago, when the
son of Bishop Kip, of California, wrote some interesting articles concerning the Indians, and other subjects,
from Walla-Walla, that he had gone pretty near to the
world's extremity. But here *now* is Walla-Walla, a
thriving, growing, enterprising city. A railroad train
from its suburbs connects daily at Wallula with the
passing steamers that at least twice a week penetrate to
the very heart of Idaho. Daily stages start from this
railway terminus for east, and north, and south, and the
busy telegraph keeps the newsmen and merchants in perpetual contact and business sympathy with San Francisco
and New York.

The journey through the rich and beautiful valleys,
threading our way among the hills, and over the spur of
the Blue Ridge, brought us back to Lewiston, then,
twelve miles further, to Fort Lapwai. A lady, the wife
of an army officer, said about it :

"You don't know how I do love Fort Lapwai, and
with what regret I left the place." It is the bright sunshine, the beautiful rolling hills and gorgeous mountains,
and valleys of every shape and description, lighted up

into attractive pictures; it is the excellent climate that
invigorates while it does not freeze you; it is these, with
good companionship, that make this most frontier of
posts dwell pleasantly in the memory of those who have
resided there. There is really no fort. There is a hollow square on the western side of the ravine; the Lapwai
flows northerly, near the eastern slope of it. The usual
officers' quarters are on the west, facing inwards; the barracks opposite; office on the south; guard-house, with its
one sentinel walking up and down in front, on the north,
and the parade between. The post-trader's and laun-
dress' houses are nearer the Lapwai; while the stables
and other outbuildings are arranged a few paces outside
the square, and up the valley. Behold any 'two-com-
pany' army-post prepared for cavalry, and you have
caught the type.

The first council with young Joseph was held at Fort
Lapwai, the 3d of May, 1877. Present: Agent Monteith, with his interpreter, Whitman; Joseph, Ollicut,
with about fifty of Joseph's band of Indians.

We had, by way of preparation for the council, a large
hospital-tent pitched in front of that one walking sentinel
at the guard-house, and extended the tent — as we were
accustomed to do with our wall-canvas houses during the
Rebellion — by prolonging and propping the ridge-pole,
and stretching over it the tent-fly, with ropes well out,
and with sides of tent looped up. This whole contrivance
was to give all the shelter practicable from the sun, and
still open everything to the free circulation of air and
sight, not forgetting to be open to the guard on the one
hand, and to the garrison of soldiers, who were to remain

at their barracks, on the other. "You were already afraid of the Indians?" Oh, no; that is against the soldiers' theory; but it is well to be prepared.

There were fifty non-treaty Nez Perce Indians, not more, arranged as usual; a long rank of men, followed by women and children, with faces painted, the red paint extending back into the partings of the hair, — the men's hair braided and tied up with showy strings, — ornamented in dress, in hats, in blankets, with variegated colors, in leggings of buckskin, and moccasins, beaded and plain; women with bright shawls or blankets, and skirts to the ankle, and "top moccasins." All were mounted on Indian ponies as various in color as the dress of the riders. These picturesque people, after keeping us waiting long enough for effect, came in sight from up the valley, from the direction of their temporary camp, just above the company gardens. They drew near to the hollow square of the post, and in front of the small company, to be interviewed. Then they struck up their song. They were not armed, except with a few "tomahawk pipes," that could be smoked with the peaceful tobacco, or penetrate the skull-bone of an enemy, at the will of the holder. Yet somehow this wild sound produced a strange effect. It made one feel glad that there were but fifty of them, and not five hundred. It was shrill and searching; sad, like a wail, and yet defiant in its close. Our ladies, thinking it a war-song, asked, with some show of trepidation, "Do you think Joseph means to fight?" The Indians swept around outside the fence, and made the entire circuit, still keeping up the song as they rode. The buildings broke the refrain into irregular bubblings of sound till the ceremony was completed.

Joseph, Ollicut, and other principal men, came up behind Colonel Perry's quarters, and walked through the transverse hall, this being to them, doubtless, the most modest and acceptable mode of approach.

I had gone to the council-tent to receive them, where were already gathered the agent, the interpreters, Mr. Whitman and James Reuben, lieutenants Wilkinson and Boyle, several officers and ladies of the garrison, and numerous "treaty Indians," standing or crouching outside of the tent. Father Cataldo, the priest of the Catholic mission, which is situated eight miles from the fort, was also present. After the usual hand-shaking and orderly seating of the assembly, the Catholic father opened the exercises by a short extempore prayer in Nez Perce.

Then I turned to Joseph, and said, through Mr. Whitman, "I heard from your brother Ollicut, twelve days ago, at Walla-Walla, that you wished to see me. I am here to listen to what you have to say."

Joseph answered, "Another band of Indians, White Bird's, from the Salmon country, are coming. They are already in the Craig Mountains, on their way. They will be here to-morrow. You must not be in a hurry to go till all can get in to have a talk."

I replied, "Mr. Monteith, the Indian agent, and I have received our instructions from Washington. They send us to your people. If you decide at once to comply with the wishes of the government you can have the first pick of vacant land. We will wait for White Bird if you desire it. Instructions to him are the same as to you. He can take his turn."

Thereupon the old Dreamer, whom I have previously described, stood up, and addressed Mr. Whitman in the most pointed manner :

"On account of coming generations, the children and the children's children, of both whites and Indians, you must interpret correctly."

A companion-piece to this Dreamer, another aged medicine-man, with a cross and querulous manner, said, "We want to talk a long time, many days, about the earth, about our land."

The answer was, "Mr. Monteith and I wish to hear what you have to say, whatever time it may take ; but you may as well know at the outset that in any event the Indians must obey the orders of the government of the United States."

Then Mr. Monteith read his instructions from the Indian Bureau to the Indians, which were slowly and carefully interpreted to them, and added, "I sent out Reuben" (then the head-chief of the treaty Nez Perces, — since dead) "and some others to your camp, and invited you to come in. [This message went to them in the Grande Ronde, or Wallowa, country, and was not heeded.] Now you must come, and there is no getting out of it. Your Indians and White Bird's can pick up your horses and cattle, and come on the reservation. Joseph can select the place he wants if he will do it at once. General Howard will stay till matters are settled."

Ollicut—tall, well-knit, supple, and graceful fellow— was now and then almost persuaded to yield to the white man's power; then, driving himself, in seeming regret, to the opposite extreme, Ollicut spoke:

"We must think for ourselves, whites and Indians. We have respect for the whites; but they treat me [their orators frequently using the first person singular when speaking for the whole band] as a dog, and I sometimes think my friends are different from what I had supposed. There should be *one law* for all. If I commit murder I shall be hung; but if I do well I should not be punished. Our friends will be here to-morrow, and I will then tell what I think."

I answered, "Joseph, Agent Monteith, and myself are under the same government. What it commands us to do, that we must do. The Indians should come on the reservation first; then they may have privileges, as the agent has shown, viz., to hunt and to fish in the Imnaha Valley. If the Indians hesitate to come to the reservation, the government directs that soldiers be used to bring them hither. Joseph and Ollicut know that we are friends to them, and that if they comply there will be no trouble."

The two old Dreamers, whom the Indians treat with great respect, and by whom they were always unduly influenced, were at this council very saucy and quarrelsome in their manner. On account of this I was obliged to treat them with marked severity, and to tell them plainly that "they must give good advice," or I should be obliged to arrest and punish them. They then took alarm, and changed their tone.

Severity of manner in dealing with savages is believed by many of the Indian's friends to be always uncalled for and decidedly wrong. It may be so ; but the manner of dealing must depend much upon the peculiarities of the people with whom you have to do.

One general principle, however, the white man may lay down : If he desires to influence Indians to comply with his wishes he must neither fear nor hate them. In the outset of this council Joseph had sought to so move, act, and talk as "to weaken the hearts" of the white folks. While he held himself in reserve, with a sour, non-committal appearance, he pushed forward his harsh representatives. Had his preliminaries been met with any sign of weakness, as he always interpreted softness of manner to be prompted by weakness, the results which we were endeavoring to bring about would have failed of the accomplishment. In fact, the long pleadings of the Washington Commission during the previous November, accompanied as they were by the most kindly manner and patient tones, were believed by Joseph and his band to indicate great weakness. Though it failed to get their consent to the most liberal conditions, it did have the effect to enlarge their ideas of their own importance. In fact the time for loving persuasion had now gone by. Positive *instructions* had come, and *obedience* was required. There was no unkindness, or even severity, in the face, manner, or words of the agent or officers of the government, except when it became necessary to meet and overcome apparent malignity and noisy opposition. Against these, fearless sternness always produced the most wholesome and immediate consequences.

CHAPTER IX.

JOSEPH AND HIS CONFEDERATES.—THE SECOND INTERVIEW.
— WHITE BIRD AND HIS BAND. — ALPOWA JIM. — JOSEPH'S
BRIEF SPEECH. — TOO-HUL-HUL-SOTE. — THE ADJOURNMENT.

THE second Indian council was held at Fort Lapwai,
May 4. It was a glorious day; the sun shone without a cloud, but its heat was relieved by a gentle breeze
which was coursing through the valley and over the
smooth hills, and causing the abundant grasses and
flowers to ripple and sparkle in long noiseless waves.

White Bird had marched into the valley with a part of
his band, the remainder, he reported, were driving the
ponies and fetching the lodges and provisions across the
Craig Mountain. The Ashotins were present, and Too-
hul-hul-sote, with his followers, were straggling in. The
trails are still difficult at this season, often obstructed
with deep drifts of snow, which, being softened by the
increasing warmth, are worse than at an earlier season,
when they are stiffened by the frosts of winter.

The Indians gathered and formed in lines, as on the
previous day. There was the same careful toilet, the
same preliminary ride around the garrison, the song being
louder and stronger, and perhaps more defiant than before; the same back-door entrance and cordial hand-shaking. We were then seated; when, at my request, one of
the handsomest and pleasantest of the " treaty " Nez

Perces, and one whom I had noticed as active and happy in the religious gatherings, called Alpowa Jim, was requested to conduct the opening service. He fervently prayed in his own language; then Mr. Monteith repeated the reading of his Washington instructions, carefully explaining them, as was done the day before. After a little delay Joseph made a brief speech. " This is White Bird. I spoke to you of him. This is the first time he has seen you, and you him. I want him and his Indians to understand what has been said to us."

To-day, Joseph, with his shining hair very carefully braided at the sides, and his face slightly rouged, sat on a low bench. His tall brother on the ground, half reclined, before him, and White Bird, with his followers, massed behind him, squatted on the grass to the left of Ollicut.

White Bird was a demure-looking Indian, about five feet eight inches tall. His face assumed the condition of impassibility, or rigid fixedness, while in council; and probably for fear that some passing event, some look or word, might surprise him into the betrayal of the slightest emotion, he kept his immense ceremonial hat on, and placed a large eagle's wing in front of his eyes and nose.

In speaking of the country occupied by the Indians I mentioned the sub-chief, who habitually encamped on the north side of the Snake River, — Too-hul-hul-sote. He held, as we have seen, some of the country between Joseph's Wallowa and White Bird's Salmon River region. He was broad-shouldered, deep-chested, thick-necked, five feet ten in height, had a heavy, guttural voice, and betrayed in every word a strong and settled hatred of all Caucasians. This man the Indians now put forward to speak for them; not, probably, that they had already decided to endorse his sentiments, but as he always counselled war, they evidently desired to see what effect his public utterance would produce upon us. He said: "There are always two parties to a dispute. The one that is right will come out ahead." This was introduced by plentiful flourish of words and illustrations, but with no attempt at conciliation even in manner. The old answer was repeated in substance: "We are all subjects, children of a common government, and must obey its requirements." Too-hul-hul-sote said, "I have heard about a bargain, a trade between some of these Indians [referring to the treaty Nez Perces] and the white men concerning their land; but I belong to the land out of which I came. The Earth is my mother."

We rejoined: "The Nez Perces did make such an agreement, and as the commission from Washington explained last fall, the non-treaty Indians being in the minority in their opposition, were bound by that agreement, and must abide by it."

The old man, more surly than before, declared; "You have no right to compare us, grown men, to children. Children do not think for themselves. Grown men do think for themselves. The government at Washington, 'cannot' [or shall not] think for us."

This method of talking, continuing for some time, was troublesome, and I saw that the Indians were evidently excited and tired. Further, I felt, from their manner, that it would be wise to have the troops that were already on the march in position; viz., the Wallowa force, about a hundred cavalrymen, at least, as near us as the Grande

Ronde; a new company at Walla-Walla; and one of the cavalry companies from Walla-Walla in our immediate vicinage.

Therefore, when Joseph asked for postponement, I proposed to Joseph and White Bird not to meet again till the following Monday. This arrangement seemed to please everybody. I remarked, as we were about to separate, " Let the Indians take time ; let them wait till Monday morning, and, meanwhile, talk fully among themselves." So, with pleasant faces, and cordial hand-shaking, the second interview ended.

There was, however, great anxiety during the few days of intermission. The " treaty" Nez Perces betrayed symptoms of fear. The extravagant speeches of young Indians were circulated by the women. Gossips came to servants of the officers and told of the sayings and the threats of Joseph and White Bird.

For a time there were at the fort, and at the agency, which is but three miles distant, much sleeplessness and terror lest there should burst out somewhere in our neighborhood a fire that no ordinary effort could quench.

The wild Indians were well armed, with many breach-loading rifles and pistols. The friendly Nez Perces had nothing but shot-guns. The former were constantly trained by their unceasing racings and firings, while the latter were cultivating their farms. The " non-treaties " had made themselves, like the irregular cossacks of Russia, the best skirmishers in the world. Like them, they are never so well off as when left to themselves. They are quick-sighted, superior marksmen, and subject to sufficient discipline when following their recognized chiefs,

to scatter, run to cover, and reassemble, without disband-
ing.

Already there were hovering about our garrison at Lapwai this well-appointed force of Indians, greater in number than the two skeleton companies of United States
soldiers stationed there; and every hour brought them
new accessions. Some one asked, " Did not General Canby trust the Modocs? and what was the result?" It must
be confessed that my reflections were not altogether
pleasant, nor such observations and questions very re-
assuring.

The interval of waiting was, however, relieved by the
lively exercises of the Sabbath. At the agency chapel the
Dreamers — men, women, and children — and the Christians filled the house, the steps, and " the borders round
about," while their songs of praise could be heard for
a long distance.

There is so much that is picturesque in the Indian costume that such an assembly presents a gay spectacle at
any time. This Sunday was not an exception. The
gloom and anxiety which, like a heavy cloud, had previously settled upon the whites in the vicinity, seemed to drift
away before the cheerful spirit of this occasion. Reuben,
the chosen head-chief, James Reuben, the teacher, and
Archie Lawyer, who read in English and preached in Nez
Perce, all prophesied *peace*. So that at night the Indians
in general were happy, and the whites in attendance became hopeful of a peaceful solution of disquieting questions. Yet, as I subsequently heard, Joseph held
himself aloof from the Christian gathering, and stirred
up many of his immediate followers by those interesting

" dreamer " ceremonial movements, drumming and song, which, subsequently, at the prisoners' camp at Leavenworth, Kansas, the following November, by their novelty, brought together five thousand of our citizens to hear and to see them.

CHAPTER X.

JOSEPH AND HIS CONFEDERATES. — THE THIRD COUNCIL. —
HUSH-HUSH-CUTE. — THE OLD DREAMER AGAIN. — HIS DEFI-
ANT TALK AND ARREST. — THE DANGERS OF A MASSACRE.
— THE CHANGE OF TONE.

THE day for the third interview with the discontented
Indians came. It was Monday, the seventh day of
May, 1877. There had been many accessions to their
numbers. They had come to Lapwai from all directions.
Hush-hush-cute, the oily, wily, bright-eyed young chief,
who could be smooth-tongued or saucy as the mood
seized him, or as he thought it would best subserve a
present purpose, had, with a number of followers, just
arrived from the vicinity of the Palouze river. Messengers had come to Joseph from the mouth of the Grande
Ronde, and declared that soldiers were already in the
Wallowa country.

The ceremonial display of the Indian bands, with
greatly increased forces, similar to that on previous
days, evidently gave the Indians courage, and those disposed to war measures were bolder in their manner and
in their demands. Mr. Monteith, the agent, who was
very kind and conciliatory toward them, told them that
they had evidently received a wrong impression with
regard to the government requirement. There was no
purpose to interfere with them in their religious rites and
ceremonies; no restraint except when a " too-at " or

" dreamer," in his mistaken zeal, occasioned a disturbance of the peace. It was added that a bad teacher, who counselled disobedience of the clear instructions of the government, would certainly have to be punished.

Too-hul-hul-sote, the cross-grained growler, was again designated as the speaker, and took up his parable. He was, if possible, crosser and more impudent in his abruptness of manner than before. He had the usual long preliminary discussion about the earth being his mother, that she should not be disturbed by hoe or plough, that men should subsist on what grows of itself, &c., &c. He railed against the violence that would separate Indians from lands that were theirs by inheritance. He repeated his ideas concerning " chieftainship," chieftainship of the earth. Chieftainship cannot be sold, cannot be given away. Mr. Monteith and General Howard, he said, must speak the truth about this chieftainship of the earth.

He was answered : "We do not wish to interfere with your religion, but you must talk about practicable things. Twenty times over you repeat that the earth is your mother, and about chieftainship from the earth. Let us hear it no more, but come to business at once."

The old man replied, in a very insolent tone : " What the treaty Indians talk about was born of to-day ! It isn't true law at all. You white people get together, measure the earth, and then divide it ; so I want you to talk directly what you mean !" The agent says very pleasantly : " The law is, you must come to the reservation ; the law is made in Washington. We don't make it."

To other similar remarks the old Dreamer replied fiercely : " We never have made any trade. Part of the

Indians gave up their land. I never did. The earth is part of my body, and I never gave up the earth."

I replied: "You know very well that the government has set apart a reservation, and that the Indians must go upon it. If an Indian becomes a citizen, like old Timothy of Alpowa, he can have land like any other citizen outside, but he has to leave his tribe, and take land precisely as a white man does. The government has set apart this large reservation for you and your children, that you may live in peace, and prosper."

The rough old fellow, in his most provoking tone, said something in a short sentence, looking fiercely at me.

The interpreter quickly says: He demands, "What person pretends to divide the land, and put me on it?"

In the most decided voice I said: "I am the man. I stand here for the President, and there is no spirit good or bad that will hinder me. My orders are plain, and will be executed. I hoped that the Indians had good sense enough to make me their friend, and not their enemy."

Signs of anger and bad blood began to appear. Looking-glass dropped his gentle style and answered me evasively. White Bird, from behind his eagle's wing, spoke mildly, but endorsed his aged spokesman, and said:

"If I had been taught from early life to be governed by the white men I would be governed by the white men. The earth sustains [or rules] me."

I now perceived that the Indians were trying to see how saucy they could be through this Too-at, and I noticed that some of them had weapons. I perceived that I must, somehow, put in a wedge of separation, and curb their unruly tendency. So I said to the old man: "Then

5

you do not propose to comply with the orders of the government?" He answered: "So long as the earth keeps me, I want to be left alone. You are trifling with the law of the earth." I replied, "Our old friend does not seem to understand ·that the question is: Will the Indians come peaceably on the reservation, or do they want me, in compliance with my orders, to put them there by force?"

He declared, in substance, "I never gave the Indians authority to give away my lands." I asked: "Do you speak for yourself alone?" He answered, with additional fierceness, "The Indians may do what they like, but I am not going on the reservation!"

Speaking as sternly as I could, I said: "This bad advice is what you give the Indians. On account of it, you will have to be taken to the Indian territory. Joseph and White Bird seem to have good hearts, but yours is bad. I will send you there if it takes years and years. When I heard that you were coming, I feared that you would make trouble. You say you are not a medicine-man, but you talk for them. The Indians can see no good while you are their spokesman. You advise them to resist, to fight, to lose all their horses and cattle, and have unending trouble." (Turning to the others.) "Will Joseph, and White Bird, and Looking-glass go with me to look after their land? The old man shall not go. He must stay with Colonel Perry."

The old Dreamer said, "Do you want to scare me with reference to my body?" I answered, "I will leave your body with Colonel Perry."

At this time I called for the messenger, but he being

away, Colonel Perry and I led Too-hul-hul-sote out of the council. [My conduct was summary, it is true, but I knew it was hopeless to get the Indians to agree to anything so long as they could keep this old Dreamer on the lead, and defy the agents of the government;] and I believed that the Modoc massacre would very soon be repeated, if I gave time for concert of action. [In fact, in dealing with Indians, my conviction is strong that the true policy is to demand obedience to the requirements of the government of the United States. The crisis had come, when either this demand must be made, or these wild Indians be allowed all the latitude and leisure that their hearts desired.]

A far different spirit now prevailed among them. Their tones changed. They spoke pleasantly, and readily agreed to go with me to examine the Lapwai, and afterward the valley of the Clearwater, at more remote parts of the reservation, where there would be good ground to cultivate, fair grazing for their animals, and plenty of wood for the winter months.

With this satisfactory conclusion, the council again adjourned.

CHAPTER XI.

JOSEPH AND HIS CONFEDERATES. — THE RIDE THROUGH THE
LAPWAI VALLEY TO LOOK FOR LAND. — THE LUNCH, AND
THE CALDWELL HOUSE. — A HORSE-RACE. — LOOKING-GLASS
AND WHITE BIRD PLEDGING THEIR LIVES. — THE DECISION
TO COME ON THE RESERVATION. — JOE ROBOSKO'S JOY. —
LOOKING-GLASS LAUGHING. — THE FINAL INTERVIEW. —
INDIANS FRIGHTENED BY RUMORS. — GOOD FAITH APPAR-
ENT, EXCEPT WITH HUSH-HUSH-CUTE. — JOSEPH CHANGES
HIS CHOICE OF LAND. — GENERAL REJOICING. — GENERAL
HOWARD'S LIFE THREATENED. — THE RETURN TO PORT-
LAND, OREGON.

TUESDAY, the 8th, Joseph, White Bird, and Looking-
glass rode with Wilkinson and myself up the valley
of the Lapwai. These chiefs were, to-day, dressed in their
best. Their swinging side-locks were braided with unusual care. Their faces were painted, as usual, with a
line of red running back along the parting of the hair
over the head. Well mounted on large-sized Indian
ponies, of divers colors, with their rich blankets dropped
from the shoulders to the saddle, they sat waiting for us
near their lodges, and what was very encouraging, they
appeared hearty and cheerful, chatting with us and with
each other as we rode along.

A lady, at Caldwell's, in the upper part of this valley,
very kindly gave us a lunch. Joseph looked over Mr.
Caldwell's house with much apparent interest. I said to
him, " Joseph, you prefer canvas houses; you don't like
these wooden-frame houses?" He answered, "Oh, no;

when I come upon the Lapwai I shall want a frame house." On our way back to the post we had quite a horse-race. White Bird wished to try his snug-built roan, and see if it could not outrun Captain Wilkinson's American bay, and all laughed and talked in the most friendly way. On one occasion during the ride Looking-glass came to me and begged me to release the old man — Too-hul-hul-sote — from confinement. He said he would make him say that he was sorry for his crossness, and that he and White Bird would be responsible to me with their lives for his good behavior. It was, doubtless, with his promise to me in memory, that Looking-glass, later, became afraid to surrender, and always said, " General Howard will surely hang us." And this promise, also, so affected White Bird that, at the final surrender, he crept out betweeen the lines rather than risk a meeting ; for he said, " We would soon begin to kill the prisoners."

Looking-glass and White Bird were told, as we approached the fort on our return, that the old man would be kept under restraint for a while, till all the land matter should be arranged. The friendly sub-chief, Jonah, and Joe Robosko, the interpreter, went with us this day, and they both, in substance, remarked, " The ' non-treaties ' have now made up their minds fully to come on the reserve. Joseph and his band of Wallowa Indians want the Lapwai, from where the Sweetwater joins it to its source, above Caldwell's ranch. White Bird wants to go to Looking-glass' country, on the Clearwater, above Kamiah. Hush-hush-cute will go to the land along the Clearwater, just above the agency." Joe Robosko was very happy about it. He said, " I didn't believe till to-day that they had decided to come." Of course all of us were very glad. Matters appeared to be taking a good turn. The beauty of the day, the exhilaration of this ride of fourteen miles, the effect of the fine lands presented to Joseph's eye, and the sight of the nice house on the Lapwai that would be his, and the breaking of bread with us at lunch, all appeared to combine to soften the heart of the young chieftain, and relieve him from the sinister undercurrent of his thought and purpose.

The next day was Wednesday, the 9th of May. We set out for Kamiah very early, before the sun arose. I never can forget that lovely morning, when the sun began to appear, touching the round hills with light, and glorifying the mountain before us, which looked like a great monarch enthroned among his humbler dignitaries and subjects.

Looking-glass rode along by my side and told of his father, long since dead, and of the old man's good advice; advice that he had not hitherto heeded, but that he now meant to follow. " What makes me feel like laughing this morning, General Howard?" he asked, in pleasant thoughtfulness.

I answered, " There are three kinds of laughter, — one from fun, another from deceit, and another from real joy ! "

" Mine," he replied, " is from real joy. I shall never forget our ride along these paths." So we talked.

White Bird took to Captain Wilkinson for his amusement. His face lighted up and broke into smiles as he talked. I believed, and all who made this journey of sixty miles with us, and all, including Rev. Mr. Thompson, of Olympia, and Mr. Monteith, the Indian agent, who went over the hills and mountains along the banks for sixteen miles above Kamiah the next day, then believed, and so expressed themselves, that these leading Indians then really meant to conform to the wishes of the government, and come on the reservation.

After the return to Lapwai the Indians came together for a final interview, Tuesday, May 14. Captain Trimble's company of the 1st Cavalry had arrived at Lapwai, and gone into camp; special news that two other companies, Whippple's and Winter's, had reached the banks of the Grande Ronde, not far from its mouth, had just come in. This news created much excitement among the Indians. Word was brought to Joseph to hurry and make terms with me, for a thousand soldiers were near his old camping-ground, beyond the Snake River. Joseph had, in consequence, very early this morning, run to my aide-de-camp, in breathless haste, and asked to have all matters speedily settled.

The white inhabitants from the Salmon River and Camas Prairie country, from the vicinity of Wallowa, and from the neighborhood of Hush-hush-cute's roaming places, had, from time to time, sent the Indian agent the most marked complaints of the unruly character of many of these Indians, and forwarded earnest entreaties that they be made to go upon the reservation. A formal entreaty of this kind, from Salmon River, was received this very morning, of which the Indians were informed. It evidently strengthened their decision to come to the reservation; yet, as subsequent events proved, these remonstrances were treasured up in memory, and made the excuse for murder and outrage.

All came together, Indians and white men, near the adjutant's office. Their petition to release the old " dreamer " had been granted. Then they each entered into formal agreement with the agent and the army to be put on the Lapwai reservation in one month, i. e., by June 14. Joseph, at last, concluded that he would rather go to the Clearwater with the others. This favor was granted, really because it relieved us from the unpleasant necessity of disturbing two white men, who, together, held some seven hundred acres of the good land along the Lapwai Creek. And as there was seeming hostility even against the friendly reservation Indians, at the town of Lewiston, twelve miles from them, it was deemed, for this reason also, a good thing to settle the new-comers seventy miles or more farther off. Hush-hush-cute was given thirty-five days. He was the only Indian who, at this time, betrayed any symptoms of treachery. His protection papers were withheld on account of it, and given to the agent, to be presented to him when the agent should be satisfied of his good intentions.

There was general rejoicing over the peaceful outcome of our councils, and long rides to locate the Indians. Other Indian agencies were notified of the results. One reliable story, however, came in, that a Columbia-River renegade had burned his stuff and had gone on the warpath, and that, according to his bitter threats, my life was in danger. This had a good foundation; but we supposed as soon as the news of peace should reach the runaway that he would return to his deserted wife, and surely one should never lie awake of nights from fear of personal harm.

The military aides, and myself, now turned homeward. We had a quick and pleasant trip down the Snake and Columbia rivers, and Saturday, May 19, found us again with our families in Portland. The eastern progress was something like that of the children of Israel towards the promised land; it had many backward as well as forward movements. We had journeyed, however, four hundred miles from the mouth of the Willamet, toward the Rocky Mountains, and returned.

The next time we set out, thanks to the enterprise of the redoubtable Joseph, we shall not turn back till we reach the Missouri River, and look into the eyes of our friends beyond, in St. Paul and Chicago.

CHAPTER XII.

JOSEPH'S ALLIES. — BACK AT THE PLACE OF BEGINNING. —
PEACEFUL SCENES. — COLONEL WATKINS, THE INDIAN
INSPECTOR. — THE FOURTEEN MASTERS. — SKEMIAH. — VISIT
TO FATHER WILBUR. — A CLEAN CHURCH. — THE MESSEN-
GERS SENT TO NUMEROUS INDIAN TRIBES. — BRANDING
CATTLE. — GOOD TIDINGS.

IF you take your map of Oregon, and look up Portland,
you will find it one hundred and ten miles from the
sea, on the Willamet, (sometimes called Willamette and
sometimes Wollamet,) but you may not realize the fact
that this cosmopolitan city of twenty thousand people is
really the centre of all kinds of activities, military and
civil; oceanward, up and down the gentle Pacific; southward, by rail and by river, to the broken mountain
divides; northward, by rail and by stage, to western
Washington Territory; and eastward, by the broad, grand
old Columbia River, with its numerous and almost endless branches, that mingle their fountain extremities with
the millions of their kind which supply the brooklets,
creeks, and rivers of the Atlantic slope.

My companion and myself came back with the feeling
that a difficult task had been done. General Mower, one
of the Union heroes of the great rebellion, used to say at
the end of a battle, which he always seemed to compass
with a fierce delight, "*Fait accompli, fait accompli*, sir."
So seemed the closing interview at Lapwai an accomplished

work. We felt almost sure that there would be no difficulties with the Nez Perces. All their history and their traditions favored this view. But we did forget, I think, that even in the veins of Joseph there was some of the Cayuse blood. The Cayuses had intermarried largely with the Nez Perces. It was, as we have seen, the Cayuses that accomplished the cowardly, treacherous, excuseless, and horrible massacre of Doctor Whitman and his helpers. "Blood tells!" Why ever forget it?

The days came and went in Portland much as usual. The streets were lively with the summer trade. The thousand children at the central school were coming out and going in with joyous, springing gait, and an almost infinite variety of plumage. The rains had pretty nearly ceased, or had been replaced by brief showers, that one enjoys as he does tears of gladness after a long sorrow. How many items of comfort in common, almost unnoticeable things, come back to the memory when the spell is over, and the perpetual conflict is joined! So were we in comfort, and peace, and hope, when Colonel E. C. Watkins, the Interior Department Inspector of Indian affairs, came into my office during this interval of rest. I was glad enough to see him, for I used to declare that I had fourteen commanding officers in the fourteen Indian agents within the geographical department of the Columbia. It is difficult to serve fourteen masters; certainly it is not Scriptural. Now here comes their civil senior. I transfer my allegiance at once. Colonel Watkins was not only able and competent officially, ready as he was to take the lead in the work of gathering in the renegade Indians scattered along the Columbia, but he

was also personally very pleasant company. He had
served acceptably during the war of the rebellion, and
had, as we all must have, a fund of anecdote relating
thereto. He had also quite an experience, country wide,
as an Indian inspector. The hair-breadth escapes of the
war were more than equalled by his peaceful raids against
whiskey frauds through Tennessee and northern North
Carolina. He is a large, full-built, wholesome man,
backed up with genuine courage in any dangerous position.

After much conversation and reflection upon the situation, Watkins and I agreed that if Joseph could secure
allies among the numerous Columbia River tribes he
might yet change his mind, should he be inclined to
treachery, — here was his leverage. It was certainly wise
to anticipate him, and if possible divert the bands that
were roaming up and down the great river.

Well, the 30th of May we made a start. It was the
national holiday. We first went to Fort Vancouver, six
miles due north from Portland, to spread flowers on the
graves of our deceased soldiers. As Indian Skemiah,
whom, we have seen, Father Wilbur had laid his hands
upon and delivered to me for temporary correction and
confinement, and conversion after the military sort, wished
much to see me, and better still, Colonel Watkins with
me, we had a formal interview with this chief. With
a clay-colored, expressionless face, and a fat, waddling
body, the old man, accompanied by a soldier to guard
him, made his appearance in General Sully's back office,
where we were in waiting. In the meagre "jargon," — a
language part French, part English, and part Indian,
once quite popular on this coast, but becoming of less

and less use as learning steadily advances, — the sergeant interpreter received and translated the assurance that Skemiah's heart had always been good; that his people had gone to Father Wilbur's reservation, and that he would gladly go there and do just right henceforth. We promised him that he, starting the next day, should go there under the escort of the sergeant. He was to accompany us to the reservation, where, if he behaved well, he would doubtless be released.

On the 31st of May, at the usual early hour of five in the morning, we set out for the Dalles. I little thought, as I took my small valise in hand, and bade adieu to my drowsy family, on that morning, that I should pass through an Indian war, and be absent five months, before I should look upon their faces again. Yet so it was to be.

Skemiah and his keeper joined us at Vancouver. Skemiah was happy, probably never happier in his life. His dull, clayey face had an eager, pleasant look this morning, and I was glad for him.

What books would be written to fill the world if what is said and done on transport steamers and other vehicles were only jotted down! . . . . Colonel Watkins and Captain Wilkinson had a fund of stories, so that the day passed quickly, as the palatial steamer, through the Hudson-like scenery of the West, ascended the Columbia.

Forty miles above the Cascades the steamer was left. As travellers, we did not tire of the hills and mountains on the north bank, opposite the Dalles, and the grand scenery, as we turned our eyes from time to time to look at the valley of the Columbia, and the twice ten thousand hills, and the old mountains beyond them. Thither we wound our way, up, up, and over into the valley, and up, and up, to the top of the Simcoe range. Near there, with weather cold as in the Alps, we camped for the night. Indians were plenty. Skemiah's little son of four years, dressed like a young prince in Indian finery, had joined us, and they condescended, as they had not provisions with them, to receive of our bounty. Indians, when they smoke tobacco, and when they eat the white man's food, always appear so remarkably contented, that it is well, when possible, to gratify them. It is hospitable, and it usually makes friends.

By eleven the next day, June 2, we were at Father Wilbur's Indian agency on the Simcoe River. The Simcoe is a branch of the Yakima, which enters the Columbia above the mouth of the Snake. The Yakima gave the name to the handsomest Indian reservation of the Pacific coast. Mr. Wilbur was away when we arrived, at a remote part of his reserve, branding cattle. That evening he and his wife returned. How strong he looked. Standing six feet in his slippers, a broad-shouldered, thick-chested, large-headed, full-voiced, manly man. Yet he tires sometimes, as age creeps on. Mrs. Wilbur said: " We had to stop by the way, and he lay down a while and took a sleep and rest." I do not wonder, for he had the care of a nation on his shoulders, and was his own cabinet, legislature, and judiciary. He did have a prime-minister, however, who was systematic and painstaking, and that was Mrs. Wilbur. The next day we looked in upon one of their churches, that one which was crowded to overflowing with Indians, and had the fences lined with their waiting saddle-horses. That church was without a speck of dirt, even a tobacco stain !

Monday, messengers were sent out to Indians along the Columbia for hundreds of miles, and they asked the bands to meet at Fort Simcoe. While we were waiting for this important gathering, Colonel Watkins, Captain Wilkinson, and I looked over this extensive and celebrated Indian reservation, so well known to benevolent people everywhere. We went even to the cattle ranch, twenty-six miles from the agency, and saw how the young cattle and calves were branded, and did not wonder that Mr. Wilbur got weary when we saw the practical way in which he taught the Indians to mark a wild steer. The animal had to be thrown down, and made to lie flat and still, while the strong man took and applied the heavy and fearful branding-iron. To catch, to throw, to fasten, to hold, to brand, then to separate the public and the private, the Indian's and the white man's, was a trying ordeal, almost like a battle in its excitements.

While Colonel Watkins and his escort were waiting on the Yakima, the mail brought only good news. Joseph, Ollicut, and White Bird were gathering in their ponies and cattle, preparatory to settling down, as they had promised. The newspapers, which are fond of sensational paragraphs, gave out good tidings. The favorable reports gladdened the hearts of the Yakimas also, for while there is an Indian war all the red men are more or less involved in suspicion and trouble.

CHAPTER XIII.

JOSEPH'S ALLIES. — THE YAKIMA COUNTRY. — FORT SIMCOE.
— JOE STWYRE. — SMOHOLLIE. — MOSES. — PAMBRUN, THE
INTERPRETER. — THE TALK OF JUNE EIGHTH. — SOLEMN
FORMALITY. — WELL-DRESSED INDIAN WOMEN. — COLONEL
WATKINS' SPEECH. — AGENT WILBUR'S SPEECH. — THE SUN-
DAY SERVICE. — A WONDERFUL OCCASION. — THE WILD IN-
DIANS' ANSWER. — THE SCHOOL CHILDREN'S SONGS. — TALK
OF JUNE TENTH. — SPEECHES OF MOSES AND OTHERS.

I RETURNED to Fort Simcoe in time to meet the
renegade Indians, should they listen to the appeal of
our messenger, and come in.

This Fort Simcoe is located about sixty-five miles
north of the Columbia, that is, by the route that must be
taken, though much less in a direct line. It is in the
Yakima and Simcoe valleys, prolonged westward, lying
close to the foot-hills of the Cascade range, in a beautiful
grove of oaks. It was built for two or three companies
of infantry, by Major Garnett, who was at one time the
commandant of the Military Academy, and who afterwards
fell in the Confederate service. He made picturesque
quarters for his officers, and good buildings generally,
and surrounded the gardens with handsome fences. The
improvements were years ago transferred to the Indian
Department, and became the headquarters for the agency
of the Yakima, or Simcoe, reservation. The great beauty
and fertility of this valley, the complete success of civil-
izing influences under Agent Wilbur, the neat Indian

houses and farms it contains, and the other evidences of progress, have long been the subject of public record. I may here add that all this ground force was brought to bear by the agent, employes, head-chief Joe Stwyre, and the friendly reservation Indians, to help Colonel Watkins in carrying out his instructions. These were to gather the renegades and wild roamers of the Columbia, and start them on the road of civilization.

White people tried to hinder and frighten Joe Stwyre. "You'll be killed *sure*, if you go to Smohollie!" "No, no!" Smohollie received him gladly, and hastened with his principal friends to set out for Simcoe. So, also, Moses, from Priest's Rapids, and the other nomads along the Big River Valley. Pambrun, the interpreter, the son of the Pambrun of the time of the Cayuse massacre, who spoke a language that all these understand, came from his home, near Touchet. All the Indians, far and near, gathered in the neighborhood of Simcoe, Saturday, the 8th of June.

It was a hot, sunny day, so that the tent stretched in the grove afforded a very grateful shade. Behold the formal grouping! I never have experienced so much solemn formality, except at the first January examination at the Military Academy, where the superintendent, and all officers of the army, came and arranged themselves in dazzling order; so was it at an Indian council. First, Colonel Watkins, Agent Wilbur, our military selves; white men and ladies arranged; then facing these are the Indians on benches or chairs, in the first row, in order of their supposed rank, from right to left, — Moses, Smohollie, One-eyed John, Calwash, Skemiah, Thomas, and

6

others.   Friendly Indians mingled with the new-comers.
Renegades came in behind, sitting or gracefully crouching.   The background was finely studded with women
and children, with bright and contrasted colors, with
straight, black hair, and black, flashing eyes.   Remember
that these women are mostly housekeepers, and have, on
such great occasions as this, clean hands, clean faces, and
combed locks.

Colonel Watkins (after the opening prayer) made the
first speech.   It was in substance :

I. Now, the government of the United States requires
you all to come on this or some other of its reservations.

II. In every possible way of looking at this matter it
is evidently better for you to come.

III. The commander of the military forces will enforce
this requirement.

Agent Wilbur talked mostly to the second proposition,
and strove to influence Smohollie particularly ; for Smohollie, the author of the "dreamer religion," is believed
to be the cause of the restlessness of the Columbia River
tribes, for it keeps alive the hope of supernatural aid,
somehow, to come through a general Indian resurrection.
As it was late, and the Indians were tired from their long
journeys, the council, after a few remarks of notice and
welcome, was adjourned to Monday.   All were invited
to stay for the morrow's religious service, appointed at
the grove where we were at the time assembled.

The next day's service cannot well be forgotten.   All
took part.   Father Wilbur, with his great spiritual
power, and Colonel Watkins, with his calm statements,
and Captain Wilkinson, with his nervous energy and

moving pathos, were followed by Indians, pleading for
the cause of Christ in the Indian's own tongue. Smohollie, and other wild ones, answered these appeals with
much apparent sincerity and feeling. The well-dressed
and happy Indian school-children cemented the whole in
joyous demonstrations of sacred song.

The adjourned meeting reassembled at eight A. M., the
10th of June. I will simply introduce the Indians'
speeches as I recorded them.

Moses (he is, indeed, a handsome Indian, neat in his
dress, full-built, muscular, his head held well up and
back, his eyes red from inflammation, — probably the
effect of wind, and alkali dust, and Indian fires) : "My
Indians are scattered over a large country. I cannot say
what they will do. I am ready to tread on any reservation. If it is better for me to go on some reservation
other than this, all right.

"The Indians above the Spokane, several tribes, have
invited me to become their chief; and if they shall have a
reservation I would like to go to them."

Smohollie, with his hunchback figure and big head,
apparently fearing that Moses may get ahead of him, even
in our favor, remarked at once, "Your law is my law. I
say to you, Yes. I will be on a reservation by September. I have but two or three hundred people."

The oldest chief, Thomas, blear-eyed, spare, tall, full
of trembling, says, "I have about fifty Indians in all. I
will go to the Umatilla Reservation by the 1st of September." He kept the promise in November.

The others, Skemiah, One-eyed John, and Calwash,
made similar promises, naming the number of Indians for

whom they were responsible. These five Indians, who spoke at the council, were chiefs of bands. They made their promises freely; and so far as joining others against the whites is concerned neither of them did so, and few of their people have since misbehaved.

That afternoon we bade our good, hospitable friends at the agency good-by, feeling as if another peaceful work had been done, and well done. Surely at least five hundred warriors, apprised that Joseph and his discontented Indians had yielded to us, were themselves deterred from all preparations for war. If any of them afterwards meditated treachery, as people who doubt all Indians claim, it was too late. The military movements prevented reinforcements from this quarter without great hazard. And really I do not think such treachery was contemplated after this gathering.

In a spring wagon, drawn by two good mules, our party followed the Yakima down its south-easterly course to near its mouth. The interpreter, and many Indians on their ponies, afforded the wagon a lively cavalcade, before, behind, and on the flanks. The heat, and finally deep sand for several leagues, prevented our arrival at Wallula the night of the 11th. We had at least twenty-five miles to go, when it occurred to me that the Indians might take us down the Columbia in a canoe. We came to near the mouth of the Yakima, where it enters the Columbia, just about sundown. Captain Wilkinson here became alarmingly ill, could eat nothing at the ranch near by, and could hardly be induced to proceed. Still, we thought it very important to be at Wallula to catch the up-river boat to Lewiston. Colonel Watkins must

go to Lapwai to inspect; and then together we were
bound for the Spokane, and beyond. So we went to the
Columbia's bank, and called loudly for the promised
canoe. At last two of Smohollie's Indians pushed out
in the darkness, and paddled over a long "dugout."
The captain was carried and assisted to a comfortable,
though narrow, bed, midway. The Indians and Pambrun
managed the boat; while Colonel Watkins and I told
stories, and sung our songs, till Captain Wilkinson was
soon sufficiently recovered to join us. Past the dark
places, past the islands, past the Homely Rapids, frightful to our small craft by their roaring, past the mouth
of the Snake, — we shot along, wind, current, and Indian
paddle, all in our favor. It was two o'clock in the clear
morning, the dawn just appearing in the east, when we
pulled up at the little hamlet of Wallula. The gang-
plank was just about to be drawn in when the night-
travellers stepped upon it, and hurried to the steamer's
deck.

"Grant me fifteen minutes for messages below and
eastward?" "Yes, yes; hurry," the captain answers.
In less time we are off for Lewiston. Our sick friend,
who was supperless at the Yakima, now is all right,
eating a hearty, early breakfast in the steamboat kitchen.
This is the morning of the 12th of June.

We again get good accounts of matters among the Nez
Perces, so that, worn out with the great fatigue of the
journey, without anything to disturb our repose, we were
soon fast asleep; while the steamer toiled on, without our
care or help, making slow headway against the powerful
current of the Snake River.

CHAPTER XIV.

JOSEPH AND HIS SURROUNDINGS. — SCENERY. — CURIOUS
FORMS. — ALMOTA. — LEWISTON. — A FRONTIER VILLAGE. —
ARMY OFFICERS. — CHARLIE MONTEITH. — PEACE. — THE
OMINOUS SIGN. — L. P. BROWN'S ADVICE. — THE LARRY OTT
CASE. — THE SECOND LETTER OF ALARM. — WEST AND THE
BROTHER OF LOOKING-GLASS. — THE MASSACRES.

THE Snake river comes into the Columbia a few miles
above Wallula. The scenery along the Snake is
unique and striking. The banks are very high and very
broken, with surfaces worn into all kinds of fantastic
forms. The snows, near at hand, the rains, the winds,
and the extraordinary risings, when the freshets from the
supplying mountains come tumbling down into this immense and crooked drain, shape the shores, and mould
into variegated forms the contiguous receding hills. It
takes but little fancy to see, as you look left and right,
sleeping giants, reclining beauties, or figures of the animal creation of all descriptions, each carved, as it were,
from the earth-masses, and lying there, covered with a
grassy spread, in everlasting repose. The scenery is
wild, untamable; in spite of immigration it will be so for
a century. Here and there we find a landing, where emigrants and prospectors are getting off the steamer.

Almota, a year ago, appeared pretty well out of the
world. The son of the famous missionary, Mr. Spalding, had here but his one cottage and his lovely wife.

Now, there are many houses. His own house has become a hotel, and he is boarding at it. Almota has become a large supply depot for a back country, fast settling. This and a few other landings make a slight impression on this large, grand, almost boundless country; but they no more remove from the traveller's mind a feeling of the vastness of the expanse around him than do a few ships at sea, as he paces, day by day, his steamer's deck.

By eight o'clock, June 14, we came into view of the distant village; we say "village," for, however large, as a mining town, Lewiston may have been, after the change of the mining interest to other centres of fortune-hunting and gambling, the city of Lewiston has relapsed into its normal condition of a frontier village. The hills behind this pretty town, and close to it, look like regularly constructed fortifications. The line of the table-land is just above the chimneys, and nearly horizontal; and the white fence of a burying-place on the top, in the distance, adds to the idea of a constructed parapet. Lewiston has a mill, a newspaper, and several well-to-do merchants.

As we neared the landing, the people of the village were seen in waiting. As soon as our boat touched the shore, Colonel Perry, Major Trimble, Lieutenant Bomus, and Charlie Monteith, the brother of the Indian agent, sprang on board, and gave us a welcome. Colonel Perry was still in command at Fort Lapwai. He has a prominent part in this history, and deserves special notice. His rank, not the brevet, is that of Captain of company "F," First United States Cavalry. He is a little over six feet in height, and very erect. He shows a clear Saxon eye, and usually wears a pleasant smile, — pleasant, but with a reserve in it. One hardly can command men, and go into battle often, and still keep an altogether sunshiny face.

Major Trimble is another who has a brevet title. His ground rank is that of Captain of company "C." His post proper was Walla-Walla. It will be remembered that he came with his company to Lapwai, marching overland, a month before. He was first brought up to Lewiston, to be where he could strengthen Fort Lapwai, or the troops near Wallowa, as need might require. But, as our councils with Joseph were in progress, he was sent on to Fort Lapwai, partly for the comfort of his men, and partly that Joseph and his Indians might see, during the conference, a larger force than the ordinary garrison. With Trimble added, we had about one hundred and twenty men, all told, to garrison the post.

Lieutenant Bomus was the post Quartermaster; afterwards to serve in a more important position at Lapwai and Lewiston. Such were the friends who came to meet the steamer at the landing.

"How is Joseph, Colonel?" I asked.

"All right, at last accounts. The Indians are, I think, coming on the reservation without trouble."

Mrs. Perry was here, to go down on the steamer to the Dalles. Young Monteith, the clerk, had come to meet Colonel Watkins, the inspector. He told the same story: "All quiet at last accounts; Indians seem to be acting in good faith; guess they will make no trouble." Mr. Coburn, and a member of the firm of Loewenburg, and several of the other citizens of Lewiston, united in similar testimony: "The Indians are all right." I said at first to Colonel Watkins that I saw no need of my going farther at this time toward Lapwai. Colonel Perry could now attend to all matters, and I would wait at Lewiston for Watkins to finish his inspection at the Lapwai agency, and he could pick me up on his return. Then we would proceed to the Spokane and Colville country, obey our Washington instructions, fulfil our promises to the Columbia River renegades, and settle the vexed questions of the up-country.

But Perry said, " You had better go with me. It will be pleasanter for you to wait at the fort."

The Colonel's kind hospitality was at last accepted, and, leaving Lewiston early in the afternoon, we rode the twelve miles together, behind his spirited and handsome horses.

After the first considerable ascent we sped away for six or seven miles, on a beautiful table-land, over the finest of roads, even and hard, so that we made excellent time. Ahead were the usual rolling hills of the Snake region, to the left the Clearwater, and beyond the almost mountain ridge that hides the new town of Moscow; behind was the Lewis River, or Snake proper, and all that vast succession of indescribable breakages of the earth's surface, with edges smoothed off and softened down; peaceful out-door pictures, too numerous for the pencil, but kaleidoscopic and pleasant to the eye.

Soon appeared the charming Lapwai Valley, always fresh and new in the sunlight. Down the long descent we whirled, then turned to the right, taking a half mile's survey of the tented post, and in a few moments were passing the gate, which had been opened by the quick courtesy of the guard. My former aid-de-camp, Lieutenant Boyle, had been promoted since we last saw him. He was here with his beautiful family, no longer Lieutenant, but Captain Boyle, in command of a Twenty-First Infantry company. He is a sturdy and loyal officer. No war-cloud now; so the meeting at the fort was most pleasant. Here was Trimble's lieutenant, a colonel by brevet, — whose title, given to honor a brave man, served rather to confuse outsiders, — Colonel Parnell, by "ground rank" Lieutenant Parnell. Here, also, was Lieutenant Theller, a generous, brave man, with a warm heart. He had quarters near the Lapwai Creek, where he and his wife were wont to give cheery hospitality to the officers of the Department, as they came and went on duty. You could see him often trying the speed of his stallion on the race-course, just west of the garrison.

On my arrival all seemed as peace-like and happy as home; but toward evening there came a ripple, a slight warning. A courier approached Colonel Perry, and handed him a letter from Mount Idaho. Here is a copy:

MOUNT IDAHO, June 14, 1877.

COLONEL PERRY: — DEAR SIR: Mr, Overman, who resides at or near the head of Rocky Canyon, eight miles from here, came in to-day and brought his friends. They are very much alarmed at the action of the Indians, who are gathered there. He says there are about sixty lodges, composed of the Salmon River Indians, Joseph and his band, with other non-treaties, and that they are insolent, and have but little to say to the whites, and that all their actions indicate trouble from them. Mr. Overman is regarded as a very truthful man, and confidence can be placed in all his statements. Some of the other neighbors have likewise moved over this way, where there are more people.

Yesterday they had a grand parade. About a hundred were

mounted, and well armed, and went through the manœuvres of a fight — were thus engaged for about two hours. They say, openly, that they are going to fight the soldiers when they come to put them on the reservation, and I understand that they expect them up on Friday next. A good many were in town to-day, and were trying to obtain powder and other ammunition. Mr. Scott told me to-day that they offered him two dollars and a half for a can of powder. Up to this time, I think, they have been buying all the arms, &c., that they could get, but do not believe they can make any purchases now. They have a strong position at the head of the canyon, among the rocks, and should they make any resistance could give the troops much trouble. I do not feel any alarm, but thought it well to inform you of what was going on among them. Early this morning one Indian came here, and wanted to know when General How-ard was coming up. As the stage came up last night, they perhaps thought we might know when he would be up. They are evidently on the lookout for the soldiers. I believe it would be well for you to send up, as soon as you can, a sufficient force to handle them without gloves, should they be disposed to resist. Sharp and prompt action will bring them to understand that they must comply with the orders of the government. We trust such action will be taken by you, so as to remove them from the neighborhood, and quiet the feelings of the people.

I write this for your own information, and at the suggestion of many settlers who are living in exposed localities.

Very respectfully yours,

L. P. BROWN.

Colonel Perry read the letter, then handed it to me. He, in substance, remarked: "Mr. Brown, who is a relia-ble man, is not greatly alarmed. I will send out a de-tachment to bring us information; that is best, is it not?"

I said, "Yes, do so by all means."

This town of "Mount Idaho" is situated at the further edge of an extensive camas prairie, near the mountain

spurs that lie between the Salmon and the Clearwater
rivers.   Its distance from Fort Lapwai is sixty miles,
in a direct south-east line.   The "Rocky Canyon," where
Joseph and the non-treaties were behaving so insolently,
the same distance, and nearer the Salmon.   This canyon
debouches into that furious river.   They were, in fact,
near the borders of the reserve, and apparently hesitat-
ing whether to go on peaceably, or stay off and fight.

At dawn, of the fifteenth, the military detachment left
the fort, accompanied by Joe Robosko, the half-breed who
had, as interpreter, just before the last interview at Lapwai, helped in locating Joseph.   The detachment moved,
probably as fast as the horses could carry them, towards
Mount Idaho.   The place where the Indians were encamped was to the right of the Mount Idaho road after
passing Norton's ranch.   It was nineteen miles from
Norton's ranch to Mount Idaho.   Craig's mountain had
to be passed before Norton's.   Our detachment met two
Indians, somewhere near Craig's mountain, and turned
back with them.   These Indians were much excited.
They arrived at Lapwai about noon.   The name of one
was Pu-ton-ah-loo, and the other was an Indian lad of
perhaps fourteen years.   We heard their story, sifting it
through Joe Robosko's interpretation.   It was to the effect
that some three or four Indians had committed a murder
near Slate Creek, where there was a scattered settlement,
some forty miles beyond Mount Idaho.   It was in some
way connected with a citizen, Larry Ott, who had killed
an Indian.   Colonel Watkins had gone directly to the
Indian agency on our arrival, and remained there.   As
was proper, then, taking the messengers with us, Perry

and I started immediately for the agency, and had the Indian authorities examine the young men through Mr. Whitman, the official interpreter. Mr. Whitman confirmed the Larry Ott story. All believed that serious trouble was coming. The interpreter and the Indian agent thought it wise to send at once the acting head chief, and Joseph's father-in-law, who still insisted that Joseph would not fight, and who volunteered to go. This party rode off at full speed. They had not been gone very long when — I think it was half past four — the party came back, running their horses, and bringing with them another communication from Mount Idaho, brought by the brother of Looking-glass, and a half-breed citizen by the name of West.

The time of busy preparation had come. As before a battle, when men are often pale and thoughtful, and little is spoken by one to another, so now, officers and men were mostly silent, but in constant motion. Arms, ammunition, provision, means of transporting, everything was being put in readiness with skilful and steady nerves, without over haste, and without confusion. Those brave, true men! How few people there are to appreciate their constancy in the days of trial! How few to mourn their loss! Because of the injustice our fathers and our rulers have done to the red men, is it not?

CHAPTER XV.

JOSEPH AND HIS MURDERS. — MESSENGERS AND EXCITEMENT
AT FORT LAPWAI. — THE GOOD AND BAD DIVIDE. — COOL-
NESS OF DEPORTMENT DIFFICULT. — A STARTLING LETTER
FROM MOUNT IDAHO. — GENERAL ACCOUNT OF THE KILL-
ING AND WOUNDING. — CALL FOR ARMS. — MURDERS ON THE
SALMON. — SECOND LETTER. — THIS MEANS BUSINESS. — WIL-
KINSON OFF WITH DESPATCHES.

THE brother of Looking-glass, was a stalwart Indian,
with a very intelligent, pleasant countenance. Mr.
West, who came with him, was a man short of stature,
with long, black hair; as I have said, a half-breed. He
spoke English freely, so that we had an account of matters straight from his lips. Other Indians, friendly Nez
Perces, came into Fort Lapwai about the same time,
among them several who belonged to the Catholic mission,
and who had gone out with the non-treaty Indians to participate in their sports of gaming, lance-throwing, running, and horse-racing. As soon as they found that these
malcontents meant war, they broke from them, and rushed
with their small herds toward their homes.

The most intense feeling now existed at the fort and
at the agency. A large group of people were on Colonel
Perry's front porch, — the officers, the ladies of the post,
several principal friendly Indians. The new-comers gathered around the steps of the porch, or were sitting upon
them. The despatch was instantly opened. One of the

essential things in war-like operations is for the commanding officer to preserve his equipoise under all circumstances, but there are times when he is likely to be moved more or less by the contagion of others' excitement. This was such an occasion. So that I made an unusual effort to be perfectly cool and self-possessed, while I read, first to myself, afterwards to the officers, the following startling communications :

MOUNT IDAHO, 7 A. M., Friday, June 15, '77.
COMMANDING OFFICER FORT LAPWAI.

Last night we started a messenger to you, who reached Cottonwood House, where he was wounded and driven back by the Indians. The people of Cottonwood undertook to come here during the night; were interrupted, all wounded or killed. Parties this morning found some of them on the prairie. The wounded will be here shortly, when we will get full particulars. The whites are engaged, about forty of them, in getting the wounded. One thing is certain: we are in the midst of an Indian war. Every family is here, and we will have taken all the precautions we can, but are poorly armed. We want arms and ammunition and help at once. Don't delay a moment. We have a report that some whites were killed yesterday on the Salmon River. No later word from them; fear that the people are all killed, as a party of Indians were seen going that way last night. Send to Lewiston, and hasten up. You cannot imagine people in a worse condition than they are here. Mr. West has volunteered to go to Lapwai; rely on his statements.

Yours truly,   L. P. BROWN.

The next letter was received at the same time. It speaks for itself:

MOUNT IDAHO, 8 A. M., June 15, '77.
COMMANDING OFFICER FORT LAPWAI.

I have just sent a despatch by Mr. West, half-breed, Since that was written the wounded have come in, — Mr. Day mortally; Mrs. Norton with both legs broken; Moore shot through the hip; Norton killed and left in the road, six miles from here. Teams were at-

tacked on the road and abandoned. The Indians have possession
of the prairie, and threaten Mount Idaho. All the people are here,
and we will do the best we can. Lose no time in getting up with a
force. Stop the stage and all "through travellers." Give us relief,
and arms and ammunition. Chapman has got this Indian [the messenger, Looking-glass' brother], hoping he may get through. I
fear the people on Salmon have all been killed, as a party was seen
going that way last night. We had a report last night that seven
whites had been killed on Salmon. Notify the people of Lewiston.
Hurry up; hurry ! Rely on this Indian's statement; I have known
him for a long time; he is with us.　　　　　　　L. P. BROWN,

P. S. — Send a despatch to town for the express not to start up,
unless heavily escorted. Give the bearer a fresh horse, and send
him back.　　　　　　　　　　　　　　　　　　　CHAPMAN.

" Well, colonel, this means business ! "

" Yes, sir."

" Are your men in readiness ? "

" Everything but some transportation that must come
from Lewiston."

" Captain Wilkinson, get ready to go to Walla-Walla
at once."

Lieutenant Bomus had his buggy at the door of his
quarters in less than ten minutes.

During the few minutes of preparation I examined Mr.
West, who corroborated all the statements of the letters,
and gave the graphic accounts of an eye-witness of the
murders and outrages which had been committed. Then
immediately the messages and letters from Messrs. Brown
and Chapman were sent to the Indian agency for the information of Colonel Watkins, the inspector, and Mr.
Monteith, the agent; and the following letter was sent
by the half-breed to Mount Idaho:

FORT LAPWAI, I. T., June 15, '77, 5 P. M.
MR. BROWN.

DEAR SIR: Your two despatches are received. I have sent forward two companies of cavalry to your relief. They leave to-night. Other help will be *en route* as soon as it can be brought up. I am glad you are so cool and ready. Cheer the people. Help shall be prompt and complete. Lewiston has been notified.

Yours truly, O. O. HOWARD.

Wilkinson and Bomus are ready to start. Wilkinson's memoranda :

I. Order through Colonel Grover, Captain Whipple's two cavalry companies from Wallowa to Lapwai by shortest route. (They march.)

II. Send Infantry from Walla-Walla and vicinity to Lapwai. (By steamer.)

III. Forward despatch to Colonel Wood at Portland, for more troops and three months' supplies, to be sent to Lewiston at once.

IV. Send despatches of information to General McDowell, San Francisco, and request twenty-five scouts.

All the details of these memoranda were set in order and executed. To do it, Captain Wilkinson rode with Lieutenant Bomus to Lewiston, and then got a special conveyance from the stage line, and kept up the most rapid riding, making his one hundred and ten miles to Walla-Walla by eight A. M. of the next morning. There he came upon a line of the telegraph, and communicated accordingly. As the information then appeared it was put into the despatch to Division Head-quarters : "Indians began by murdering a white man in revenge for a murder of his, killing three others at the same time." [This statement will have to be modified now, though there

7

seems still to be some connection between the first murder
and the death of the Indian previously killed by a white
man in the Salmon River country.] " Since then they
have begun war upon the people near Mount Idaho.
Captain Perry started with two companies of cavalry for
them. Other troops are being brought forward as fast
as possible. Give me authority for twenty-five scouts.
Think we will make short work of it."

The work did not appear short to the impatient country. Yet, as the history shows, a month's battling on
fields wide apart, and three months' pursuing, brought
us through.

Lieutenant Theller had been added to Perry's command, — four resolute young men, including Trimble and
Parnell. They were all married. Mrs. Perry had just
gone down the river, and was sent by her husband's
despatch to Mrs. Howard, at Portland. Mrs. Trimble
and her children, and Mrs. Parnell, were at Walla-Walla ;
only Mrs. Theller was there to suffer the added trial of
parting with her beloved husband for battle, or it might
be for death. Perry and I stood there in the doorway
of his hospitable home, and looked into each other's faces.
How tall, strong, and confident he appeared. He set
out with one hundred cavalry men less ten, — too few for
the work ahead, but the best we could do. We cannot
wait even a few days for reinforcements, for if we do the
murders will continue. " Hurry ! hurry !" is the citizens'
watchword and earnest call. We could not send more
from Fort Lapwai, for no smaller force than the twenty
men of Captain Boyle would answer for defence of goods
and home and agency and Lewiston. The best we could
do, these ninety men !

" Good-by, general ! "

" Good-by, colonel. You must not get whipped."

" There is no danger of that, sir." And, indeed, there did not then seem to be much danger of such a catastrophe, with trained and disciplined troops against these Indians as yet unused to war with white men.

When the husband buckles on his armor and sets out for war, it is the wife left behind who requires patience and fortitude. She busies her fingers to keep the blood in motion, and keep it from stopping at the heart at every ring of the door-bell. To her the ruthless newspapers are a terror, a cruelty.

It was my duty, at this time, to remain and wait for the soldiers to come together from distant places, and carry them forward should they be needed at the front, and watch against other firebrands of dissatisfaction and outbreak among the thousands of savages apparently at peace. To remain behind and wait — it awakened in my heart unusual sympathy for other watchers, nay, a painful feeling hard to bear.

So, to busy myself, find relief for anxiety, I read and wrote, studied maps, counted days for the marches, paced my room, and watched every flying rumor.

Stoicism is properly condemned. Imperturbability is a suspicious accomplishment, akin to deadness of love. Still the exhibition of these qualities is very properly demanded of the soldier. They are not so hard of acquirement in danger ; but to remain at home and wait, amid the pulsations of extreme anxiety — who but woman is equal to the task?

CHAPTER XVI.

JOSEPH AND HIS LODGES. — A CHAPTER OF HORRORS. — LARRY
OTT. — SAMUEL BENEDICT. — AN INDIAN KILLED. — HARRY
MASON. — TWO INDIANS WHIPPED. — MANUEL'S RANCH. —
THE INDIANS' CAMP. — MR. JARRETT'S ALARM AND ESCAPE.
— RICHARD DIVINE KILLED, JUNE 13. — HENRY ELFERS AND
OTHERS KILLED, JUNE 14. — AUGUST BACON AND OTHERS
KILLED, THE 15TH. — MRS. MANUEL KILLED. — CROOKS' IN-
TERVIEW WITH MURDERERS. — THE NORTON FAMILY AND
FRIENDS KILLED OR WOUNDED. — CRUSHING A CHILD.

L IKE an arrow shot into the air, that may return and
wound you; like a plunge to save life, which may
cost you your own, such was the venture in the quick
movement of Perry's command toward the hostile camp.

A fine body of men they appeared as they rode away
that night. A few horses plunged, and reared, and
"bucked," but the men soon mounted, and had them
under control. They rode off into the darkness, toward
the Camas Prairie and Mount Idaho. While they toil
along the muddy, hilly road, for the seventy or eighty
miles before reaching their enemy, let us look through
subsequent glasses and see if we cannot make out, and set
down, what had really been happening in that Salmon
River country, and on the extensive and fertile Camas
Prairie.

Until very recently the testimony had been uniform
that "Young Joseph" had nothing to do with the perpetration of the following chapter of horrors. Of late it is

asserted by Arthur Chapman, the interpreter, that other Indians, who were engaged with him in the war, accuse Joseph himself of killing Mrs. Manuel, with his own hand, after others had left her wounded, and entreating for her life. I believe that this charge is not true. His wife was ill, and separated from the main camp. Joseph, it is proved by our own scouts, remained there with her, protesting, till he believed it too late, — till he felt, like many who joined the great southern rebellion, — that in a war already begun he must identify himself with his own people.

The first day of March, 1875, Larry Ott, who lived on the south side of Salmon River, had a quarrel with an Indian, which terminated in the death of the latter. The grand jury had the killing of this Indian by Ott under consideration, and being unable to find sufficient evidence of guilt, brought in no bill. Ott was not killed by the Indians, as reported, but is still alive.

In August, 1875, Samuel Benedict, who then resided with his family at the mouth of White-Bird Creek, killed an Indian. The circumstances under which the killing took place were as follows: Late at night, several intoxicated Indians came to Benedict's house, and demanded admission; and, upon being refused, commenced breaking the doors and windows of his residence. The wife of Benedict and her two children made their escape under cover of the darkness, through a back window, waded White-Bird Creek, and found shelter in a neighboring house.

Benedict fired, and killed one Indian and wounded

one or two more. He is accused of having sold liquor to the Indians.

Another citizen, Harry Mason, whipped two Indians early in the spring. A council of arbitration met to decide who was in fault, Mr. Elfers, a white man, (I believe chosen by the aggrieved Indians,) being a member of that council. The decision of the council, as one might have predicted, was unfavorable to the Indians.

On or about the 1st of June, 1877, the Salmon River Indians collected on White-Bird Creek, near Manuel's ranch. Soon after, Joseph and his band appeared on Camas Prairie, ten miles west of, and nearer Mount Idaho. The white settlers, who had never seen anything like an armed hostility on the part of the Indians, except in a few individual cases, were not at first alarmed, but supposed that the Indians were collecting preparatory to going on the reservation. About the 10th of June, however, the Indians made such warlike demonstrations as to seriously alarm Mr. Jarrett, and others, who lived near the Indian camp, and they took their families to Mount Idaho for safety.

The outbreak commenced on the afternoon of June 13, by a small party of Indians killing Richard Divine, an old man, who lived alone on Salmon River, eight miles above Slate Creek. The next victims were Henry Elfers, Robert Bland, and Henry Beckroge, the killing of whom took place between the hours of six and seven o'clock the following morning, June 14. These Indians then mounted the horses of the murdered men, and rode off down the Salmon River. They soon met Samuel Benedict, who was out seeking for his cattle, shot and wounded him.

He managed to get on his horse, and succeeded in reaching his home, where he was followed and put to death on the afternoon of the same day.

It is stated by the Indians that but three were engaged in the perpetration of the above murders, to wit, the killing of Divine, Elfers, Bland, Beckroge, and the wounding of Benedict, two of whom were Salmon River Indians, named Mox-Mox and Wall-Tits. The other was a strange Indian, said to belong to Joseph's band.

After the three Indians had wounded Benedict, they left, and came up to Camas Prairie, where Joseph's main band was encamped. The three Indians referred to were here joined by about seventeen more, and immediately returned to Salmon River. . . . On their way they shot and wounded J. J. Manuel and his little girl, killed James Baker, and upon arriving at Benedict's place, they discovered Benedict in the attempt to escape across White-Bird Creek. They fired at him, and he fell dead. At the same time they killed a Frenchman named August Bacon. On the following day, June 15, they killed Mrs. Manuel, William Osborne, and Harry Mason. This is the time when Joseph is accused of participating.

June 14th, Mr. J. M. Crooks, of Grangeville, (four miles from Mount Idaho,) rode to Joseph's camp at Rocky Canyon, and asked the Indians whether they intended to fight. They told Crooks that they would not fight the settlers provided they would not help the soldiers. . . . The alarm about this time became general, and families came rushing into the village of Mount Idaho, from all directions.

On the evening of the 14th, Arthur Chapman, who

lived on the Camas Prairie, east of the Lewiston road, came to Mount Idaho, his horse covered with foam from hard riding, and reported that an Indian boy had come to his place and informed him that the Salmon River Indians had commenced killing the settlers. Lew Day immediately volunteered to go to Fort Lapwai for military aid. He had proceeded on his way about twenty-five miles, when he was fired upon by the Indians and slightly wounded. Seeing the impossibility of reaching Lapwai, he started back, and when he came to the Cottonwood House (proprietor, B. B. Norton) he found there Mrs. Norton, Hill Norton, Miss Bowers, Joseph Moore, and John Chamberlain with his wife and two children. Day informed these people of the threatening danger, and caused them to make immediate preparations for flight to Mount Idaho, distant eighteen miles.

They set out in a wagon, with two on horseback, about ten o'clock at night, and had gone on their way to Mount Idaho about ten miles, when the Indians came up in their rear, and began firing at them. Soon Norton and Moore, the horse riders, were badly wounded, and compelled to abandon their horses and get into the wagon. Their team-horses, however, were soon shot down, and the wagon came to a halt. Miss Bowers and little Hill Norton got out of the wagon, and made their escape unharmed. Mr. Chamberlain, his wife and two children attempted to escape in the darkness, but had gone only a short distance when they were discovered by the Indians. Chamberlain and his little boy were killed. The boy was murdered, according to the mother's statement, by having his head placed beneath the knees of a powerful Indian, and so

crushed to death. The other child was torn from its
mother, and dreadfully wounded, a piece of its tongue
being cut out, and a knife run quite through its neck.
Mrs. Chamberlain was repeatedly outraged by the Indians, and received severe injuries. The remainder of
the party sought shelter behind the dead horses. Here
Norton was struck by a ball, and killed. Moore was shot
through the hips, Day through the shoulder and leg, and
Mrs. Norton through both legs. The Indians kept up a
desultory firing until about daylight, when they left.
Miss Bowers, in the mean time, having reached Mount
Idaho, the alarm was given, and several men started for
the scene of the massacre. The wounded men were
brought to town. Day died the following afternoon.
Moore lingered for about six weeks and died. Mrs.
Norton, Mrs. Chamberlain, and her child, in time recovered.

After the first murders had been committed, while Joseph was absent, having a separate lodge, the murderers
rode into his camp, followed by White Bird and several
of his men. One of them made a wild, characteristic
speech, as he galloped around among the tepees: "Look
here; see this fine horse! Behold this rifle, this saddle,
and all these good clothes! Why do you remain here
talking and talking? The war has begun! I am mad!
I have killed the enemies! Up! Get your horses and
come on; there is plenty of everything, if you only
work for it!"

White Bird took fire, and rode around through the camp,
and cried for war. "All must join now. The white
men will never believe you if you ask for peace. There

is blood — You'll be punished if you wait. Everybody get ready to fight."

After a few hours' delay Joseph is said to have joined the malcontents. The peace men escaped, as we have before seen.

When the purpose of war had become general, Indians from all the bands of non-treaties except that of Looking-glass proceeded to commit the last terrible massacres, which we have related. Then, doubtless fearing the swift approach of the troops, Joseph's lodges at Rocky Canyon were taken down, and he concentrated his whole force ten miles further away from Mount Idaho, in the White-Bird Valley, where stirring events were soon to transpire.

CHAPTER XVII.

JOSEPH AND HIS ENEMIES. — THE DISTANCE TO SCENE OF MUR-
DERS. — THE CAVALRYMEN ON THE WAY. — THE PACK-MULE
TRAIN. — NIGHT MARCH. — EXCITED CITIZENS OF GRANGE-
VILLE AND MOUNT IDAHO. — VOLUNTEER AID. — WHITE-BIRD
CANYON. — SECOND NIGHT MARCH. — THE SALMON DESCRIBED.
— ALSO THE SCENE OF CONFLICT. — MEET MRS. BENE-
DICT AS THE TROOPS DESCEND THE CANYON. — A SAD
PICTURE.

THE distance from Fort Lapwai to Mount Idaho, by the
road usually travelled with wagons, is sixty-two
miles. The people near Fort Lapwai said it was twenty-
four miles to the " Old Mill," thence nineteen miles to Mr.
Norton's ranch, thence nineteen miles to Mount Idaho.
Grangeville is three or four miles nearer, so that there
are fifty-eight miles from Fort Lapwai to Grangeville, and
sixty-two to Mount Idaho. The road is quite direct, and
running south-easterly.

Let us look now for a few minutes at our little squadron of cavalry. They are toiling steadily along this road.
The column appears long. That irregular moving mass
behind is the mule train. The mules, with ammunition
and supplies of every kind bound to their "aparejos," —
a large, soft, packing-saddle, — run in and out of the
column, get now a little ahead, and now behind, feeding
by the roadside when it is light enough to see, — a restless set of creatures, yet always obedient to the sound of
the bell attached to the neck of the trained white mare,

who, herself, never seems to forget her place or duty. Horses unaccustomed, as these have been, for some months at least, to journeys, soon fret themselves, and many of the stanchest and smartest of Perry's, that were the most restive at the start, soon became weary. Add to the ordinary difficulties a hilly, or mountainous, road, as this is, and plenty of wet, miry places, that cannot be avoided, and the cavalry will even sooner show signs of flagging.

Packers, with their trains, always find the first day out a difficult one. So was it with our column. But it toiled bravely on all night, over Craig's Mountain and across Lawyer's Canyon, and succeeded in reaching poor Norton's now deserted ranch by ten o'clock of the 16th of June. It was near night when the next fifteen miles had been accomplished.

Here the excited citizens gathered around the welcome soldiers. The Indian horrors which we have tried to describe had to be recited, and great excitement prevailed.

Frontier men are very apt to undervalue the fighting ability of Indians. In times gone by, when we have been better mounted and better armed than the Indians, and as well trained as they, we have beaten them in our conflicts, whether we have been grouped together as soldiers or citizens.

"Oh, colonel, you can easily whip the scoundrels!" "They are cowardly wretches. We could destroy them if we only had the arms!" "You will have to hurry up, or you will not be able to overtake them!" "We will go and help you, as many as have arms and horses!"

Such were some of the expressions that saluted the

colonel's ears as he halted at Grangeville, and tried to take cognizance of the situation.

Grangeville is a small settlement; consisted of a mill and two or three dwelling-houses. After a talk with some citizens and volunteers the commanding officer gave orders for a night march to White-Bird Canyon, distant about sixteen miles.

A few citizens, perhaps ten, went with them as auxiliaries, to show the way and to help shoot the foe, as yet much despised, much underrated.

They came to the top of the canyon about an hour before the dawn. Here Colonel Perry called a halt till dawn. Our men had been one day and two nights now without their accustomed rest, and yet they were on the very verge of a battle, as we shall soon see.

I have before tried to give some idea of the Snake River; also the Salmon, one of its tributaries. From the entrance of White-Bird Creek to the mouth of the Salmon the distance is perhaps forty miles by the windings of its course. Colonel Perry, in the dim dawn, could not detect the valleys. His eye beheld nothing beyond the river but a succession of steeps, with pointed or rounded tops. These were covered with verdure, and behind them rose snowy peaks, which were indistinctly mingled with the clouds.

The Salmon is a torrent with mountain shores. Its feeders, the creeks coming in on the right and left, are short, and channel out the mountain masses transversely. White-Bird is no exception. The top or head of the Canyon is where the scooping begins. A horse-trail, rather broad for a trail, but narrow for a road, leads from this "top" down, down, by a long descent, to the rolling country that forms the bottom of the canyon. When the light has come how plain it all looks! A slight smoke from the Indian camp, not more than four miles off, as it seems, down in the smooth-looking bottom. The sides of the canyon are steep, but they have numerous crosscutting ravines, by which you could ride up if you should be repulsed!

When daylight came a few individuals were seen stirring at the Indian camp. As they came slowly out of their lodges, each wrapped his blanket round his neck at one end, and allowed it to stretch to his feet, so as to get all the protection against the dew and chill of the morning. Some moved to the war-horses, which were picketed near at hand, to change them to better grass. Some sought the herd to relieve the night watchmen, and others, in order to scan the horizon, which everywhere appeared above them, went quietly to the tall pile of rocks that flanked their encampment, and lay down beside the sharp crags.

Among the latter observers were Joseph and his tall brother. Suddenly, as the sunlight, descending steadily from the highest peaks, where it first appeared, began to tinge with warmth and beauty the broad edges and sloping surfaces of the west side of the canyon, the brother's quick eye caught sight of a stationary, motionless group of horsemen.

They looked as if they were painted on the sky, just where the hills touched it. "Hu-hugh! Horses!" says Ollicut. Joseph gazes steadily at the group.

"Get the white man's glass. Tell White Bird. They are Indians up there ; Jonah's men ! "

Ollicut ran down the steep with long, springy strides, sat down a moment by White Bird's blanket, wakened him without disturbance, and told him that the young war-chief wanted him at the rocks. Then he went to his lodge and returned quickly, fetching the field-glass to his brother. The purchase of this glass at some village or trading-post, just before this outbreak, perhaps indicated an intention to begin the war, but perhaps not. These glasses ena-ble drovers and rangers to distinguish their herds miles away. Old Blackfoot, one of White Bird's men, had exten-sive herds of wild cattle, and he was quick to fall in with any improvements in their care and control. He doubt-less imitated the Chapmans, the Crooks, and others who herded cattle on his ranges. They were never without the glass, and why should he be?

The three Indians now crouched, silent and motionless, among the rocks. Joseph used the glass, passed it to White Bird, and said :

" Indians there ! " pointing to a bluff to the west.

White Bird took the glass, and quickly calls out :

" Mox-Mox is coming."

Two horsemen were running their horses from a low height a mile distant. They constituted the outpost. Mox-Mox and another Indian had watched together. Now, as the glass was pointed toward the northwest, White Bird and Ollicut exclaimed, at the same moment,

" Bostons ! Bostons ! "

Colonel Perry had finished his brief rest, and was lead-ing his little squadron, in close order, over the crest of

the first slope of the canyon, along the trail, while his
friendly scouts of Jonah and Reuben were watching on the
distant and commanding hill further toward the Salmon
River, where the quick, piercing eye of Joseph had discovered them.   Mox-Mox, having dismounted and
ascended the crags, confirmed the tidings already revealed through the field-glass.

Joseph then gave his instructions for the first battle.
Ollicut was excited, though he had been fierce for war.
The number of Perry's command now appeared to him
great as they filed over the hill and down into the shadows of the ravine.   He said: " Cross over the Salmon !
It is big and swift; they cannot catch us ! "   White Bird
gave a grunt of satisfaction at this safe proposal, but
Joseph said, " No; their horses are new; they will not
wait.   They will scatter at the sound of the firearms.
Get the people all ready, — women, children, and the
stuff over there ! " pointing down the White-Bird Creek.
" White Bird, take your men and turn the Bostons when
they get to this ridge, turn around that upper butte.   I
will get over there behind the rocks and wait.   Let every
Indian be ready to mount.   Mox-Mox and the women
must take care of the herd, and give us horses, if ours are
shot down.   Ollicut must stay with me."

Soon there was busy preparation throughout the village.   The lodges were mostly taken down; the pack-
animals loaded.   The three main groupings were formed
as Joseph had directed.   At first there was heard, in all
directions, the noise of hallooing and loud talking by women and men.   Children screamed as they partook of the
common excitement, but it was not long before every-

thing of this kind was hushed. With arms and ammunition in readiness, with ponies standing patiently behind their lariats, which were not fastened, but simply thrown on the ground, the Indians remained quietly waiting the attack of the soldiers.

Joseph had managed to conceal in the hollows, and behind the buttes and rocks, which formed for him a natural defensive line, every sign of his force, particularly from any one coming along the approaches to his front. Were it not for the telltale smoke arising from the late Indian village his arrangement would have been a very complete ambush.

Let us return to our weary soldiers at the head of the canyon.

With daylight Perry's command began the descent. Before reaching the more level ground a white woman, Mrs. Benedict, made her appearance from the slight brushwood cover by the roadside, holding a baby in her arms, and having a little girl about six years old by her side. The Indians, some of them, had released her from her horrid confinement, and she was hiding against recapture by the more brutal. She was burdened with her little ones, and still more heavily with grief at her husband's death, shivering with exposure, hastening, as best she could, to a settlement, the nearest being at least twelve miles distant.

8

CHAPTER XVIII.

JOSEPH. — HIS WARRIORS AND HIS ENEMIES. — PERRY'S FIGHT
AT WHITE-BIRD CANYON. — THELLER IN ADVANCE. — HEADS
APPEARING. — DEADLY SHOTS. — THE INDIANS FLANKING. —
BATTLE JOINED. — ALL GOING WELL AT FIRST. — HORSES
FRIGHTENED. — BUGLER SILENCED BY DEATH. — RETREAT.
— FIRST RALLY. — RETREAT AGAIN. — MUCH CONFUSION. —
THE ROUT. — THELLER'S DEATH. — BEARING TIDINGS.

THE little column continued its march till it neared
two small knolls, — the people here call them
"buttes"; the Indian camp beyond these buttes was
thought to be only a portion of the Indians who were on
the war-path, for the talk of the citizens at Grangeville
was, "They are getting away." "They are crossing the
Salmon several miles further on."

As the cavalry approached the buttes, this was the
order of the march, all with carbines loaded:

A hundred yards before the main force, with a little
squad of eight brave men, was Lieutenant Theller.
Colonel Perry with the citizens, followed by his own
company, was next; and then Trimble, some forty or
fifty yards' interval being left between the companies.
All were marching in column of fours, — four men abreast.
Suddenly the Indians appeared "in skirmish order,"
stretched out in an irregular line. Their heads popped
up from behind stones, from gulches, ravines, and other
cover. Those on foot took deliberate and deadly aim.

Between the left butte and the creek an interval of at least two hundred yards appeared to be full of them — mounted, and galloping well to the left. It was White Bird, obeying Joseph's orders, with his flanking party. Indians always try to effect a flank movement.

While Theller began the work, — to meet skirmish by skirmish, — the citizens ran to the left butte, covered themselves by the inequalities of the ground, and prepared to shoot all Indians that they could see, the leading company of cavalry coming into line near them, taking position to their right. Trimble's company was ordered forward into line, and it was done quickly, without closing the interval. Away the men went to the next butte, and broken, stony ground; and Trimble, looking after his exposed right flank, (for there were, it seems, Indians enough to get beyond even this,) went himself to the extreme point where at dawn Joseph was crouching and watching. The disposition appeared good under the circumstances. These cavalrymen will have to stay here now, and fight it out as the Seventeenth Army Corps did when its line was enveloped in the same way at Atlanta, fighting on one side of the cover, and then jumping over and fighting from the other side. For, with the cavalry under fire, and spread out in a line, it was too late to plunge ahead, and go through the Indians' line and camp towards the Salmon River.

Perry's men were firing, some of them over the horses' heads. The air was full of noise and smoke. Some of these horses proved wild and unmanageable at this time. Just here, while Parnell watched the space between the companies, Indians began to press up to a still higher point, to the right of our whole line. They were ascending the same kind of ledgy, rocky knoll as that now occupied. First a sergeant and six men went thither against them, and fired rapidly. Those Indian flankers were driven back. All this moving, so thrilling and exciting, had not taken ten minutes. Perry and Trimble seemed to be together for the moment. Their left flank was now suddenly turned. Two of the citizens at the butte were wounded; then their companions gave way and began to fly. Some of the cavalrymen, too, had already taken the trail to the rear, at a run. Companies were badly broken. Colonel Perry endeavored to close all in together, for mutual protection. The bugler, who sounds the calls, and makes orders plain amid noise and confusion, was already dead, being the first man shot.

"Can't go on to Salmon River, Trimble."

"No, that's annihilation." Retreat was ordered, and was commenced in pretty good shape. Whether Chapman, of the volunteers, or Trimble, or both, suggested it, is not certain; but the word was, "Good position yonder; high ground among the rocks can be held."

Perry said, "We might try that."

The little column, now moving rearward, turned to the left, and sought this position. But the Indians, too quick for them, were around them, and more to spare! The men were panic-stricken, and began to cry out, —

"Can't stay here! Get back from here! Take ridge farther back!" Horses were galloping without riders. Lieutenant Theller's horse was gone; probably a panic had seized the soldier holder. Trimble and Parnell helped him to mount another, bareback. Probably the

balking, plunging, kicking animal had been freeing himself from his saddle in a furious way, thus adding to the
terror and confusion, if anything could.

All soon became broken, and the rout was general, — a
kind of Bull Run, on a small scale.

Perry and Parnell again found each other; bearing
over a little to the left, Trimble was soon separated, and
held by the right bluffs. There was rallying, and short
resistance, from knoll to knoll, up the creek. Indians
pressed along faster and faster, gaining the well-known
trails up the flanks of the White-Bird Canyon; while the
American horses which our men rode were every now and
then put to their speed, to prevent a complete cutting off.

A tough struggle for life was made, just as the soldiers
came to the steep and narrow trail. Here, it appeared
by the location of the bodies of the men who had been
killed, one after another, and by the place where Lieutenant Theller finally fell, that the Indians had succeeded
in heading them all on the trail, and that the most who
were not already shot down, dead, or left to die, had
deviated into the first available ravine to the left. At
any rate, here, where they so thickly lay, must have been
the last resolute stand made by our men in the valley of
the White-Bird. Defeated, losing their brave officer,
Lieutenant Theller, the men who were still alive rushed
to the top of the canyon ridge, as fast as their horses
could carry them. Here Perry and Parnell succeeded
in getting better order of movement with the remnant.
Perry, in an informal letter, written the evening of the
battle, said, "It was only by the most strenuous efforts
of Colonel Parnell and myself in organizing a party of

twenty-two men that a single officer or man reached camp.

"The Indians fought us to within four miles of Mount Idaho, and only gave it up on seeing we would not be driven any farther, except at our own gait."

The first account of our loss, brought me at Fort Lapwai, showed over one-third of the one hundred souls that entered into this Indian battle killed and missing.

Only two or three of the missing ever came in. The closing words of Perry's note were, "Please break the news of her husband's death to Mrs. Theller." It is easier to go into a battle than to do this. I endeavored to control myself, and break the tidings gently. But Mrs. Theller read them in my face before I could speak, and words had no place.   "Oh, my husband!"

Surely, peace is better than war; is it not?

Joseph, Ollicut, and White Bird, each followed by squads of Indians, pushed their pursuit to within sight of Grangeville. Then they drew off, and slowly rode back to White-Bird Canyon. It was a wild and jubilant set of lodges that day! Clothing, arms, and ammunition were now abundant.

The first thrill of victory is animating, is sweet to those who conquer; but the humiliating, chastening defeat is ever hard for men to bear.

CHAPTER XIX.

THE WAITING. — THE PREPARATION. — HOW TROOPS ASSEM-
BLED FROM ALL QUARTERS. — THE FRIGHT AT KAMIAH. —
THE STORY OF JONAH'S WIFE. — PERRY'S LETTER.

FOR a time we leave the victorious Indians at White-
Bird, and our discomfited squadron at Grangeville,
where Colonel Perry collected, reorganized, and put in as
good condition as possible, for defence, his scattered fragments, and return to Lapwai.

It is usually troublesome to turn back and begin a journey anew. It is doubly so at this juncture. How much
more satisfactory if we could say that Perry and his comrades had finished their task, and afterwards returned with
victory perched upon their banners! And what joy to us,
if the brave Lieutenant Theller, and thirty other gallant
soldiers, who went out on Friday full of hope and life,
could ever have come back! Still, such is the fortune of
war. The hour of trial must precede the hour of triumph.

It will be remembered that I remained at the Lapwai
garrison.

As the cavalry companies departed in one direction, Captain Wilkinson, with despatches for Fort
Walla-Walla, and for the telegraph, had hastened in
another.

Early on Saturday morning, as we said, he entered

that garrison, having accomplished the journey during the night, and startled everybody with his nervous messages. Then off sped a courier across the Blue Ridge to Whipple's camp at Indian Valley, near the famous Wallowa. Thus the message was carried a hundred miles more before Sunday was over.

Colonel Whipple, ready at call, left a small squad to take charge of all luggage, except the bare necessaries, and set his column of two cavalry companies in motion. " Slow," say the excited citizens, and " Slow," say those furious scouts, who kill a horse every two days. May be it is slow, but when I said to the waiting people at Lapwai, " Colonel Whipple will be here by Thursday night," even an experienced officer thought not, because the horses were fresh and not hardened to marching. My faith was pinned to the man in charge. Dark-browed, strongly built, apparently forty years of age, Colonel Whipple (called colonel from volunteer remembrance, more properly the Captain of Company " L," First Cavalry), was a reliable man. Neither reluctance nor delay was in the man, nor in the three or four officers associated with him. Not hurry; a kind of breathless double-quick for an hour, with a lagging slowness the next hour, — no, not that ! But that steady, care-taking, walking of men as well as horses, tramp, tramp, from before the dawn till evening twilight, day after day. The heart says, " Faster, faster, Colonel," but the judgment remembers the proverb, " Too much haste makes waste ! " So that the steady pull is kept up. The few soldiers that are at Fort Walla-Walla, those near Wallula, where the up-river boat touches, the available men from forts

Vancouver, Stevens, and Canby, Townsend, Klamath, and Harney, are also in motion; some towards Boise and the Weiser River northward, but the most towards me, at Lapwai. How quickly the mind fixes upon points that must be occupied! Soon Lapwai, or Lewiston, draws like a loadstone; not only these, but the artillerymen, on the wing from Alaska, hurried on to the field without stopping to breathe; and further help from California and Arizona; and Boise draws its accessions from all the forts within the range of three hundred miles, yes, even from the harbor of San Francisco. So, afterwards, Lewiston calls loud enough to be heard in Georgia, and the Companies of the Second Infantry come flocking together, and take the railway flight thitherward. But during all this excitement and movement a very few of us were only patiently waiting at Lapwai, and estimating the time before relief could come.

You can only get suggestive glimpses of the past; for the fullest memory only yields detached pictures, leaving the blanks between them for the imagination or other memories to fill.

The diary for June 16 says: "A request from Colonel Watkins for relief for Kamiah."

The immediate answer from me is a pictorial glimpse, not flattering, but truthful. "Despatches just received and noted. Captain Perry actually has with him less than man for man. I depend on the superior skill and the experience of the soldiers to overcome the odds. Wilkinson reached Walla-Walla at ten in the morning, to-day (actually a couple of hours sooner). Steamer lies at Wallula, and can return to Lewiston as well as not. I shall expect troops to-morrow morning, and will send relief to Kamiah as soon as it will do to detach; but think the best possible relief is the vigorous push against the forces of Joseph at Cottonwood. We shall probably hear from Perry soon."

Second diary item for the 16th: "10 p. m. Jonah's wife (Jonah having gone with the cavalry to the front) came to the garrison with the woman who ran in from the hostiles; believes Jonah killed, and all the troops."

This night was a peculiar one, and remarkable, as it gave a view almost accurate of the general and particular features of the subsequent engagement and disaster at White-Bird Canyon; an account given some sixty miles from the scene, and, at least, six hours before they happened.

I was awakened by loud talking in front of the porch at Lapwai, and went out. Jonah's wife, a large-sized Indian woman, sat upon her horse. She was accompanied by another woman, the one that, as I understood, had just come from the hostiles. One of the half-breeds interpreted. She spoke so emphatically and so excitedly that she awakened everybody, and she declared:

" The Indians had fixed a trap. All our troops had run straight into it. They (the hostiles) had come up on every side, and killed all the soldiers and all the scouts, including the friendly Indians."

The Indian scouts were for the most part unarmed, and fortunately were not taken down into the dangerous part of White-Bird Canyon. The next morning, while Colonel Perry and our soldiers were actually fighting at the front, as the Indian woman had predicted, I was writing to Perry the letter, of which I give a few extracts:

"DEAR COLONEL: We have been intensely anxious here; for we had not heard a word, till the arrival of this messenger [the first one who had come, announcing their safe trip to Grangeville]. Rumors have reached us that you were ambuscaded, and all killed. Jonah's wife came at ten o'clock last night in great distress, with a story that a woman brought from the hostiles. The Kamiah people send messenger in great terror. Reports put hostiles, men, women, and children, at or near the mouth of Cottonwood Creek, — Looking-glass' camp. Take it for what it is worth. As the steamer can come up from Wallula as well as not I expect re-enforcements of two companies, perhaps three, to-day or early to-morrow. Will forward supplies just as soon as troops arrive. . . . . Be careful about THOSE TRAPS. Of course you will. They, the hostiles, have placed several for you, as this Indian woman explains them to Jonah's wife."

In these times of actualities, when it is difficult to make even Christians believe in special providences, we do not attribute prevision to the two Indian women.

What, however, is made plain, is this, that the Indians, or rather a part of them, had a clearly defined plan.

The Indians were to begin the war by a series of outrages, in the usual style.

This would force the troops from Lapwai before they could be reinforced from distant points. It would also unite the malcontents themselves. The grouping of Indian lodges suited this view; viz., to separate for the warfare upon the scattered inhabitants, then to assemble near the mouth of White-Bird, in order to meet the soldiers of Lapwai.

The ambuscade, which the women described in detail, was made, as we have now seen, beyond the well-placed buttes, the rocky heights, and the favoring ravines of the White-Bird Creek. The soldiers and citizens came; the Indians sprang their trap. Defeat and death on the one hand, victory and savage joy on the other, were the results.

CHAPTER XX.

JOSEPH'S FIRST BATTLE, AND ITS EFFECTS.—EXCITEMENT AT
LAPWAI AND AT KAMIAH.—JAMES LAWYER AND THE
FRIENDLY INDIAN ESCORT.—MISS MACBETH'S STORY.—
CHRISTIAN INDIANS REMAIN TRUE THROUGHOUT.—FEVER-
LIKE PANIC AT LAPWAI.—BUSY PREPARATIONS.—GENER-
OSITY OF FRIENDLY INDIANS.—GENERAL HOWARD'S MARCH.
—THE FIRST DAY.

AT the beginning of an Indian war, while waiting for
re-enforcements, one has little idea of the fearful excitement which prevails at a military post like Lapwai,
almost denuded of troops. Citizens from all directions
flocked thither for protection, including friendly Indians
and their families, who, without arms or ammunition, came
from great distances to us. There, too, were very early
gathered the Kamiah inhabitants, sub-agents, teachers,
and other employes. They were escorted across the
prairie by James Lawyer and his people. The excellent
and successful lady teacher at Kamiah, Miss MacBeth,
gave an interesting account of the journey: " The Indians
[friendly ones, of course] treated us with great delicacy.
They rode well ahead. They watched sharply to the
rear. Some of them cantered off to round hills on our
left; and they searched out all possible hiding places
where an enemy could lurk, or jump upon us suddenly,
and they have brought us all without harm these sixty or
seventy miles."

The Christian young men, Indians whom Miss Mac-Beth had so successfully taught, remained true to the friends of the government throughout the struggle.

On the eighteenth, quite early in the morning, I wrote Colonel Perry : " Reports are not favorable, but my confidence in you, your officers, and men, makes me distrust the stories of those who ran away from the field just as the battle began. I want a report, as soon as possible, from some reliable person."

Then follows in the record other communications, fuller, of the sad events now already familiar to the reader.

Lewiston was made the depot and base of operations. Every available man was set in motion. The able and experienced Colonel of the Twenty-first Infantry, General Alfred Sully, was called to Lewiston for counsel, and to the field if his precarious health would permit. He was informed : " About thirty citizens reported murdered so far. . . . Shall not feed the enemy with driblets, but had to start the two companies to stop the murder of men and women, and keep the attention of Joseph and White Bird while I concentrated my troops."

I had great experience of panics in the east. The first was that of Bull Run, where the cry of " Black-horse cavalry !" would in an instant clear the road, and fill the woods alongside with thousands of flying stragglers. The next was that from Vienna to Chain Bridge, after McClellan's return from the peninsula, where, in a dark night, a whole division of General Sumner's was thrown into complete disorder. Everybody fired at random, killing and wounding comrades by the scores and hundreds. All this was brought on during the silent marching through a wood, by an accidental musket-discharge, or, as some say, by a quarrel arising from the cavalry running their horses upon the infantry. But nothing there was so continuous and feverish as the panics which took place at our small fort while we were waiting for the troops. On one occasion two friendly Indians, who had been chased and fired upon by some unruly white men, men who were jealous because these Indians had better arms than themselves, rushed toward the fort with the utmost speed of their ponies, and cried out something which the excited people of the garrison took to mean "Indians are coming." Defences were made; the little garrison was arranged for its best resistance. Some of the officers were at the top of the hill, in two minutes, looking out. Laundresses and children, wild with fear, and with hair flying, came running to the officers' line of houses. A resolute army lady gathered and took charge of a large number of women and children. Some incidents had a comic and ludicrous side, and, in the retrospect afforded much merriment: as ladies seizing rifles and pistols, barricading doors and cellar-ways, stepping into water-pails in dark passages. The alarm was serious for a short time, until the frightening cause was made known through the interpreter, who had bravely met the incoming Indians, friendly ones we knew, and learned the truth.

It appeared that some wicked white man had pretended that these friendly Indians belonged to the hostiles, and so ruthlessly fired upon them, and sought to disarm them.

Oh, how angry the Indians were. Explanations and apologies, after a while, appeased them.

On one of these interval-days the ladies and the children who had come to the garrison for protection were sent away, by the seemingly harsh Department Commander, to Lewiston. It was a hard order, and caused much gossip, and, I fear, the feelings of many friends were deeply touched; but it was necessary, for we were getting ready for vigorous war.

Mule trains were hired, supplies of all kinds put in motion, couriers were coming and going; Indian messengers and escaping soldiers, with their mouths full of exciting rumors and bad tidings, were arriving from a field seventy miles away. By the 21st of June eight new companies of regular troops — little companies they were, for the whole made up but a few over two hundred souls — were on the green plat near the Lapwai post. A small organization of volunteers, under Captain Paige, joined themselves to Whipple, who was in command of the cavalry, and were on hand for Indian fighting.

The friendly Indians (Nez Perces) generously brought in their ponies for the infantry officers to ride; and, in order to mount the soldiers of the infantry and artillery, they were ready to drive in their herds, but officers of experience in Indian warfare remonstrated. Colonel Pollock, of the Twenty-first Infantry, for instance, said, " No ; the ponies are Indian-trained, and always go to their friends. A pony will buck and run away, and always carries off a good soldier with him?" To such speeches I replied, " It is good, indeed, to have your feet on the firm ground; but ponies' feet will speed faster than yours for the long marches. At last, using the ponies, we will wear them out."

The time from the first news of the terrible disaster at White-Bird Canyon till the morning of the 22d of June seemed long indeed. It appears long even in the retrospect. Still it was only four days. Our effective men for the front, now at Lapwai, numbered but few more than two hundred.

Captains Whipple and Winters had arrived from their circuitous and tedious march from Wallowa. Captains Miller and Miles had reached Lewiston, by steamboat, and marched to Lapwai with several companies of the Fourth Artillery and the Twenty-first Infantry under their charge. The volunteers before mentioned, a little more than twenty strong, under Paige of Walla-Walla, had also joined us. Lieutenant Bomus, the quartermaster of the post, had improvised a supply train. The numerous miners, employed in different directions about Lewiston, had been thrown out of employment by the Indian outbreak, so that their means of transportation, "the mule pack-train," and their packers, became available for our use.

The moment of starting is solemn. The air is full of rumors. The Indians who began the war, and who virtually have raised the black flag, are still more numerous than our column. The road winds over hills and mountains, through ravines, past the mouths of cross canyons, which are full of pits and rocks; a wild range which is covered in places with forest trees, and often with thick underbrush. The few daring messengers had skulked through by night from Colonel Perry to Lapwai. They had chosen the most roundabout and unlooked-for paths, and they naturally magnified the dangers in order to demonstrate their prowess. Our whole force numbered

9

about one-fifth of a full regiment, such as those we took into the rebellion. Still this body of resolute men made a fine appearance. The cavalrymen sat on their horses waiting the word; the infantry, firmly grasping their rifles, were in line, ready to move; the artillery, who are really foot soldiers, with a bright uniform, presented their perfect ranks, slightly retired from the rest.

The mountain howitzer, heretofore used for the morning and evening gun, old and worn, but " fixed up " for the occasion, and the two gatlings, with their, as yet, restless animals, flanks the picture on one side, while Bomus's train, now an irregular body of noisy mules, going backward and forward, hither and thither, unstable as water, filled the space on the other. The few last loads of commissary supplies were being strung to their appointed *aparejos*, already upon their backs, while they remained grouped around the storehouse door. As I moved out with my staff officers, received the salutes, and listened to the orders that put the small mass in motion, a little of the old thrill of war came back to me.

There was another notable spectacle when the column wound its way up the foot-hills of the Craig Mountain. The cavalrymen led their horses two abreast; the infantrymen followed, arms at ease, talking, smoking, and apparently light hearted as boys are when on a holiday tramp.

The mule column lumbered along, one and another of these indefatigable burden-bearers darting out and in, now ahead, and now behind, to catch a bite of grass; while the bell-mare kept up the unending ding-dong call, occasionally relieved by the packers' oaths. These oaths,

I fear, are believed, by the train-men, to be essential in mule-driving, and adapted to the stubborn and eccentric natures under treatment! The column was stretched out, and, including its intervals, covered more than a mile in extent. Doubtless, Indian scouts from Joseph were watching it from the wooded crest of the contiguous mountain. Artillery, infantry, and cavalry, were pressing toward them. When Ollicut had, a month previously, seen two companies of cavalry on the banks of the furious Grande Ronde River, he hurried to his brother, then at Fort Lapwai, and said, excitedly, "There are a thousand armed men coming!" So, probably, at this time, these sleepless scouts hurried off to the White-Bird hostiles, and reported, "More than a thousand armed men are coming." I soon found it the part of wisdom, for producing effect upon Indians, to elongate a column, or stretch out a line, to its utmost capacity. They never once attempted to break across a column, or an organized line; but always tried to shower their skirmishers upon our flanks.

The memorandum of this day was very brief. It records the hour of starting, the length of the march, and the camp for the night. It does not mention the orders, reports, and preparations for departure, the storings at Lapwai, the last messages to friends at home, nor the abundant news that went rearward to furnish the eager journals. It gives no idea of the camp in the woods, at the cross-roads, where we might be attacked before the next morning; no idea of how the guns are put into artillery positions; of how the men encamped in line of battle; of the great carefulness in locating the outposts and

pickets; of the manner of grazing the animals in the openings, and then securing them at picket lines, or fettering
the mules and the bell-mare during the night; of how,
when all this is done, the officers, hitherto so solemn in
manner, and authoritative in tone, sit around the small
" mess kits " and unbend.   Camp fires must be small
here, and early extinguished; but this did not hinder the
sounds of mirth as the story went around the mess-table.
Our wives and daughters at home sometimes declare that,
" while they are nearly dying of anxiety for us, we are
having the best of times."   Isn't it well for hearty work,
and clear-headed thinking, that it is so?

CHAPTER XXI.

JOSEPH AND HIS WAR.—MARCH CONTINUED.—COLONEL MIL-
LER.—REVEILLE ABOUT 4.30.—NORTON'S.—A CONSEQUENCE
OF RIOT RUN MAD.—SUNDAY.—AN HONOR UNEARNED.—
WAITING FOR TROOPS.—THE COUNTRY DESCRIBED.—WELL
WATERED AS EDEN.—THE NORTH PACIFIC.—THE FORWARD
MOVEMENT.—VISIT TO GRANGEVILLE AND MOUNT IDAHO.—
THE WOUNDED.

HERE is the record of the 22d of June: "Left Lap-
wai at 12 M. Column under command of Captain
Miller. Make camp at Junction Trail (Mount Idaho and
Craig's Ferry Trail) at 5.30."

Who is Captain Miller? If I turn to the Army Reg-
ister I find, "Marcus P. Miller, a captain in the 4th
Artillery, with several brevets, the highest of which gives
him the appellation of Colonel. He was appointed from
Massachusetts, and graduated from the military academy
of West Point in 1858. He served with distinction in
the war of the rebellion, and heightened his reputation
by his brave work in the Modoc war." He was with me
then: of middling height, well knit for toughness, with
light beard and lightish hair, handsome forehead, blue
eye, and a pleasant face.

There are two classes of good soldiers: one that always does the work because it must be done; and another that manages to take a sincere pleasure in every
loyal duty. Miller belongs to the latter class.

Next day the reveille was sounded at a little past four. We breakfasted at five, and were on the march at six. Norton's ranch will be recalled by the reader. Mr. Norton, the late owner, was the man who was trying to get to Mount Idaho with his family, when he and others were killed, and his wife sadly wounded. We came to his house about half-past one o'clock, having marched nineteen miles. Mr. Norton had kept a sort of hotel. His house was now deserted. The Indians had rummaged everything; what the family had left here was found in complete disorder. Who can realize what it is to have savage warfare break upon a family with little or no warning; to kill and wound and scatter like this? It was worse than the desolation spoken of in the Scriptures, where one shall be taken and another left. None were left! There were the clothes, cut and torn and strewn about; the broken chairs; the open drawers; the mixings of flour, sugar, salt, and rubbish, — the evidences indeed of riot run mad. Do we wonder that those who have passed through such experience have been slow to forget and forgive " mad Indians"?

The force was ordered to encamp here. The next day, the twenty-fourth, was Sunday. As I did not move my main body this day the story was circulated, and published, that I halted because it was the Sabbath, and spent precious time in giving religious exhortation to my command, and in the distribution of some three hundred Bibles! Of course this would not hurt my reputation with a vast number of my Christian friends were it literally true, and under ordinary circumstances would have been proper enough.

But as it was not the case, I may speak of the occasion of the halt. First: I was not then quite sure of the position of the Indians. This I must ascertain beyond question, in order to determine the direction of my movement.

Perry, from Grangeville, came to us during the day, and brought us the desired information. The Indians were still in or near the White-Bird Canyon, not far from the scene of the disaster.

Next: I wished to send Captain Trimble, with his cavalry company, beyond the hostile Indians to Slate Creek. They were obliged to move by a difficult and circuitous route. I knew it to be wise for my main column to remain quiet, so as not to "flush the game," and press it upon a small company of brave citizens, who had been standing on the defensive in a little fort of their own construction, and sending to Mount Idaho for help. Again: I meant that there should be no question, when at last I should take the offensive against the savages, of my having a superiority of numbers. Therefore, for the additional reason that the troops at Lewiston might come up, I gladly delayed.

Mark well this place: Norton's ranch is to be historic, a central point. The broad and beautiful Camas Prairie opens out before you as you set your back to Craig's Mountain, and look towards the south-east. The straight road in your front leads from you to Grangeville and Mount Idaho. What a beautiful stretch of rolling prairie land! Where is there richer soil, or finer prospects? Towards the right is the "Snake country." The Salmon, which flows north-westerly, empties into the Snake not more than twenty miles to the south-west. The Cotton-wood, heading near by, runs easterly into the curvilinear Clearwater, twenty miles off; and the Rocky Canyon Creek, close by, shoots out south-west, to join the Salmon; while White-Bird, before described, makes its remarkable canyon, and empties into the Salmon, a few miles further up that river. This country is as well watered as Eden, and as fertile as any garden which has been much longer under cultivation.

When the Pacific railroads shall be completed, the Camas Prairie will not be despised. These wicked Indians have loved these broad acres, which they have not been wise enough to cultivate.

Joseph and White Bird understood the disabilities of their people, and how they were letting everything valuable to them slip through their hands. But, bright as they were, they had not sufficient ability to rise above the influences around them. Who, indeed, can do so?

If Colonel Perry could have anticipated the results which were to follow his haste to the White-Bird Canyon, and had halted here at Norton's, and stood on the defensive till I came up, it would have been a good thing, in a military point of view; but that would not have had the effect, like his bold advance, of stopping the Indian murders.

The superior officer could not have known all the facts until he reached the scene of operations.

Defeats are always deplored. They naturally fill the hearts of the vanquished with great chagrin. They are usually interpreted against the commander. But every eminent commander has had his lessons of defeat. They are often the essential stepping-stones to subsequent victories.

Perry's defeat at the White-Bird Canyon reminds one of the rout of Mackay at the celebrated battle of Killie-crankie. Lord Macaulay says of the civilians, who lost confidence in him, and made loud complaint:

"The truth seems to be that they, after the fashion of men who, having no military experience, sit in judgment on military operations, considered success as the only test of the ability of a commander. Whoever wins a battle is, in the estimation of such persons, a great general. Whoever is beaten is a bad general; and no general has ever been more completely beaten than Mackay."

Perry, too, had hard work to make head against his accusers, till two courts of inquiry had, by favorable findings, put the subject matter at rest.

It should always be remembered that in a combat both parties cannot be equally successful.

On Monday we made a brisk movement forward. The infantry, bearing off to the right, went to "Johnson's ranch." It was the farm where Perry made his first considerable stand, where he was able to check his swift pursuers, and enable his stragglers to catch up and close in. Deviating from the infantry's route, I took the cavalry to Perry's position at Grangeville, a little hamlet, it will be remembered, four miles short of Mount Idaho, on the road leading to that town. The soldiers who were left alive of Perry's command here met us. How different they were, in numbers and appearance, from the brisk and hearty troopers that had left Fort Lapwai the week previous! But our people rally quickly after defeat.

They were glad enough to see us. The officers declared
to Whipple and Winters, "You have made the long
march, and reached us sooner than we thought possible."
The soldiers and the restless citizens, gathered in from
the neighboring country, or come from Mount Idaho, to
meet us, were soon telling to our men the story of the
massacres, and of the last battle. I delayed for an hour,
to examine the supplies that the principal citizen had in
store, and which he gladly put to our use; also to gather
all the information known here concerning the enemy;
his position, number of warriors, and intentions. Then
leaving the cavalry to rest and feed till my return, I
made a hurried visit to the already famous town of Mount
Idaho.

A little rivalry, like that between New York and
Boston, existed between Grangeville and Mount Idaho.
Each village must have its own volunteer company; each
must have its guns for defence. If one has a fortification,
or a cannon, the other clamors for a like favor. The
mounted citizens began to swarm around me as I proceeded. A prominent one — Mr. Croaesdale, an Eng-
lishman, who had recently put a nice farm under cultivation in the neighborhood, and brought hither a beautiful
young wife, of refinement and culture — rode ahead, and
guided us. On a knoll to the left of the town he had
thrown up rough barricades, and improvised a few quite
creditable field-works. He manifested soldierly instincts
and enthusiasm. I found that he had made a citadel on
this knoll, which was already occupied by families, for
shelter and protection, whose fears had sent them in from
the country.

Engaging, after a time, to dine with Mr. Croaesdale, I passed down the principal street to Brown's Hotel. Before entering this building the crowd of curious, eager, solemn-looking men closed around me, and expressed a desire that I would speak to them. So I said, in substance, what I had already written Mr. Brown: "We have now taken the field in good earnest; more troops are on the way to join us. I propose to take prompt measures for the pursuit and punishment of the hostile Indians, and wish you to help me, in the way of information and supplies, as much as lies in your power. I sympathize deeply with you in the loss of life, and in the outrages to which your families have been subjected, and you may rest assured that no stone will be left unturned to give you redress, and protection in the future."

There is always risk, on such occasions, of promising more than one is able to perform. My brief speech, however, appeared to give satisfaction, and I passed into the hotel, with Mr. Brown and others, and went from room to room to see those who had suffered outrage at the hands of the Indians. Poor Mrs. Norton was there, very sadly wounded through her limbs. A lady lay in another room, pale as death, and suffering from a gunshot wound, and from other savage and repeated violence. Her little child was playing, to all appearance quite happy, on the outside of the bed, but a part of its tongue had been cut off. There was an unusual number of people gathered in this place, shut up by a sense of danger, and full of feverish excitement.

We dined at Mr. Rudolph's, with Mr. and Mrs. Croaesdale and others. How patient and helpful were the ladies gathered here, yet how uncertain, how depressing were all the circumstances of this horrid Indian war! From the peaceful beauty of life in rural England, to the appalling butchery in the wild canyons of Idaho, the transition was sufficiently abrupt.

CHAPTER XXII.

JOSEPH AND HIS WAR. — JUNCTION OF TROOPS AT JOHNSON'S
RANCH. — A WORD FROM HOME. — EFFECT OF EXAGGERAT-
ED REPORTS. — HOW A SOLDIER PEOPLES THE HILLS AND
RIDGES WITH TROOPS. — NEIGHBORHOOD OF PERRY'S DIS-
ASTER DESCRIBED. — A DESERTED CAMP. — A RECONNOIS-
SANCE. — THE BOISE MOVEMENT UNDER GREEN. — BURYING
THE DEAD. — LIEUTENANT THELLER'S BODY. — JOSEPH AND
HIS WARRIORS BEYOND THE SALMON, WATCHING THE
TROOPS. — JOSEPH'S GENERALSHIP COMPLIMENTED.

THE village realities passed before our officers as vivid
pictures. Their sympathies were enlisted, amid the
terror and the suffering, but they could not delay over
them. After a march of eight miles, by southerly routes,
we rejoined the main column at Johnson's. Here a messenger came, with the news that our re-enforcements were
on the way ; and he also bore welcome words from home.
How wonderfully news can spread. It is like the cloud
no bigger than a man's hand, when it leaves us ; it is
magnified several times before the journals at Lewiston
and Walla-Walla have put it into type, and by the time
it has reached Portland and San Francisco it has become
a heavy cloud, overspreading the whole heaven. About
this time, the disaster at White-Bird Canyon had shown
this speedy and terrific increase. A friend told me that
at Fort Colville, where he was then stationed, two hundred
and seventy miles from Joseph's field of battle, he heard

a story, with complete and graphic details, of the death of Colonel E. C. Watkins, the Indian Inspector, and myself, with other exaggerated horrors. All the people there believed the account, as it was so connected and so circumstantial. It was pleasant to us to find that our home people were not afflicted with these frightful stories. The stories existed, but the correction was ever at hand.

I remember that after the war of the Rebellion, whenever I travelled, particularly on horseback, I used to continue, in imagination, peopling the hills, ridges, groves, forests, and ravines with soldiers, and laying off everything, for purposes of offence and defence, into military positions for cavalry, artillery, and infantry. In just such groupings does that whole region around "Johnson's Ranch" lie in my memory to-day. South-eastward was a gradual slope, four or five miles in extent, to the head of the Big White-Bird Canyon, an open, rolling country; southward, one rougher and rougher, filled with deep ravines, extending to Salmon River, which was boiling and rolling on, in mad fury, at the bottom of mountain banks. The largest transverse ravine in this direction was "Rocky Canyon," at the head of which, three or four miles off, was, as we have seen, one of the Indian camps at the time when the first murders were committed. The lodge-poles, and many of the lodges without their skin or canvas covering, were still there, giving indications of the recent sojourn of six or seven hundred persons. To the north, twenty miles away, in the direction we came, were the Cottonwood Creek and Canyon, "Norton's Ranch," with the Craig mountain, fringed with

trees, behind it, as a fine background to a beautiful landscape; to the east, and sweeping around to the northeast, the rugged hills that border the Camas prairies, and
are opposite Craig Mountain, and near Mount Idaho, and
all the vast, charming expanse, which people come hither
to occupy and to cultivate, lying spread out between
mountains and hills, like an unrolled map, for your inspection.

We left camp on reconnoissance at 6 30, A. M., and our
column moved directly to the hill at the head of White-
Bird Canyon. This reconnoissance was for an important
object. "Where are Joseph and White Bird?" "How
many warriors have they with them?" Our march was
occupying their attention, and keeping them together.
It was, further, the best method of gaining time for the
companies now *en route* to overtake us, and for those
moving northward from Boise City, some two hundred
miles to the south, to get into such a position as would
prevent an escape of the hostiles in that direction. This
Boise movement, under Colonel Green, was intended to
keep the disaffected Nez Perces and the Wieser Indians
apart.

A reconnoissance which does not bring on an engagement, gives one the information he seeks, and does not
drive off the foe, has to be well conducted. Ours was
thus successful.

We had another desire. It was to look up and bury
our dead soldiers, who had been lying exposed for more
than a week, upon the hill-sides, or in the ravines where
they had fallen. Miller commanded the footmen, increased by a company of cavalry, under the diligent

Captain Winters. These proceeded cautiously down the Canyon trail, preceded by the watchful skirmishers, and covered by vigilant flankers. Whipple stayed with our artillery and company of cavalry, at the head of the canyon, where the trail just begins to descend. Perry accompanied me to a good post of observation, near the transverse ravine, where, the week before, the greater number of his living men had, at their extreme peril, ascended from the canyon below to the broader space above.

The brave volunteer, Captain Paige, of Walla-Walla, with his little company of men, and Arthur Chapman as guide, skirted the hills to the right of the canyon. The scene was so vast, the hills so high, and the ravines so deep, that our small numbers seemed even smaller by the contrast. As we peered down into the canyon the bottom seemed level as a plain, though, in reality, there were many hills, knolls, and buttes between us and the battle-field. Little by little, the troops uncovered the ground. The burial parties followed closely, and behind the moving columns, and, as soon as they came near enough, sheltered with their blankets the poor boys who, stripped of clothing, were still lying there in death. It was quite late in the day before Lieutenant Theller's remains were found and identified. He was then carefully buried on the spot. Afterward the afflicted wife was gratified in her wish to have the body removed to the neighborhood of her home in San Francisco.

Paige and Chapman, pushing well forward, at last, from a promontory at the end of the ridge, which they had followed almost to the Salmon River, discovered the Indians. Joseph, keen-eyed and active, was now, with all his warriors, his women, children, and baggage, well across the swift river; and there, from some curious, sharp-pointed hills on the other side, was watching our movements.

A citizen, half starved and twice wounded, was brought to us. From him we gathered additional information. We learned the names of the poor settlers who had suffered most by the robberies and by the flames. We were told that Joseph's first intention was to have given me battle before going over the Salmon; but that he had changed his mind, and wished to draw us into the vicinity of those snow-clad peaks called "Seven Devils," where our troops would be further from supplies, and more easily handled.

The full purpose of this forward movement having been accomplished, in the midst of a heavy rain, the command, slowly toiling up the muddy trail, gathered at the head of the canyon, and returned to Johnson's for the night.

The leadership of Chief Joseph was indeed remarkable. No general could have chosen a safer position, or one that would be more likely to puzzle and obstruct a pursuing foe. If we present a weak force he can turn upon it. If we make direct pursuit he can go southward toward Boise, for at least thirty miles, and then turn our left. He can go straight to his rear, and cross the Snake at Pittsburg Landing. He can go on down the Salmon, and cross at several places, and then turn either to the left, for his old haunts in the Wallowa Valley, or to the right, and pass our flank, threatening our line of supply,

10

while he has, at the same time, a wonderful natural barrier between him and us in the Salmon, a river that delights itself in its furious flow.   We shall see next how it was sought to solve the problem presented us by this shrewd savage.

CHAPTER XXIII.

JOSEPH AND HIS WAR. — SKIRMISH AT THE SALMON-RIVER
CROSSING. — CAVALRY SKIRMISH WITH THE FAMOUS LOOK-
ING-GLASS. — THE CAVALRY SKIRMISHES AT THE COTTON-
WOOD, NEAR NORTON'S RANCH: INCLUDING THE ACTION OF
THE SEVENTEEN VOLUNTEERS, AND THE MASSACRE OF
LIEUTENANT RAINS AND PARTY.

THE troops were gathered near the mouth of White-
Bird Canyon. The main canyon forks a couple of
miles back from the Salmon. One tine of the fork is the
White-Bird Creek, running directly into the river; and
the other holds the main trail, which bears off to the left,
and leads to the river a couple of miles farther up stream.
A very high bluff lies within the triangle thus formed.
Standing upon this bluff you could see, hundreds of feet
below, the restless Salmon, and, beyond it, the irregular
mountain valley held by the Indians. Their sentry-posts,
on pointed hills, were scattered along between us and the
mountain slopes.

They were shouting back and forth. We could hear
the voices of Indians giving their orders. While we were
preparing a ferry, by collecting boats and crossing a
cable, the Indians suddenly started from the hill-tops and
from ravines, and rushed towards our position. Paige
and I were sitting near the right of our line, on the bluff
overlooking the White-Bird. It seemed, for a moment,
that the little silvery thread, far below, that we call the

Salmon River, could really be no obstacle. I sent Wilkinson and others for long-range rifles, and got ready with what artillery we had, to fire as soon as the Indians should be within range. Paige became more and more resolute, shouted loudly to the approaching foe, fired his rifle rapidly, while other rifles were coming. Some shots appeared to whistle among them as they drew nigh the river. Away they turned, and down the river they ran, like wild cattle just let loose from the corral; and in fifteen minutes they had disappeared. Surely all was ready for them had they re-swam the swift river. It was partly a ruse, and intended to make me think that they designed to turn my flank at Rocky Canyon crossing, and partly the usual bravado of Indians, who, by their wildness of movement and defiant yelling, hope to inspire surprise and terror. But our field-glasses had shown us ponies grazing, and figures sneaking behind the hills, and I was confident that the hostiles had returned under the cover of the rough ground, and would go in another direction when they were ready.

Now that we were together, Miller had the artillery battalion, Perry having been sent to the rear for supplies, Whipple had the cavalry, Trimble was still at the Salmon River crossing near Slate Creek, and prevented a turning of our left in that direction.

Chief Looking-glass, in the rear, was already beginning to give trouble. "Forty bucks have just left him to join Joseph. He is only waiting his favorable chance." Such was the information from our friendly Indians. As he was behind us, and at the fork of the Clearwater, we must take care of him. "Captain Whipple, go with your

cavalry and gatling guns, arrest the Indian chief Looking-glass, and all other Indians who may be encamped
with or near him, between the forks of the Clearwater,
and turn all prisoners over, for safe-keeping, to the volunteer organization at Mount Idaho."

It may, perhaps, add to the interest of the narrative to
give Whipple's account of the execution of those instructions.   He says : " On account of the distance, greater by
ten miles than was supposed, and the difficult approach,
the village was not reached at dawn, July 1, as contemplated ; but soon after sunrise such dispositions were
made as seemed most practicable, under the circumstances,
to carry out my instructions.   An opportunity was given
Looking-glass to surrender, which he, at first, promised
to accept, but afterwards defiantly refused, and the result
was that several Indians were killed, the camp, with a
large amount of supplies, destroyed, and seven hundred
and twenty-five ponies captured, and driven to Mount
Idaho.   .   .   .   About twenty citizens, under lead of a
volunteer officer, Captain Randall, [killed near Norton's,
July 5,] accompanied me on this expedition."

Of course we thus stirred up a new hornet's nest, and
did not get Looking-glass and his treacherous companions
into custody.

While my men, those immediately at hand near the
Salmon, were pulling some small boats over the torrent, and
whirling into port by an eddy, and then, in column, (the
Slate-Creek detachment, Hunter's and McConville's volunteers, and all,) were winding their way up the almost
interminable " hog-back " in a rain-storm, and following
along the trail of the departing Joseph, down the Salmon,

toward the Snake country, for twenty-five miles, to the raging crossing-place at Craig's Ferry, Whipple, having completed his instructions, was waiting and watching at Norton's; because, under our chase, Joseph might, after swimming the river, turn again that way across the Camas.

These Indians excited our admiration by their despatch in crossing rivers. James Reuben, (an Indian,) who brought me a message at Craig's ferry, told me how it was done: "Make skin rafts, and load them; tie four horses, abreast, to the rafts with small ropes; put four Indians, naked, on the horses, and then boldly swim across." He gave us a practical demonstration by swimming his half-breed over to us and back across the fearful torrent. Brave Scout Parker attempted the same, but failed to get many yards from shore.

While this was going forward, after he had made the remarkable crossing, Joseph did turn back upon the Camas Prairie, towards Norton's ranch, and threatened Whipple and the others.

I must try to afford a few glimpses of this detachment, with their doings and surroundings.

Captain Babbitt, ordinance officer of my staff, had met Whipple at midnight, near Mount Idaho, with orders: "Proceed, without delay, to Cottonwood, (Norton's,) and form junction with Perry." The object being to gain the earliest information of the movements of the enemy, should he, as was thought probable, re-cross the Salmon." Such were the orders. Whipple tells how he fulfilled them:

"I marched," writes Whipple, "to Cottonwood, July 2,

and, on the following morning, sent out two citizen scouts, named Foster and Blewett, to examine the country in the direction of Craig's Ferry, the place where Joseph and his party swam the river, for indications of the presence of the Indians.   Toward evening Foster returned rapidly to camp, and reported that he had seen Indians, about twelve miles distant, coming from the direction of Craig's Ferry ; that they had fired a shot or two at him ; that he last saw his comrade about that time." . .

Whipple immediately prepared for action, delayed a little by unloading and distributing ammunition, and, following his report again, " I directed Second-Lieutenant S. M. Rains, of my company, with ten picked men, and the scout, Foster, to proceed at once toward the point where the Indians had been seen, for the purpose of ascertaining the strength of the enemy, and to aid young Blewett.   I particularly cautioned Rains not to precede the command too far, to keep on high ground, and to report the first sign of the Indians.   The command was in motion very shortly after the detachment had started, and firing was soon heard on our front.   A rapid gait was taken up, and, after a couple of miles, Indians were discovered about a half mile distant ; and, on approaching nearer, it was found that they were in large force, and that Lieutenant Rains and EVERY MAN of his detachment had been killed."

These were dreadful tidings !

This young officer was of the same mould as the famous Winterfield of history, who was killed in just such fashion under Frederick the Great, — prompt, loyal, able, without fear, and without reproach.   Frederick lost many brave leaders, but "only one Winterfield;" we, but one Rains. Whipple continued a short distance, deployed, and dismounted for battle. The enemy, it seems, took the back track for a few miles on meeting the larger force, and, at dark, the captain very properly retired, with his men and guns, to Cottonwood. During the night couriers arrived from Perry, coming from Fort Lapwai, with the pack-train.

The 4th of July, at dawn, the command from Cottonwood set out bravely toward Lapwai, to meet the escorting detachment, now in great danger; marched toward it eight miles, and returned in safety with Perry's escort and supplies. But this exciting morning ride was not enough for our Cottonwood celebration of the Fourth of July?

"About midday Indians began to gather, and but a short time elapsed before the camp was surrounded by them, and for hours they made the most frantic efforts to dislodge us. Every man of the command was kept on the lines this afternoon (rifle-pits having been dug at a little distance from the Cottonwood house) until about sundown, when the enemy withdrew for the night."

This is very calmly described, but there were, doubtless, plenty of flags flying; plenty of firing from carbines and gattlings, which made the old Craig Mountain ring. Add the Indian yellings and shoutings, and the day we celebrate was here thoroughly, if not formally, honored.

Cottonwood, July 5. Perry, being the senior, was in command. Whipple was constructing some defences, east of Norton's, when two mounted men were seen approaching at full speed. They came, pursued by Indians, from the direction of Johnson's ranch. These two were the messengers sent to me beyond the Salmon; their mission having been performed, they had thus returned; but nothing befell them except the hot chase. Not so with the next party which immediately followed them! On the same hill where Whipple had constructed the defences, a short time after the couriers rushed in, Whipple was standing. He says :

" Noticing that there was some commotion at the brow of the hill, where a few citizens had gathered, and that Captain Perry was walking towards me, I turned and met him, asking, at the same time the cause of the excitement. He replied, ' Some citizens, a couple of miles away, on the Mount Idaho road, are surrounded by Indians, and are being all cut to pieces, and nothing can be done to help them !'

" ' Why not ?'

" ' It is too late !' "

Still it is decided to try, and the entire force is ordered thitherward.

Here is another picture :

"Arrived at the ground where the attacked party was I found it to be Captain Randall's company of volunteers, numbering seventeen men. Randall had been mortally wounded, one man killed, and two slightly disabled. . . After I reached the point where the citizens were attacked, and remained, Randall having been wounded at the first onset, I took position close at hand, so as to relieve the volunteers from all duties but the care of their wounded comrades. A few shots were fired at us by the hostiles, small parties still hovering around, but no damage was done, except that one horse was slightly wounded."

Lieutenant Shelton, First Cavalry, volunteered, with his detachment of seventeen men, and, in a spirited manner, drove the Indians from his front.

Then all returned to camp, bearing the wounded. Much complaint, as before noticed, arose because the officer in command at Cottonwood was not more prompt with his relief, whom a court of inquiry, after long sessions and much labor, exonerated. After the return to camp the Indians had the prairie to themselves, and leisurely crossed the road between the Cottonwood forces and Grangeville, and continued on eastward. Doubtless Joseph did so in order to pick up Looking-glass, as, in this, we had not succeeded in anticipating him.

A little after sunset two companies of mounted volunteers reported from my main column, which was yet on the other side of the Salmon.

On hearing of Lieutenant Rains' desperate struggle I had sent these volunteers from us by the way of Rocky Canyon.

Let us return to our pursuing troops on the table-land beyond the Salmon. I pressed this column after the Indians to Craig's Ferry. Lost our raft in attempting to cross. Too much of a torrent to cross troops and supplies without it! James Reuben, the scout, had brought clear accounts that Joseph had not turned south toward his old haunts in the Wallowa, but northward and eastward, to gather up Looking-glass and re-enforcements, catch small parties like Rains' detachment, and do what mischief he could. Therefore, by turning straight back, recrossing the Salmon at Rocky Canyon, or White-Bird, where there were boats, and going *via* Grangeville, where I could bring the Cottonwood force to me, I had a short line, and hoped to get a decisive battle from our doughty chief. This difficult work was promptly attempted.

The 9th of July, by some night-marching, and by getting alternate "lifts" to our infantry in country wagons, saw our advance, at evening, at Grangeville; and the remainder was not far behind. The enterprising volunteers, who had become a little disgusted with the slowness of regulars, and angry at their own fearful discomfiture near Cottonwood, had suddenly left us and started on an independent movement. They had crept to a lofty height, overlooking the fork and ravines where the Indians now were, near, if not in, Looking-glass' old camp, that Whipple had stirred up a few days before. The volunteers sent an officer, whose message was, " Come straight to us." Shearer, a volunteer major, with a few men from Mount Idaho, went thither for me and explained why I had borne off to the right, crossed Jackson's Bridge over a branch of the Clearwater, and worked my way down toward the fork, which was to be the battle-ground.

Joseph, in consequence of his success at White-Bird, his eluding me at the Salmon, his massacre of Rains, and his escape from Whipple, and his skirmishes with the volunteers, as well as his aiding Looking-glass in avoiding arrest, had come to boast of his prowess, so that he was rather inclined to try his hand with me. Probably he did not believe it possible that I could get my force concentrated, so as to bring the whole of it to bear at once. But, on our part, we were decidedly inclined to battle, and so hastened with all our might thitherward. The chief advantage on the part of the savages lay in the toughness, and swiftness in flight, of the Indian ponies.

CHAPTER XXIV.

JOSEPH AND HIS WAR. — BATTLE OF THE CLEARWATER, THE
11TH OF JULY. — LIEUTENANT FLETCHER DISCOVERS THE
ENEMY. — RAPID MOVEMENTS OF INDIANS. — QUICK CHANGES
OF TROOPS. — FOOD AND POWDER IN DANGER. — CHARGES
ON FOOT AND ON HORSEBACK. — BANCROFT AND WILLIAMS
WOUNDED. — MILLER'S CHARGE. — HOW AIDES-DE-CAMP AS-
SISTED. — INDIANS CAPTURED SPRING OF WATER. — THE
SECOND DAY. — SPRING RECAPTURED. — JACKSON'S AP-
PROACH. — MILLER SENT THROUGH THE ENEMY'S LINE. —
AN OFFICER OF GENERAL McDOWELL'S STAFF. — THE FINAL
ATTACK. — THE VICTORY.

OUR infantry, artillery, and cavalry having passed
without delay through Grangeville, the volunteers
being already at the round hill beyond the Cottonwood,
and looking down into valleys filled with wild men,
women, children, and ponies, the small army, bearing to
the south, crossed by Jackson's bridge. It delayed at
the crest of a height beyond the bridge until the ammunition train, the baggage, and infantry, that had been somewhat separated by the forced marching, were closed up.

The 11th of July was a day ever memorable to us and
the people in North Idaho, even if such little affairs do
not disturb places more remote. This midsummer day
saw us creeping down carefully, hunting our way through
the extensive forest, through the deep ravines, over the
sightly hills, on toward the confluence of the two Clear-
waters. About noon, Lieutenant Fletcher, my aide, who

had galloped away a few minutes before, and was already
a quarter of a mile to my left, discovered the enemy in
a deep ravine, near the mouth of Cottonwood Creek.
Numbers of horses, and a few Indians, were seen.

Let us try to sketch the picture which presents itself.
We have just emerged from the forests into a country
comparatively open. We are looking northward. One
branch of the river, the Clearwater, which is running
parallel with my course, some half mile to our left, sweeps
around in its swift flow two miles ahead, and crosses our
path, and is then flowing easterly. The surface of the
river is down at the foot of high bluffs, and gives us only
occasional glimpses of its current.

Trimble's troop, accompanied by an aide-de-camp, was
sent forward to watch, toward the front and right, while
I rode to the bluff at the left, where Fletcher was, and
saw plainly the hostiles, who, judging from their motions,
had just discovered our approach. By one o'clock a howitzer and two gatling guns, manned by a detachment under
Lieutenant Otis, Fourth Artillery, were firing towards
the masses of the Indians below. The Indians were running their horses up the south fork of the Clearwater, on
both banks, near the river, and driving their stock, as
fast as possible, beyond our range. In ten minutes more
it was impossible, with our artillery, to reach them, owing
to the craggy mountain-shores back of, and close by, the
river border. My guide, Mr. Chapman, assured me that
they could escape only by a canyon on our left, which
made a small angle with the river, and led toward the
rear.

The next bluff, in that direction, was beyond a deep

and rocky transverse ravine, perpendicular to this canyon. Instantly the howitzer battery and gatling guns, supported by Winter's cavalry, were ordered to go thither with all speed. Around the head of the ravine our distance was over a mile, the enemy having less than a third to go. So beyond the second bluff we found Joseph and his people, dismounted, and already in position, on our approach, while some thirty or forty mounted Indians had galloped just beyond range, to compass our left. Just in time Colonel Mason, the Department Inspector, appeared at hand, with Burton's company of infantry, which deployed, stretching off to the right, and enabled Winters to take care of his left. They all now pressed forward, in an open line. Firing became very brisk. My line I extended to the left by the cavalry, and to the right by the infantry and artillery battalions, gradually refusing my flanks, until the whole bluff was enveloped. Four hundred men, necessarily much spread out, held a line two and a half miles in extent. Our main pack train had passed by this position. Another small train, with a few supplies, was on the road near us. The Indian flankers, by their rapid movement, struck the rear of the small train, killed two of the packers, and disabled a couple of mules, loaded with howitzer ammunition. The prompt fire from Perry's and Whipple's cavalry saved the attendant ammunition from capture; luckily, the main supply train was saved by the quick work of a messenger, guiding it within the lines.

Beyond this Clearwater stream to the north is the high, round hill, five miles distant in a straight line, where, we mentioned, that the volunteers were located; farther off is the Craig mountain, which recedes to the left, and rises up as a background. From its nearest slopes the Cottonwood ravine makes its dark and crooked course toward us, and disappears behind our shore of the Clearwater. The very steep and very high banks of the river are roughly cut with numerous transverse ravines. The Indian camp, from which, on our approach, the hostiles emerged, yet hidden from view, was beyond the river, and hundreds of Indian ponies were herded in ravines, close to the camp. The warriors, the greater part of them mounted, under cover of the bluffs, had forded the river, near our flank, and, when discovered were racing up a transverse ravine, whose shallow head we had some time since passed. Between these transverse ravines, some of which would be called canyons, there were large, level flats of open land. These were filled with rocks and gullies, and their sides lined with small trees. We were obliged to work back toward the head of any one of them in order to cross it with howitzers, or with horses. Our skirmishers were just sweeping over one of these plateaus, formed by the river and the canyon, when the quick, covert movement of Joseph, which we referred to above, was revealed to Fletcher's field-glass.

For a few moments it was feared by lookers-on that the Indians would destroy all our food and our powder. The messenger had run his horse with all speed, and to good purpose; for a loss here would have been a calamity indeed.

The fierce onset of the Indians requiring great haste, Wilkinson, aide-de-camp, being now sent, quietly gathered the trains, and brought them under cover of Rodney's artillery and Trimble's cavalry companies.

The enemy manifested extraordinary quickness and boldness, planting sharpshooters at all available points, making charges on foot and on horseback, accompanying the charges with all manner of savage demonstrations. At one time, an Indian paraded himself in plain view, beyond our left flank, and beyond the easy range of our rifles. He would dance around, and leap up and down in a strange way, with arms outstretched, swinging, as he did so, a red blanket. Doubtless this was done with a view to encourage others to follow him in the bold work of attacking the flank of the position.

These attempts were successfully resisted at every part of the line. At 3 30, P. M., a spirited counter charge was tried on our right, down into a ravine. Captain Miles, commanding the infantry battalion, led in this charge. Captain Bancroft, Fourth Artillery, and Lieutenant Williams, Twenty-first Infantry, were seriously wounded at this time. A number of Indians were killed, and several wounded, in the charge, and the ravine was thoroughly cleared.

Miller, a little later, led a second charge near the centre. He succeeded, at first, only in putting the Indians on their guard, behind the barricades of stone which they had hastily thrown up. Wilkinson, with a view to a diversion, meanwhile led a demonstration on the right, using artillery and infantry, and every available man from the cavalry, including horse-holders, orderlies, extra-duty men, and train. Fletcher, also, pointing a howitzer dur-

11

ing the battle, did effective service by lodging shells within the enemy's barricades.

Miller's charge at last gained the ridge in front, and secured the disputed ravine near Winter's position. Further spasmodic charges on the left, by the enemy, were repelled by Perry's and Whipple's cavalry, dismounted, and Morris's artillery. Yet a few Indian sharpshooters, finding hiding-places, managed to so annoy every man who approached the spring, our water supply, that, in spite of our successful charges, the situation at dark was still uncomfortable.

During the night, additional stone barricades and rifle-pits were constructed by ourselves, and by the enemy. Thus each party, still hopeful of a final victory, spent much of the night in the hard work of preparation.

In the darkness, a few officers, in spite of the extreme danger from Indian bullets, went several times quietly to the spring, and carried away full buckets of water, and took them to the lines to refresh their thirsty men. Promptness and courage had, in the outset, saved the ammunition and food; gallant self-exposure during the darkness saved the water-supply.

At daylight, the 12th, every available man was on the line. I directed that food should be cooked, and coffee made, at the centre, and carried to the front. This was not so easy to do; for we had first to get complete possession of the spring, as sufficient water was not secured in the night. This feat was executed, with great spirit, by Miller and Perry, using Otis's battery, and Rodney's company, on foot. As soon as the battery had made a rapid firing, it ceased, when a prompt charge at a run, with shouting, was undertaken by the men in support. The Indian sharpshooters were thus driven from their hiding-places, and the spring secured by our riflemen against recapture.

As soon as every man had been provided with food, I directed that the artillery battalion be withdrawn from the lines, thin though they were already, and that the whole stretch be held by the infantry and cavalry. This gave a reserve force to employ in any offensive movement. It should be remembered that the number of our men on the lines, and the number of the Indian warriors that Joseph marshalled, were about equal. Miller withdrew his battalion, and at 2 30, P. M., the time I had selected, was preparing to execute a peculiar movement, viz., to push out by the left flank, piercing the enemy's line just left of the centre, cross his barricaded ravine, then to face suddenly to the right, and charge, so as to strike the Indian position in reverse, assisting himself meanwhile by a howitzer.

Miller was fully ready and about to move, when beyond the Indian position, toward the south, a dust appeared in the distance. Our glasses, quickly catching every new appearance, revealed it as an expected supply train, escorted by Jackson's cavalry company. Immediately the artillery battalion, which was waiting for the other work, was sent out to meet the new-comers. This occasioned considerable skirmishing, and the delay of an hour, when the train was brought in in safety. To our joy, Major Keeler, of General McDowell's staff, accompanied the escort, and brought us cheering words from his general, at San Francisco, as well as welcome re-enforcements. At the time of these arrivals I had ridden out a few yards, to secure a fair view of the field.

Upon my invitation, Major Keeler came forward to see the battle, and took a place by my side.

Captain Miller, instead of returning with the train, was marching slowly in column by the right flank towards us, when, as he crossed the enemy's line, just at the right point, he faced to the left, moved quickly in line for nearly a mile across our front, and repeatedly charged the enemy's positions. This manner of striking at an angle, and following up the break, is called "rolling up the enemy's line." This Miller accomplished most effectually. The usual attempt to double his left was made by the Indians, when a reserved company, Rodney's, in Miller's rear, deployed, and flanked the flankers, and drove them back.

For a few minutes there was a stubborn resistance at Joseph's barricades; then his whole line gave way. Immediately the pursuit was taken up by the whole force, infantry and artillery, Winter's troop dismounted, and the remaining cavalry as soon as they could saddle and mount. This movement was decisive. The Indians are completely routed, and flying over the rugged banks, through the ravines, swimming and wading the river, and our forces are in close pursuit.

CHAPTER XXV.

JOSEPH AND HIS WAR. — BATTLE OF THE CLEARWATER. — A
BRIEF PURSUIT ACROSS THE RIVER. — THE CHARGE DOWN
THE STEEP AT KAMIAH. — INDIANS CROSSING THE CLEAR-
WATER. — A BRISK SKIRMISH. — JOSEPH'S POSITION. — THE
BEGINNING OF THE LOLO TRAIL. — RECONNOITERING. —
JOSEPH'S DIPLOMACY. — SURRENDER OF A PART. — MASON'S
EXPEDITION. — SPRINGING AN AMBUSCADE.

JACKSON'S cavalry, just arrived, moved off quickly
along the plateau, followed the gatling gun, in support, at a trot, as far as the bluff overlooking the river.
The howitzers were brought to the same point, with
Trimble's company, and shot and shell poured into the
retreating masses of Indians and ponies. They were
closely pursued through the ravines into the deep canyon,
thence to the river, over rocks, down precipices, and
along trails, almost too steep and craggy to traverse. The
footmen pressed them to that part of the river opposite
the Indian camp. The river being too deep and rapid for
the men to ford, they here waited for the cavalry under
Perry. The cavalry worked its way as rapidly as it
could from its position on the left, down the rugged
mountain steeps, to the deep ford, and crossed slowly
into the Indian camp. But Perry, instead of pressing
after Joseph up the bluffs on the other side, strongly
posted his force near the Indian lodges; meanwhile, the
gatling guns and the howitzers, near which I was observ-

ing, were doing their best to reach the Indians, who were fleeing in every direction up the heights, and disappearing to the left of Cottonwood Creek. At this time, about five, P. M., I was following up the movement, descending a steep trail down the mountain side, when I discovered a number of the warriors, apparently returning toward their camp from the Cottonwood ravine. They were, at the time, at least three miles from us. I warned Perry, and directed him immediately to ferry over the footmen with his horses.

While doing this time was consumed, and the Indians, instead of returning to attack us, as they appeared to meditate, had turned eastward, crossed the Cottonwood Canyon, and, under cover of a ravine, had gone far in advance, and out of sight. It being evidently impossible to overtake the fugitives before dark, further pursuit was postponed until the next morning.

The Indian camp, abandoned in haste, had the lodges still standing, filled with their effects, — blankets, buffalo robes, cooking utensils, food cooking on the fires, flour, jerked beef, and plunder of all descriptions. The many wounded and dead horses in and near the encampment showed that our artillery had reached it.

We had, on our side, put into the engagement, for these two days, four hundred fighting men. The Indians, under Chief Joseph, over three hundred warriors ; also a great number of women, who assisted in providing spare horses and ammunition,—as did our "packers" and horse-holders, — thus forming for them a substantial reserve. They had twenty-three killed, about forty wounded, many of whom subsequently died, and some forty that fell into our hands as prisoners. Our loss was thirteen killed, and twenty-two wounded.

The Nez Perces fought with skill, and with the utmost obstinacy. Nobody could complain of our men on that field. "A small battle!" Yes, if we estimate by the numbers engaged. But the forces were quite equally matched, and it required just as much, perhaps more, nerve to do one's duty there, where the loss of a battle involves the direst consequences; and wounds and death were the same to those who suffered as in engagements where more lives are at stake.

The next morning we were early on the march. As soon as we reached the heights above Kamiah we saw that the enemy's families, their stock and effects, were already mostly across the Clearwater, a mile above the ferry. Our little force, now in hot pursuit, pressed down the trail as rapidly as possible, and moved in two columns, at a trot, to the place of crossing. When the river was reached by our skirmishers the last warrior was already over, and well up the other bank. The gatling guns and musketry were quickly located, and noisily used; but with little apparent effect, except, perhaps, to increase the rapidity of Chief Joseph's retreat. As Perry's and Whipple's cavalry neared the enemy's crossing, and were passing the flank of a high bluff, which was situated just beyond the river, a brisk fire from Indian rifles was suddenly opened upon them. It created a great panic and disorder; our men jumped from their horses, and ran to the cover of the fences. Little damage resulted, except the shame to us, and a fierce delight to the foe.

We learned that the enemy had intended to make a halt

and a firm stand before going over the river, and from behind barricades and natural cover, to meet us; but our rapid descent of the Kamiah hills, and resolute approach, coupled with their defeat of the day before, they could not stand; so that when our columns came in view, on the heights, they sprang upon their skin rafts, already overloaded, and swam over, occasioning the loss of many of their supplies, which their women had saved, and brought off from their abandoned camp near the field of battle.

Joseph, with the same quickness of judgment which he had displayed at White-Bird, the Salmon, the Cottonwood, and the Clearwater, took a position at the beginning of the Lolo trail, and beyond the reach of our longest guns. Here his scouts, from every elevated point, watched the unfolding of our plans, so that the wary chief was always ready to conform his motions to ours. There was a junction of trails beyond him, fifteen or twenty miles off. Could I but get there! Perhaps I could, by going back a little, and then down river and across; quick, indeed, if at all; and secret!

The fourteenth was spent in reconnoitering. The fifteenth I started a column of cavalry with intention of ascending the heights to the rear, as if en route to Lapwai, but really to move in an easterly direction twenty miles down the Clearwater to Dunwell's Ferry, and crossing there to attempt to gain the trail to the rear of the Indians, as they were still encamping in plain sight, and not more than four miles from Kamiah. But their eyes were too sharp for the success of this manœuvre; for I had not proceeded more than six miles before the Indians began to break camp, and to retreat, in good earnest, along the

Lolo trail, toward Montana and the east. Therefore, leaving Captain Jackson and his company, and a few volunteers, who had just returned to me, to watch Dunwell's Ferry, I returned at once to Kamiah and prepared to move, as quickly as possible, my entire command over the river. My own return to Kamiah was hastened by a request, said to be sent in from Joseph, asking on what terms he could surrender. While I was talking to his messenger, not far from the river, a shot was fired from the enemy upon our picket, which struck near the consulting parties. The messenger himself, his family, and some others, subsequently surrendered, but not Joseph.

It was doubtless a ruse, intended to delay our movements, but fortunately it did not affect them.

The seventeenth I sent Colonel Mason, of my staff, in command of the cavalry, Indian scouts, and McConville's volunteers, which force, with great labor, had been ferried to the other bank, to pursue the hostiles for two marches. The trail was exceedingly difficult, and passed mostly over wooded mountains. The woods were filled with fallen timber. This condition of things enabled the Indians to form ambuscades with ease. Mason followed the enemy rapidly, as directed, for the two marches condensed into one, to within three miles of Oro Fino Creek. His scouts first ran into the enemy's rear guard. Three of the scouts were disarmed, one was wounded, and one killed. One of the enemy was killed, and two pack-animals captured. Having accomplished, as he believed, the object of his movement; viz., to ascertain Joseph's intentions, and to engage him if he could do so to advantage, and having found the trail unfit for action with the cavalry, where a small rear-guard, having covered themselves with fringes of thick trees, could easily throw our people into confusion, he concluded to return; so that at eight, A. M., the eighteenth, the pursuing column was again at Kamiah. This really ended the campaign within the limits of my department.

The Indians had been well led, and well fought. They had defeated two companies in a pitched battle. They had eluded pursuit, and crossed the Salmon. They had turned back and crossed our communications, had kept our cavalry on the defensive, and defeated a company of volunteers. They had been finally forced to concentrate, it is true, and had been brought to battle. But, in battle with regular troops, they had held out for nearly two days before they were beaten, and after that were still able to keep together, cross a river too deep to be forded, and then check our pursuing cavalry and make off to other parts beyond Idaho. The result would necessitate a long and tedious chase.

Still, on our side, the Indians had been stopped in their murders, had been resolutely met everywhere, and driven into position, and beaten; and, by subsequent pursuit, the vast country was freed from their terrible presence. As it has since been proven, by means of these few months of hard work, and some attendant abuse, the whole extensive region of eastern Oregon and northern Idaho was completely delivered from perpetual conflicts and just causes of alarm.

CHAPTER XXVI.

JOSEPH AND THE LONG PURSUIT.—FIRST PLAN.—WHY ABAN-
DONED.— SECOND PLAN ADOPTED.— LONG MARCH BEGINS.—
GREEN'S ARRIVAL. — AN INDIAN RELIGIOUS SERVICE. —
RIVER CROSSING. — TROUBLE WITH INDIAN SCOUTS. — BUF-
FALO HORN. — ROBBINS' TRAIL OBSTRUCTED. — CAMP DE-
SCRIBED, WITH DETAIL. — DIFFICULTIES OF THE LOLO. —
SPURGIN AND THE PIONEERS.

I HEARD a quaint newspaper man once say, with regard to a congressional report, "I never read that
kind of literature except under compulsion!" Military
reports, with their technical terms, unembellished language, and their wearisome monotony of style, are
equally forbidding to the common mind, else I would
venture to introduce here one or two military orders,
which were extracted from a campaign report; but I
forbear, if the reader will but allow himself to be detained by a few dry statements of plans, in order to give
him his bearings, before he plunges into the wild forests
which he must cross in passing from Kamiah, Idaho, to
the Bitter-Root River of Montana.

First plan: To leave a small garrison at Kamiah, go
back to Lewiston, pick up supplies, press on to Missoula
at once; consign Camas Prairie and thereabouts to Col.
Green, who would be on hand from Fort Boise in about
ten days; and entrust all else to General Wheaton, with

Second Infantry, now fast coming from Georgia, by railroad, steamship, and steamboat, to Lewiston.

My first plan was abandoned; because of some just reasons for alarm among whites and friendly Indians, who feared that Joseph would come back before we were half way to Lewiston. Though I had halted my troops on change of plan, still, during a delay for supplies, I went in person to Lapwai. After sending despatches, and taking a brief rest, I turned back to my command. From a story that had reached me I had hoped to have met my wife. The story proved false, and the disappointment real. On the return Lieutenant Pierce, of the Twenty-first Infantry, who had been detained at the fort as ordnance officer, was my companion. His conversation was pleasant and refreshing during the long and tedious ride. In ascending Craig's Mountain, on the Kamiah trail, with a view to relieve our weary horses, we dismounted and walked together. It was a tough climb, and the lieutenant was extremely fatigued when we had reached the summit. I then turned, with the main force, to Croacsdale's farm, situated on the famous Camas Prairie, and remained for some days looking towards Kamiah, to support the little garrison which was left there if Indians should indeed turn back; looking towards Mount Idaho for Green's head of column; wishing it to annihilate space; waiting there eight days, while a fearful newspaper clamor came from the rear, of, "Slow! Slow! No ability; will never catch the Indians!"

Second plan evolved: Hostile Indians, with few exceptions (their rear guard back stealing ponies, causing the late alarm), had gone off by the Lolo trail. My dispositions were to form two columns and a reserve; to accompany the right column myself; the left column to be in charge of Wheaton; and the reserve to stay on Camas Prairie, under Green. The right column to take up the direct pursuit along Lolo trail; the left column to go eastward by Mullan road, look after old "Columbia River renegades" and malcontent Indians, keep the peace if possible, and, at first, like the right column, set out for Missoula, Montana; the reserve must watch out on all trails, keep inter-communication, be ready for hostile Indians, should they double back, and give heart to all neighboring farmers, miners, prospecters, and friendly Indians, by the show of protection at hand.

This new order of things being established, and understood, we, of the right column, began the long march, Thursday, the 26th of July, 1877. The first stage, sixteen miles, to Kamiah, was a rolling prairie, with excellent grazing, and wood and water in the canyons.

July 27. The infantry, artillery, and Jackson's company of cavalry crossed the Clearwater.

The 28th (Saturday). I took what few there were of McConville's volunteers and made a reconnoissance to what is called the "Little Camas," marching a distance of ten or eleven miles through the rough, thicket trail; found no signs of Indian families, no stock of any consequence belonging to the hostiles; and then returned to Kamiah. It was pretty evident that the wild ones had left the department. This day the head of Green's column, from Boise, reached us. Major Sanford was in command. He brought three companies of cavalry under Bendire, Carr, and Wagner, and twenty Bannock

Indian scouts. Two companies of infantry, with Green himself, were reported still far back, at Florence; but we could not, properly, any longer wait.

Next day, (Sunday,) while the troops were finishing the slow crossing of the Clearwater, at Kamiah, closing up the supplies, and getting everything ready for the long journey, James Lawyer, the Nez Perce head-chief of the friendly people, called his Nez Perces together, near the river, and invited the Bannock scouts, and all of us who could come, to participate in a religious service. Archie Lawyer, who had been so faithfully taught by a worthy Christian worker, Miss MacBeth, stood forth and preached an earnest sermon to the Indians, in the Nez Perce language. He frequently turned and spoke to us in English. He held a Bible in his hands, and translated its words readily into the Indian tongue. Many officers and men were present, and manifested much interest in this meeting. The singing was quite good. After service I made to the people some remarks, which were translated by Archie Lawyer, for those who could not understand the English.

Many Indians can follow a short conversation who cannot keep up with a connected discourse in English. I was glad enough to have this service of prayer, singing, and speaking, before we left. I think many besides myself felt as I did. There is a stern reality in going from all you love into the dread uncertainty of Indian fighting, where, perhaps, the worst form of torture and death await you. It is very wise and proper to ask God's blessing, and particularly so in these turning-points of life, when about to plunge into the dark clouds of any warfare.

On the 30th of July we were up before the dawn; the headquarters were moved across the river at four, A. M.; and the whole column was in motion by five. It rained heavily, the mud increased, and the path was narrow, steep, and slippery as we ascended the heights beyond Kamiah.

We found an abrupt descent at the Lolo fork; none but old frontiersmen and Indians could ride down, so we slipped and slid, fell, and scrambled up again. The pine trees were abundant, and, most of the way, filled in with a thick underbrush. We had, this day, our first trouble with the Bannock scouts. They had come from Boise; were tired, and did not mean to go any farther. Buffalo Horn, a young Indian, very handsomely decked off with skins and plumage, fortunately, for this time, took the side of their white chief, Robbins, and induced all but three to keep on with us for the present.

At the "We-ipe," the glade which we have before described, there was quite a lengthy opening in the forest, and plenty of water and grass. The hostile Indians had pastured this plat pretty well, and had dug over much of the land for the camas roots, which are often used by the Nez Perces for food. They are shaped something like onions, but more elongated, and have a sweetish, clammy taste, which is quite palatable.

The weather cleared up before sundown, and we gladly put our weary soldiers into camp. They had marched sixteen miles up mountain-heights, by narrow, crooked horse-trails, where the mud was deep, and there could be no firmness to the tread, but it was slip, slip, all the day. Sixteen miles are equivalent to thirty on a good road, and in fair weather. Our trail ahead, we learned, was much obstructed by fallen trees. It is wonderful what vast numbers of trees, of all sizes and descriptions, were uprooted by the winds; and they had fallen in every possible troublesome way, so that, matted together, even when small, it was very perplexing to get them out of the path. Nothing but axes would do it. We were, therefore, looking anxiously for our " pioneers." Some forty or fifty of them, with axes, were coming from Lewiston. We named this glade-like opening in the almost endless forest for our commander of the cavalry battalion, " Camp Sanford." This was his first day with us. Miller continued in charge of the foot artillery, Otis of our howitzer battery, which is mounted on muleback, and Miles had command of the infantry battalion.

Every day's record of a march like this becomes monotonous; so that, for the benefit of patient readers, after giving a brief picture of one camp and headquarters, we will only add here and there a scrap from the journal.

The camp was generally rectangular in form. One battalion covered the front, usually, encamping in line, and sending guard and pickets well out. A second covered the sides or flanks, and a third the rear. The battery took its place at will, selecting as good a position as the nature of the ground afforded. For headquarters a place was sought of easy communication, and having a neat plat of ground, with wood and water convenient. On coming to the place selected for the night's halt, Colonel Mason distributed the troops, guards, and outposts.

The "big tent" was a common square tent. Mason had a smaller one of special make, with joint and hinges in the uprights and in the ridge-pole. This arrangement enabled him to fold all in compact bundles for packing on the mules. His was put beside the big one, on one side; a tent-fly was pitched, with open front and back, on the other. These now were made to house Dr. Alexander, the army surgeon, Lieutenant Fletcher, aide-de-camp, and the news correspondent, Mr. Sutherland, who had joined us at Salmon River. I took Lieutenants C. E. S. Wood and Guy Howard, aides, into my tent. The quartermaster, Lieutenant Ebstein, pitched still another tent-fly for himself and his clerks. A small pack-train, under Louis, the Mexican, came up promptly after the night's halt was called.

The kitchen was placed some twenty paces off, to the left rear, near a stump, or clump of trees. The kitchen consisted of our mess-chest and one or two canvas bags, one or two mule-loads, according to the state of the supplies. There were one man for cook and one for helper. Our cook had the suggestive name of "Kid." He had, in himself, a mine of practical helpfulness for tent life. At first we had no chair, none until Captain Pollock, — reluctant to admit the claims of age, insisted upon giving me his camp-stool. When the nights were damp or cold we always had a large fire made in front of the big tent. Our beds were common blankets or robes of skin, the buffalo, fox, squirrel skins, and the like, placed on the ground. Our table consisted of a square piece of canvas, spread near the "kitchen," in fair weather, and within the big tent when it was rainy. One soon learns, when his

12

goods have to go on aparejos, fastened to mules' backs, that "man wants but little here below."

A more cheery, hearty, happy company than ours at headquarters is seldom found. Sometimes the officer is worn with anxiety, weary with long and tedious marches and loss of sleep, still he unbends at the mess-table, and tells lively stories to the circle around the camp-fire. There is no more intimate association among men than that, during a lengthy campaign, at a common mess. Generally we gave two hours in the morning, from the waking to the starting. Reveille at three or four, breakfast at four or five, and march at five or six.

On Thursday, the second day of August, the journal record was as follows: "The command left Camp Winters at seven, A. M. Artillery at head of column. Day clear and pleasantly cool. Captain Spurgin came into camp at six, A. M., bringing us news of his company of pioneers, still several miles behind. He was left, that morning, at Camp Winters, to bring them up. The trail led through woods of same general character as before; rather a 'slow trail,' owing to mountainous country and fallen timber. The summit of the hills was covered with rough granite boulders, making the path quite difficult. There was a plenty of excellent springs on trail; our men travel it well, and are in good order. We march sixteen miles, and encamp on a slope of the mountain. Poor grazing, indeed, here. The only feed consists of wild dwarf lupine, and wire-grass. Several mules were exhausted, and some packs of bacon were abandoned by the way. Robins, in charge of scouts, reports that 'loose Indian horses, broken down always, were seen along the trail.'"

We went into camp, named "Evan Miles," at about four, P. M. Spurgin, with pioneers, arrived at dark.

Such was the record of a day. If one could stand on Mount Washington, in New Hampshire, and look off northward toward Canada, he could see, in a clear day, much such a country as this through which we were wending our way. It does not appear far to the next peak. It is not so in a *straight* course, but such a course is impossible. "Keep to the hog-back!" That means there is usually a crooked connecting ridge between two neighboring mountain-heights, and you must keep on it. The necessity of doing so often made the distance three times greater than by straight lines; but the ground was too stony, too steep, the canyon too deep, to attempt the shorter course. Conceive this climbing ridge after ridge, in the wildest kind of wilderness, with the only possible pathway filled with timber, small and large, crossed and criss-crossed; and now, while the horses and mules are feeding on innutritious wire-grass, you will not wonder at "only sixteen miles a day."

"Didn't the hostile Indians go here?" the reader inquires. Yes; they jammed their ponies through, up the rocks, over, and under, and around the logs, and among the fallen trees, without attempting to cut a limb, leaving blood to mark their path; and abandoned animals, with broken legs, or "played out," or stretched dead by the wayside.

Our guide, Chapman, says, in frontier parlance, "No

man living can get so much out of a horse like an Indian can." Had we, for three days, along the Lolo trail, followed closely the hostiles' unmerciful example, we would not then have had ten mules left on their feet fit to carry our sugar, coffee, and hard-bread.

CHAPTER XXVII.

JOSEPH, AND THE PURSUIT. — A BREAK IN THE STORY. — BUF-
FALO HORN IN A NEW LIGHT. — AN EFFORT TO LOCATE ON
LOLO TRAIL. — MESSENGERS. — NEWS FROM MONTANA. —
HOW THE INDIANS FLANKED CAPTAIN RAWN. — LOUD FIR-
ING AHEAD. — ANOTHER RIVER-CROSSING. — NO FORAGE. —
FISH ABUNDANT. — MULES FASTING. — THE OASIS. — WARM
SPRINGS. — A HORSEMAN IN SIGHT. — DISPATCH FROM GIB-
BON. — SERGEANT SUTHERLAND. — HE GOES OUT AT NIGHT
WITH AN INDIAN GUIDE.

SINCE the Nez Perce war, another has come and gone.
Though covering a smaller region, it was a more
complicated affair, and the windings and twistings made
the sum of our journeys quite as long.

In the last chapter I mentioned the good conduct of
Buffalo Horn, the chief Bannock scout. This trusted
Indian, who never received from white men anything but
kindness and confidence, the next year became the leader
of the Bannock war.

Let us imagine that we have toiled on over those
mountains lying between Idaho and Montana, two-thirds
of the way across; that we have met Mr. Curley, the
messenger who went from Mount Idaho to Missoula, and
was returning, with an Israelite for a companion: Mr.
Curley's face was cheery, but he brought us bad news.
Joseph and Looking-glass, with their hordes, had come
up to the hastily-constructed fort in the Lolo Valley;
had promised good behavior, in consideration for a safe

conduct through to the "Buffalo Illahie." "Let us alone," according to Jeff. Davis, "and we will disturb nobody." Captain Rawn was there at the time, in command of a few regulars, and many volunteers. It was judged best by him and those with him to let Joseph's band go by, close on the right flank, and the whites promise not to fire. Who can think of the apprehension of a scattered population and blame these citizen-volunteers for letting " General Howard's Indians " go on, provided they promised to do no damage?

Yet it was to us bad news that the Indians had gone; for the pass where the fort was situated was reported to be narrow, the cliffs on either side high and difficult, and therefore we hoped that these Indians would be stopped until we could come up and help the fort, by attacking from the west and rear. It might have saved us a long march, much public abuse, and perhaps have secured to us the enviable reputation of being good Indian-fighters. We had passed the last tine of the Clearwater, where at night, after twenty-one miles of the roughest country, with Spurgin's pioneers ahead, cutting out the trail, we came into camp in the twilight, where we had heard loud echoes of firing by the advanced scouts, and thought they had come upon Joseph's rear-guard. Then we spurred up the weary animals into a tired trot, and, along this narrow trail descended for miles through the almost impenetrable forest, till we came to the narrowest of valleys, to find not a mouthful of food for horse or mule, but the nicest of salmon for the men, in water about knee-deep, — water clear as crystal, rushing and plashing over the rocks. The echoes which deceived us into thinking the enemy near, were from the scouts' carbines, shooting the bigger fish, as they were swimming up the Clearwater. Glad were we to get beyond that valley where the poor mule was obliged to fast all night, and tremble and sway himself back and forth as he undertook to take his load up the steep exit at four o'clock the next morning.

How strong and firm his step became seven miles ahead, when he came into a mountain glade, where there were little swampy lakes, and the greenest of grass in plenty. Here was the place where mule and man enjoyed a rest and a breakfast far more satisfying than in inhabited regions which are replete with abundance. Yes, we have passed this lovely oasis in the wild Lolo wilderness, and have come to an opening in the mountains, which makes us feel almost as if the tug of war was over. But we must not be sanguine, for appearances are deceptive. Our journal says: "Warm Springs, about four, P. M. Nine miles from Summit Prairie — (where the mule and man had the early breakfast) ; sixteen miles from our last camp. Fine camp here at Hot Springs, (sulphur water) ; good grazing, and mountain brook."

It requires but a little imagination for the reader to fill out the picture: Several beautiful pools of steaming water, at the foot of a gently-sloping, thinly-wooded hill. Down the hill, sweeping swiftly over ledges, and throwing up the spray, which sparkles in the sunshine, from fissures and crevices in the ledge, glides a broad, shallow stream. It was a charming place. The wilderness was speedily changed into a beautiful village. Horses and mules were feeding on the green, as quiet and contented

as if it had always been their home. The camps of the
men were promptly arranged in order. Blankets and
clothing were spread for airing, and already the under-
clothing was being wrung out by the half-naked owners,
in the hot water of the pools, and waving gently on the
bushes, as the sun and the breeze caused the speedy dry-
ing. This peaceful scene of rest and comfort, heightened
by the statuesque forms of the bathers, of whom we had
glimpses from the more distant sulphur pools, was disturbed by the cry, from the outer picket-post, "A horseman in sight from the East!" A tall frontiersman soon
appeared, riding rapidly into our camp.

"My name is Pardee. I bring a dispatch from General
Gibbon to General Howard." Pardee, as well as Curry,
who had passed us a couple of days before on the trail,
had brought us tidings of General Gibbon. He, Gibbon, had left his headquarters at Helena, hastened in our
direction to Missoula, and arrived after the Indians had
left Rawn's fort; he had with him less than two hundred men, but with these had pushed forward on Chief
Joseph's trail. His command rolled on in wagons up the
Bitter Root Valley, as fast as horses could be made to go.
He needed a hundred men more, and hoped that I might
send them by forced marches to overtake him.

Having left my infantry tramping along the crooked
trail, I had already set out with my cavalry, and was
about a day ahead, when this 6th of August message
arrived. I had but two hundred souls, all told, and I
had a fancy that *I* myself could push on more miles in a
day than one less spurred by the sense of responsibility.
Gibbon had then one hundred miles the start, and was

marching fast. We could not, of course, with tired animals, overtake him till he began a slower progress, which
he must do to cross the Rocky Mountain divide, or until
he stopped, as he would doubtless do, if the Indians discovered the fewness of his numbers, and decided to give
him battle. In any case, he might delay somewhere for
the needed accession of force.

A trusty sergeant, by the name of Sutherland, and an
Indian scout, were selected to go with him. They left at
once with the answer, having been instructed to travel
night and day until Gibbon should be overtaken.

"General Howard is coming on, as fast as possible, by
forced marches, with two hundred cavalrymen, to give
the needed reinforcement." Such was the substance of
Sutherland's message.

Conceive of a brave man starting out at night, in this
wild country, with only an Indian to guide him! The
way was rugged, the night was dark, the distance was
great, and he a stranger; but he was resolute, and a
soldier.

CHAPTER XXVIII.

JOSEPH AND THE PURSUIT. — SUTHERLAND'S PROGRESS. — THE
TRAIL DIFFICULT AND OBSTRUCTED. — SHELVING ROCKS. —
THE COYOTES. — LIEUTENANT FLETCHER AND GIBBON'S
TALL MESSENGER. — SUTHERLAND DESERTED BY HIS IN-
DIAN GUIDE. — HIS HORSE "PLAYS OUT." — BUCKING HORSE
DESCRIBED. — THE MOVEMENT OF TROOPS FOLLOWING THE
MESSENGER. — TWENTY-TWO MILES EQUIVALENT TO FORTY.
— GENERAL SHERMAN'S PROXIMITY. — COLONEL MASON LIKES
A WAGON-ROAD. — THE MOUTH OF THE LOLO. — THE SOL-
DIER'S CRITICISM. — THIRTY-FOUR MILES IN A DAY WITH
TREMBLING HORSES. — BITTER-ROOT VALLEY. — THE DOC-
TOR. — ROSS' HOLE. — A SPY.

STILL pursuing the famous Lolo trail by the rugged
passes of the mountains between Idaho and Montana,
Sergeant Sutherland and his Indian guide, who, at evening, the 6th of August, left us at the hot sulphur springs,
fifty miles from the town of Missoula, found no easy
task. The Indian only knew the country generally, and
cared little about the character of his pathway, provided
his pony held out; not so with the soldier. He liked,
above all things, a good, strong, active horse, one that he
could depend upon. And he was not quite satisfied to
follow faint trails, and go merely by the stars. Sutherland, however, plodded on with his already weary horse,
now in a dense forest, and now emerging, in the starlight,
into a hill-country, more bare of trees. For a time the
trail was pretty good, occasionally interrupted by the fallen
trees, which were too long to get around, and too tiresome

for the animals to stride over. Of a sudden he came upon a mountain spur, that blocked the way. The path turned to the right, and wound along a steep acclivity, and over a knife-edge crest. By dismounting, and slowly leading the animals, the sergeant and the guide, without slipping off the shelving rock into a deep chasm below, managed, at last, to creep around to the other side. One difficult obstacle like this was overcome, and the night wore away. When the dawn appeared, the valley of the Lolo had opened out into broader proportions; the grass-fields gave sign of cultivation, and an occasional hut showed that, at some time not far back, this region had been inhabited; still, for miles, there was not a domestic animal, not even an Indian dog, to howl back defiance to the terrific and multitudinous cries of the coyotes.

When Lieutenant Fletcher, who will be remembered as the officer who discovered the whereabouts of Joseph's people just before the battle of the Clearwater, and who was still supervising the engineering work of the campaign, and who has since issued a series of beautiful maps, and multiplied them, by the photographic methods, for the use of all of us, — when Fletcher, with Gibbon's tall messenger, set out for Missoula, the next morning at four o'clock, Sutherland had scarcely traversed twenty-five miles. The lieutenant's stock was rested, fed, and fresh, and he had daylight, so that he gained rapidly on the sergeant, and the latter was but a few miles ahead, when Fletcher and his companion turned away from his course, northward, down the Bitter-Root Valley, toward Missoula.

The Indian guide deserted Sutherland at the most convenient point and time, and also went off toward Missoula. His poor horse trembled in his joints, sweat at every pore, and had his sides, near the sergeant's boot-heel, stained with blood from the often used, though reluctant, spur, when he dragged himself into the yard of the first settler that he encountered in ascending the Bitter-Root River.

" Good-morning, Mr. A."

"Good-morning, stranger," says a jolly-looking man, emerging from the farm-house.

" 'Pears you've had a tough ride, by the look of ye' horse?"

" Yes; I'm bearing dispatches from General Howard to General Gibbon. I've authority to get a remount, and am told you have some horses."

" Oh, yes, yes, stranger. You'll have to go right smart to catch Gibbon, for he streamed it with his men in wagons. He's got three days the start on ye!"

" Well, well, sir, I'm in a hurry. Will you let me have a horse? The quartermaster will settle. I must have one."

" I reckon I can; not tamed much, but you look like a spunky feller."

A colt is soon brought forward.

After a little food and coffee, that Mr. A. kindly gave him, the sergeant mounted. Did you ever see an Indian pony " buck "?

Once several officers of us were quietly taking our lunch when a dozen voices at once screamed, " The horse! The horse!" The girth had, somehow, been loosened, and the horse, a half-breed, — i. e., part Indian and part American, — began to gallop in circles, now

leaping into the air, and now shaking himself and round-
ing up his back like a cat; sometimes going one way,
and then reversing and tearing off in another direction.
The horse made for us at first, the cries giving us just
time to keep out of the way. He continued his fury un-
abated, till he had cleared himself of his pad, blanket,
and saddle, and then quieted down, and looked as modest
and innocent as does the mule, who, often thus docile,
watches his opportunity to revenge himself on his faithful
packer because he has loaded and girt him too tightly.
With this " bucking horse " picture before the reader, he
can easily imagine the scene when Sergeant Sutherland
sprang into the saddle, and undertook to proceed. There
was first a stiff " I won't go ! " then the leaping, jumping,
shaking process ; the girt-band gave way, and the rider,
being hurled to the ground, strained his back. Still,
after a time, he managed to mount again, and to break
in his pony, so as to proceed. Though in considerable
pain, and quite lame, he got over much ground before
night.

Thus our messenger has gone ahead, followed by Lieutenant Fletcher, who had turned to Missoula for supplies.
The latter was to meet us, on his return, with the necessary food for men and animals, before reaching the point
where we were to turn off southward, in this Bitter-
Root Valley, in order to follow the trails of Joseph and
Gibbon.

To return to my cavalry column : At half-past five,
A. M., Spurgin, with his axemen, was already out on the
trail, working hard, to get well ahead of the command, so that it might make, to-day, the utmost distance

over this terribly rough and obstructed pathway. He cleared away the fallen trees, made bridges across chasms, and, when there was time, by side-digging, or walling with fragments of the rock, he improved portions of the break-neck trail.

At half-past six, A. M., with some reluctance leaving these hot-springs and this charming camp, we set out, and made twenty-two miles. If this is considered a short distance for a forced march, it should be remembered that it was equal to forty miles on a fair roadway.

We had just heard of General Sherman's proximity to our line of march, and of his intended visit to the Pacific coast. Our camp was so good a one, and so fine a wagon trail here began, on hard, level ground, that, coupling our good luck with Sherman's welcome name, we designated the field of this one night's sojourn, "Camp Sherman."

August 8. Intent on reinforcing Gibbon our two hundred cavalrymen were off betimes, just as the sun was peeping over the ridge ahead. We can truly say we enjoy the march over this excellent road. Both men and horses were more cheerful. By nine, A. M., we reached the mouth of the Lolo. The narrow pass, where the temporary fort had been made by the men from Missoula, and where the Indians had stopped to parley, was inspected by our command. And as the excellent barricades of logs appeared in our front, the question arose, " How could the Indians get by?" All eyes were turned to the high hills on the right and on the left.

" Why did not Rawn and the volunteers stop them here?" " Joseph was too smart for them!" "Looking-glass is always a good Indian here, in the Bitter-Root country." Such were remarks that I heard from one and another as we worked our way crookedly past these obstructions in this famous Lolo pass. At the mouth of the Lolo, a tributary of the Bitter-Root, while resting and grazing the animals for a couple of hours, Fletcher came up with the needed supplies. Then on we went across the river, which, with its broad and beautiful valley, delighted the eye, passed the town of Stevensville, and kept on till seven o'clock in the evening. Between sun and sun, with horses which had hitherto been staggering and trembling on the stony and log be-ridden paths of the mountains, we had accomplished thirty-four miles. So much for a good wagon-road.

Soldiers who are pressing on toward an expected battlefield are very eager for news. Ears and eyes are wide open. Every sound is caught, and accounted for. Every man met is stopped and questioned. Every unusual stir of cattle and horses, in the distance, is searched with eyes of the longest range, and with glasses. To-day, the 9th of August, on this level, hard, wagon-road, we tramped along the Bitter-Root Valley, with few incidents to break the quiet of the column. It was a fine grazing country on our right and left, — plenty of stock. The inhabitants appeared to thrive well between Stevensville and Corvallis, the next village above.

As the cavalry approached Corvallis we met a gentleman in a buggy. Yes, a covered buggy in the Rocky Mountains, far away from anywhere! It was the doctor of the region. Cautious, careful man! We did not learn from him that citizens had kindly remembered these Indians who had made, through their country, so many parallel paths, — remembered them as very friendly and profitable traders, as, year by year, they had come and gone, while en route to the buffalo illahee. We do not draw from him that some very kind neighbors carried provisions into the Indian's camp, in wagons, and sold them for money; that their old and worn horses had been traded off for fresh ones; and that for these kindnesses, and this show of fraternal feeling, the entire valley had been spared by the placable Joseph. No; these facts crept out from other sources. The doctor told us where, and when, the Indians swept by, — over yonder, across the Bitter-Root, next to the mountain-shore, beyond that fringe of cottonwood; also when General Gibbon rapidly followed. "He must be at ' Ross' Hole ' by this time." " Ross' Hole ! " Strange name. It is some kind of crater in these highlands, we think, or short canyon, too deep for the ordinary name. We shall see.

Soon are met citizens on horseback, and some in wagons. They had started to catch the Indians, but travelling two days at ten or fifteen miles a day did not suit them. Their saloons, their stores, their farms, were needing their constant care, "The Indians are already well out of the way; can run as fast, or faster, than we can follow; so that we came back."

Why shouldn't they? These citizens were not employed as soldiers, and the danger to them and their families was past.

No reliable news can be gained from these returning citizens.

A crowd watched for our cavalcade at Corvallis. It was composed of men and boys, roughly clad, with here and there a sprinkling of the brighter colors of female dress, and a few hatless Indians, standing listlessly with their red blankets wrapped around them. One such, a young Indian, sat quietly upon the flattish roof of an old shed, near the outskirts of the town. He appeared like the rest. "Who are these Indians?" A most respectable-looking trader vouches for them. "They are all friendly Flat-heads!"

As soon as the command was well out of the way, beyond the town, this Indian, who was mounted on the roof, slid easily to the eaves, sprang to the ground, mounted a Cayuse pony, standing near by, and made straight eastward. He reached the foot-hills of the eastern range of mountains, which, in that direction, wall up the Bitter-Root Valley, almost before he was suspected. Several young men gave chase, but could not find him. He sped away to the mountains, and then turned south, toward Joseph's trail. He was a spy. As successful spies no men can excel these Indians, and none was swifter than this spy-messenger, and none ever did greater service to his chief. His power of endurance was wonderful. The distance was, probably, one hundred and fifty miles, by the route he took to enable him to overtake his people. Through the forests, over the mountains, across the stretches of prairie, the Cayuse never ceased to trot or canter till thoroughly exhausted; his legs bruised and bleeding, wet with foam, the trembling, staggering animal stumbled and fell. No coaxing, no whipping and kicking will restore his courage. So the spy, having slipped off the saddle and bridle, and "cached" them close at hand, took careful observation of the place of concealment. Then he stalked away at a swift, steady walk till he had gained Gibbon's trail over the Rocky Mountain range. It was a real range at this crossing; not so very high, but plain to be seen and felt as you ascended from the west.

CHAPTER XXIX.

JOSEPH AND THE PURSUIT. — MANNER OF MARCHING. — THE
OAKS. — CAMP JOHN GIBBON. — LIEUTENANT BACON. — CHIEF
ROBBINS. — THE ESCORT. — A TROT ALL DAY. — NAME "ROSS'
HOLE" ACCOUNTED FOR. — DAY'S JOURNEY 53 MILES. — AS-
CENDING THE ROCKY MOUNTAINS. — SCOUTS RETURNING
WITH SEVEN CITIZENS. — FIRST NEWS OF GIBBON'S FIGHT. —
HOW THE CAMP WAS FIXED. — BONNY'S RETURN RIDE. —
THE SPY. — SUTHERLAND AGAIN. — GIBBON WOUNDED.

TURNING from the dismounted Indian spy to our command, we find them still wearily working their way
through the mountains. It is wonderful how much distance can be made in a day by a steady pace. Walk your
horses as fast as you can, keeping them together, the
men chat with one another, and rest themselves occasionally by a puff or two from short clay pipes. At the end
of fifty minutes, call the halt, dismount, and if there
should happen to be short intervals, do not close them.
Rest just ten minutes. Then mount and go on again, for
another fifty minutes. After just ten minutes' halt, proceed as before.

Where, in the southern part of the Bitter-Root Valley,
the mountains appeared to be shut in, and it seemed no
longer possible to move southward without climbing, was
a broad, level space, covered with trees, not altogether
the usual cottonwood, but mostly fair-sized oaks. Our
camp (August 9) was chosen close by the one lately
occupied by General Gibbon, so we named it "Camp

John Gibbon." It was a fine camp; the swift water, with its lively mountain impulse still in it, shot over bowlders in the shallow river bed; and a greensward strewn with the changing autumn leaves, that had begun to fall, invited weary men and horses to a pleasant night's refreshment.

I had become so anxious about Gibbon, with his small force, that I resolved to pick twenty of our best horses, with their well-seasoned riders, put them under Lieutenant Bacon, a tall, well-built man, of light hair and light-grayish eyes, slow of speech, but always clear-headed and brave, add seventeen scouts, under Chief Robbins; take also Lieutenant Wood, and the quartermaster's active clerk, Mr. Bonny, with me, and ride as fast and as far in search of Gibbon as the animals would carry us. Mason remained in charge of the remainder of the cavalry, to follow as rapidly as possible. In the cool, clear morning, just as the dawn appeared, in a column of twos, we moved out of camp; took a steady, firm trot, and, except in a few instances where the roughness of the trail prevented speed, kept at that gait all day. We rested at mid-day for one hour, after passing the famous "Ross' Hole." Our northern people would call it broad swamp land, hemmed in by hills; the Mexicans would name it a "cienaga;" the frontiersmen say, "Hole." It is dry now, but doubtless when Ross and his party of emigrants went this way, their wagons and horses mired, and they indignantly named the cienaga, or swamp, a horrid hole, and in time, by the proper reduction of history, we have "Ross' hole."

We could not trot up the mountain ridge; it was as

much as we could do to walk. Horses and men toiled up
the winding ascent. There were many paths. Every
new climber tried to find an easier way. But if you took
the left, through the close trees and thick underbrush,
you wished you had taken the right, or another, between
the two. There was no dodging that abrupt six miles of
mountain-climbing. Only fifty-three miles, as we came
to this nice stream, and broad, glade-like opening! We
were already in the canyon that marks the eastern slope,
and we wondered whether or not this Trail Creek sent
its waters into the far-off Atlantic.

Having halted at dark, Robbins and some scouts returned at a trot, with seven citizens on foot. You do not
often see this sight — citizens dismounted on a frontier
road! In fact, you do not often see any human being in
these mountains.

"Well, my men, what have you to tell us?" One of
them replied, "General Gibbon had a fight with the Indians yesterday morning; has lost half his men. It was
going hard with him when we left. We haven't had anything to eat for two days." So we invited them to our
intended camp, and fed them. General Gibbon and the
Indians were not twenty miles from us. As these citizens talked much as men are apt to do who early in the
conflict run from the field of battle, it is not fair to the
gallant soldiers who remain and fight it out to give their
story too much weight. Our horses were too much exhausted to move another league that night (that 10th of
August). We were so near the enemy, — just how near
we did not know, — and there were so few of us, that we
barricaded a little with logs, and built fires, to make it

appear that we had many troops. Mr. Bonny was started back to Mason at once with the news. How could he get his horse through thirty miles more, back beyond Ross' Hole?

A short time ago we saw the Indian spy in swift motion across the rocky range, first on horseback, and then on foot. He had come into the wagon-road just ahead of my brilliant camp, wherein we forty pretended to be five hundred. Our scouts found his plain moccasin tracks, and hence we felt sure that Joseph had already received timely warning. The spy doubtless took a good look at our camp-fires, and then pressed on. We shall see what was the probable result of his message.

The seven countrymen who dropped in upon us the night before were a sorry-looking set. They gave us a graphic account of the fight; of their own part in it; their progress, their escape. One had had a brother desperately wounded. The troops had done nobly, but were fearfully outnumbered. General Gibbon had shown wonderful gallantry, and, with many others, was severely wounded.

They enumerated those who had been killed in the battle; but, even after they had been comforted by a night's rest, and a warm breakfast, they gave us but gloomy views of the final situation at the time they themselves, for dear life, were making their escape to the brush. Now, no offer of favor or money, not even the attraction of a brother wounded and needy, could induce one of those brave men to go back, and guide us to the battle-field.

While we were making our forced march, and taking the needed rest, others had not been idle.

Gibbon's messenger had passed near us in the early morning of the 10th. There was a part of the distance, just before that Ross' cienaga, where there were two roads. The messenger was galloping along the left, while we were trotting over the right track. The high ground between prevented us from seeing this horseman, and him from seeing our cavalcade. It was too bad; for just the sight of him would have saved the brisk Mr. Bonny from the night ride of thirty miles, the poor horse under him being even more to be pitied than the man. The official dispatch which General Gibbon's messenger was bearing made matters appear very serious. The message, written in pencil, on a square piece of paper, of the size of a visiting card, reads:

GENERAL: We surprised the Nez Perce camp at daylight this morning, whipped them out of it, killing a considerable number; but they then turned on us, forced us out of it, and compelled us to take the defensive. We are here near the mouth of Big Hole pass, with a number of wounded, and need medical attendance and assistance of all kinds, and hope you will hurry to our relief.

GIBBON, Comm'd'g.

Aug. 9, '77.

The swift messenger, though he passed me, met Mason, with the cavalry, and the medical officers, who were so much required. These tidings put them into swifter motion, and the news was sent flying to the infantry, which was one day's march behind the cavalry.

How messengers do speed, with news from the battle-field! From the days of old *Ely*, waiting at the city gate, till now, messengers from the bloody field run and outrun each other, with tidings both good and bad.

Strange as it may seem, another messenger passed my

little troop without seeing us, and Mason, now pushing forward, first received him. This man brought a note from the sergeant, who, we remember, was deserted by the Indian guide, and nearly killed by the "bucking horse," and yet, with his aching back, kept in the saddle. The note is so good, and it is so seldom that readers hear from an enlisted man, that I will insert a few extracts:

ON THE BIG HOLE TRAIL, ABOUT 20 MILES FROM ROSS' HOLE, 12 M., Aug. 9, '77.

GENERAL: I arrived here en route to General Gibbon's command ten minutes ago. I find the train of General Gibbon in camp, with a guard of about eighteen men, citizens and soldiers. General Gibbon left here last night, with a force of (say) one hundred and eighty men, and has been fighting all day, but his exact whereabouts not known to party here.

In conformity with orders from General Gibbon a party of three non-commissioned officers, and seven privates, started from here at daybreak, (with a 12-pounder mountain howitzer, and ammunition,) and were attacked about three and a half miles out; one corporal killed, two sergeants wounded, and two men missing. Howitzer lost, with fifteen rounds of ammunition; also two thousand rounds calibre .45; pack-mule killed. As near as I can learn, the sergeant in charge scattered and destroyed the ammunition for howitzer; fired three rounds at Indians. It appears, from the attack, that Indians are between General Gibbon and this camp. I find the men here somewhat uneasy, but determined to stand off the Indians, at all hazards. I take two men from here, and start in five minutes, to endeavor to reach General Gibbon. . . . .

Would respectfully state, in explanation of seeming delay on my part, that I was thrown from an unbroken horse at ———, and my back severely hurt, my progress from that point being attended with severe suffering. I am, General,

Very respectfully yours,
O. SUTHERLAND,
Sergeant Company "B," 1st Cavalry.

I am glad to preserve this brief record of a brave and deserving man.

On the margin of my note-book is written, "1877, August 11. Saturday;" "Clear and cool." Think of it, just over the highest ridge of the Rocky Mountains. "We sent our Indian scouts ahead at 4, A. M., and proceeded about eighteen miles, by a trail through thick woods and underbrush, — good ambuscades." It means excellent places for traps, such as the Indians sometimes set, — traps like that set for General Braddock and Colonel George Washington, before we became a republic. "We arrived at Gibbon's fortified camp at 10, A. M., and found the command all right, and cheerful. The Indians had left at 11 o'clock, night before. Gibbon's final position was on a wooded ridge, with heights above it, and willow bottom, a creek, and table-land below it. He had no surgeon with him. The wounded were doing well, however. Gibbon's wound was a flesh wound, above the knee. Sent courier to Deer Lodge with telegraphic dispatches to Terry and McDowell." The above is explicit enough, and suggestive, to those of us who were ever on the ground; but as this Indian engagement of General John Gibbon has, from various sources, gone into history, I will, in the following chapter, give the story substantially as I had it from his own lips.

CHAPTER XXX.

JOSEPH AND THE BATTLE OF BIG-HOLE. — THE APPROACH OF
ESCORT TO GIBBON'S CAMP DESCRIBED. — ARE THEY IN-
DIANS? — ARE THEY SOLDIERS' HORSES GRAZING? — SOL-
DIERS BATHING. — GIBBON'S CAMP. — THE HOSPITAL AP-
PEARANCE. — INDIANS SLIP OFF IN THE NIGHT. — BATTLE-
FIELD DESCRIBED. — WOMEN IN THE STREAM ASKING FOR
PROTECTION. — GIBBON'S STORY.

BEHOLD our cavalcade of forty riders, with Indian
scouts ahead, as they descend the Rocky Mountain
trail! Chief Robbins sees the smoke of a camp, and
animals grazing down there in the Big-Hole bottom.
The Indian scouts, with Robbins, had stopped on a bare
knoll, to the left of the road, and, from their manner
and gestures, appeared to be excited, till I came up.

"What is it? Are they our men yonder?"

"They are soldiers, going from the smoke there, under
that hill, back and forth to the creek."

I knew, at once, that they were soldiers. It was a
party bathing in the stream; some dressing, some sitting
on the bank, and others moving about, wading in the
shallow water. I had hardly said "They are soldiers!"
before our horses were in brisk motion toward the smoke
that was rolling up from the short pines, just to the left
of the thick willows, which, from the smoke to the high

ground beyond the creek, appeared completely to cover the broad bottom-land.

We passed rapidly along the trail, around another bluff, when the little camp came full in view. "There it is!" "It is Gibbon's camp!" A thrill of delight passed through our little party, and it found a voice.

"Hurrah! hurrah!" It did look like a hospital at first, though there were lines of rifle-pits, and well soldiers enough to give one the impression of a heavy hospital guard. So many wounded; nearly half lying cheerful, though not able to move; many white bandages about the head and face; some arms in slings; there were roughly constructed shelters from the heat of an unrelenting August sun. Quite on the other side, in the northeast corner of the camp, reclined the wounded commander. His face was very bright, and his voice had a cheery ring as he called out,

"Hallo, Howard! Glad to see you."

"Well, Gibbon, how do you do?"

"Oh, I'm not much hurt; a flesh-wound in the thigh."

After a short time I asked: "Where are the Indians?"

"They drew off at eleven o'clock, last night," Gibbon said. "You'll dine with me?"

"How can I? You've no supplies."

"Oh, that was a mistake; we have bread, and to spare."

"Where was the field," I asked. Then he pointed out to me the ground.

We were standing on the north side of the valley. The willows, with grassy spaces between them, came next to us, below the bluff. Across the level willow-land, rough and spongy in places, with a few water-holes, for, perhaps, three hundred yards, you approached the main "Big-Hole" Creek. It was twenty or thirty steps across it. Then there was an open grassy bottom, that now looked as if it had been mowed. There was a strip of this grass-land, from fifty to seventy yards across, before you touched the foot of the high ground, constituting the other shore of the valley. It was on this grassy bottom that Joseph had pitched his lodges, before the battle. Behind us the hilly hither shore rose rapidly into a mountain. Farther down, on our side, was a spur of the mountain, open and covered with grass, where Joseph's herd was feeding when Gibbon's men first approached; and a big herd it was. To our right, up the creek, the mountain was of easier ascent, and, though covered with pines, it was only at intervals, so that the enemy had a plunging fire, from two or three picket posts, straight into Gibbon's camp. After the General and his generous staff had refreshed us with a dinner good enough for a soldier, he proposed to ride over, show us the battle-field proper, and explain the situation.

"But you cannnot ride, Gibbon?"

"I think I can. I'll try, at any rate."

So, with some pain, he mounted. We rode to the place, where many lodge-poles were lying. We found, just under the river bank, a part of the Indians unburied, and fresh marks of the hasty burial of others. He pointed to where women, during the battle, with their little ones in their arms, had waded into the deep water to avoid the firing; and told me how it touched his heart when two or three extended their babies toward him, and looked as pleasant and wistful as they could for his protection; this was while the balls where whistling through the willows near by.

Now, my reader, if you should take up your skilful pencil, I think you could picture that touching scene, and would sadly ask the question, "Is there no substitute for war?"

Let General Gibbon tell the story after his return to camp; for he is too lame and sore to dismount on the field, or to stay long enough to satisfy my curiosity. The excellent Doctor Fitzgerald, and his assistants, had arrived. The wounded were already attended to. The messages had been sent to the outer world, and the plans for further pursuit were agreed upon. The General reclined under his bush cover, favoring the sore leg as much as he could. I took a camp-chair, also within the homely bower, while our respective staff officials, grouping themselves at hand, sat, half knelt, or squatted, upon the ground, attentive.

"You know, Howard, when the Nez Perces had avoided Rawn, with his small force, there in the Lolo, they ascended the Bitter-Root. At first they travelled slowly enough, delaying to trade with the inhabitants. Wasn't it a shame in those Bitter-Root people to traffic with the horrid murderers, giving them fresh horses, and all sorts of provisions, as readily as if they had been the best friends in the world? I am glad to say that one man had courage enough to shut his store in their faces. [Gibbon mentions him in his report. His name is Young, of Corvallis.] I set out with a little short of one hundred and fifty rifles, on the fourth, [August, 1877,] from

Missoula, using wagons, to make all the distance possible. I don't think we could have got through to this place if I hadn't been most lucky in running across Mr. Blodget, a frontiersman, who had piloted wagons over this country before. The packs were on hand, if we had failed with the wagon train. Wasn't it a rough road, though? It took us a long time to get over the divides, but in the bottoms we made grand time.

"We ran across a number of the Indians' camps, and they made some twelve or fifteen miles a day; so that, by doubling on them, I knew I would, in time, catch up. But we were delayed, beyond measure, at the Rocky Mountains. Our men had to draw the wagons up with ropes. It took us hours to get to the top. Well, we accomplished it, and worked our way down this slope, into Big Hole; rested a while; then leaving a small detachment, three or four miles back, with the howitzer, where you saw the camp, with the remainder I came on, slowly and silently, under cover of the night. We heard the sound of Indian ponies on the next spur, over there, to my left. Pushing along quietly between them and the bottom, we at last discovered the Indian lodges.

"Here I halted my command, for it was altogether too dark to move to the attack. We could catch sounds from the tepees; occasionally a dog would bark, or a child cry, but, evidently, our presence was not discovered.

"On the edge of the bottom I deployed my companies into line, putting the citizens on the left, for quite a number of them had volunteered to come on and help us. You notice the big sloughs there beside the creek. The willows are thicker in spots. The command now moved forward rapidly. But the Indians discovered the attack as soon as we had started, and several of them put themselves across this creek, into that bend, and, using the bank as a cover, opened fire. Some of our men swept past these, and through the tepees, driving the Indians before them.

"At first we had passed the low ground, and had taken the camp, and appeared to have carried everything; but I soon found that the Indians had not given up. Some were in the willows, working as skirmishers. Some rallied up yonder on that hill, and started across the bottom to retake their herd, while others got behind trees and rocks, and were picking off our men, one by one, and you know we couldn't well spare any; some of my officers were wounded already, and myself among the number.

"At last I ordered the move back to this side, and we took this wooded point. Here we were a good deal exposed to the sharpshooters, and several officers were wounded; but we drove them back, defeated every attempt to assault our camp, and inflicted great loss upon the Indians. Of course they yelled, crept up close at times, fired, and set the grass on fire; but all that time we were digging those trenches, and barricading, and giving to the hostiles as good as they sent.

"Next day, until night, parties of them were lurking about, between me and my train. The attempt to fetch up the howitzer brought on a severe skirmish, and the howitzer was lost; but that night (evening of the 10th) the last of them gave us a sharp volley, about eleven o'clock, and cleared out. And here you find us, some killed, many wounded, but in no way discouraged. It was a gallant struggle. Who could have believed that those Indians would have rallied after such a surprise, and made such a fight?"

CHAPTER XXXI.

THE engagement, the outlines of which I have heretofore given, was a bloody one indeed, whether viewed from our own or the Indian side. "Captain William Logan, killed!" It is a short notice. Strangers are not much interested. "War is his business, general." He takes his chances. A brief biography; a two days' notice; the regular army record! But I am not satisfied with this. Heroic devotion to duty in Indian warfare saves lives by interposing one's own. Let the reader write the name of William Logan on the tablets of his memory, and think again of those that loved him, and have ever since suffered on account of his loss.

Again, Lieutenant James H. Bradley fell in action, to rise no more. You do not know his face? His photograph is not known to the reader! Never mind. He was a manly man. As Mr. Lincoln, looking over those

14

silent graves at Gettysburg, said, "They gave here the last full measure of devotion." So with Bradley; in order to punish guilt, to secure peace, and serve faithfully his country, he gave the full measure, — his life.

Lieutenant William H. English was wounded severely. All hoped that he might recover, but he did not. He lingered for several days, but before the campaign was over the news of his death came to us. Several other officers were wounded, some being hit two or three times. I do not name them in this narration lest I extend too much, though I feel toward them a strong desire to honor their service in some practicable way.

There were twenty-six others, soldiers and citizens, who laid their bodies away in this place of sepulture. Their names are not before us; but, thank a kind Providence, comrades talk of them, and somebody keeps a place of love fresh and warm in remembrance of them.

"What does this matter to them?" We may ask, in reply, what does anything matter? The honor of a nation is precious. That honor is impossible except through the loyalty and devotion of her sons. When Phillips, of Minnesota, was killed by robbers because he would not surrender the key to the safe which contained his trust money, he did not die for money, but for honor. Logan, Bradley, English, and the twenty-six other men who fell at Big Hole, Montana, died for duty, for the honor and faith in them and in us, which, aggregated, make up the honor and faith of a nation.

Look on the other side. See these women's bodies disinterred by our own ferocious Bannock scouts! See how they pierce and dishonor their poor, harmless forms, and carry off their scalps! Our officers sadly look upon the scene, and then, as by a common impulse, deepen their beds, and cover them with earth. Poor Jack Carleton hardly dared own his motive for his hard work in the burying of so many people, with poor instruments, and too little help. "Oh, general," he says, "let us bury them; the settlers on the Big Hole below will desert their ranches if we leave 'em here."

"But," says one, "aren't you disgusted with war when you walk thoughtfully over the bloody field, after the battle?" Yes, yes, deeply disgusted, horror-stricken; but it is the same with railway accidents, and with fire and pestilence. Indian warfare is horrid; but Indian massacres, outrages, and brutality, and Indian rule, which is war, are a thousand times worse.

Some such thoughts passed through my mind while we waited for the troops. It was Sunday (the 12th of August) that the different groups of bodies were counted and buried, or reburied. We had two Nez Perce scouts, or herders, drawn from the loyal Indians of the same name. These loyal ones, it should be remembered, though they constitute seven-eighths of the tribe, though industrious and true, though far in advance of the renegades, still are too often forgotten. Two of them, "Captain John," and "Old George," will be remembered by all who went across the continent in this long and persistent pursuit. They were capital herders of broken-down horses; could recruit their strength, and fetch them on when such a thing seemed possible. "Old George" had an Indian look, but kept his hair short, and always was good-natured. On all occasions when you spoke to him, his under lip, like that of some attentive and aged listener to a sermon, would drop. "Old George" was caught, some days after Gibbon's battle, by the enemy, and held a prisoner for a few hours. When he had made his escape, and returned, he told me that Joseph's men said: "Your men kill our women and children; your men are worse than the Indians." "Werte! werte! werte!" cries George; i. e., "No, no, no! my chief is kind. I saw him and his staff officers, and Mr. Carleton, tenderly bury the women and children with their own hands. They don't want to hurt the women and children." George said his captors were pleased to hear his account, and when he told them he carried no gun they simply robbed him of his horse, and let him escape.

We were ready to push on the 13th, turning southward, yet still keeping to the left of the main hostile trail. Our scouts had followed Joseph over a level stretch of country, till they struck a spur of the Rocky Mountain ridge which divided the "Bannock City" valley from the Horse Prairie valley. Across this ridge the hostiles had gone by an ugly gap, or pass, probably hoping to surprise our small advance detachment, had it ventured on the direct pursuit. But we were too wary for them this time, and I had a firm belief that this southward turning of Joseph was only a feint, to get me hopelessly in the rear. The Indians were as industrious as was General Lee after Gettysburg in attempts to deceive us as to their intentions. "We are going back by Salmon City," they gave out; or, "we are going back by a more southern trail." Always, going back! Old "Captain John" shook his head. "Werte, werte," he said. "Buffalo illahee, Joseph, Looking-glass, White Bird!" I agreed with "Captain John;" so I moved forward, keeping far to the left of the Indians' trail, and did not forget that the said buffalo country was still eastward.

Captain Browning, with Lieutenants Wright and Van Orsdale, and fifty men of General Gibbon's command, volunteered to accompany us a few marches. Gibbon's wagons, going northward, lumbered off, — hard, shaky things they were, at best. They were carrying some thirty poor, wounded men, whom Doctors Alexander and Fitzgerald had made as comfortable as possible. Cheerful sufferers these. They were sure their friends would appreciate their gallant work and their sacrifice.

The first night towards Bannock City we named our clean and pleasant camp from Lieutenant Bradley, "Camp James H. Bradley." Our men hoped that the Bannock City people, whose appearance was unusually prepossessing, would retain for the spot the honored name we gave it.

At this camp we had word from two excited messengers, that eight men, citizens, had been murdered by Joseph's Indians in Horse Prairie.

The women and children had all been previously carried to the mining town just mentioned, for safety. The Indians had also gotten two hundred and fifty of the finest American horses. This made us look despondingly at our poor cavalry, which had begun to mope so much as to excite the contempt of our frontiersmen. "Why don't you ride? Why not put your cavalry ahead every day? You never can catch Joseph, if you don't!" How truthful, yet how sad, these very apparent facts. Still I never felt these taunts so deeply as I did those eastern witticisms, which I read afterwards : " One day ahead ! " "Beautiful panorama ! Joseph and his Indians, Howard and his soldiers, running a race for the amusement of mankind ! " The issue put it all right.

The 14th of August we had almost a review ; women and children came out and watched the column for a mile, to the road junction, where we turned away from Bannock City toward the Horse Prairie country. These people were so happy to see us, so pleasant in their manner and speech, that I could not resist the temptation of stopping for a few minutes' conversation. Old people took me by the hand, and pointed me out to their children as a soldier who had seen service. That little girl at Gettysburg town, in July, 1863, who waved her white kerchief to the passing troops, inspired them anew with heartiness ; so did the Bannock City ladies cheer our little band by their happy faces and welcome words, such as before and afterwards, during the campaign, we did not often have the privilege of enjoying. The Bitter Root people, on the other hand, had stoutly blamed us for chasing the Indians to their neighborhood.

We were, the 15th, in that famous Horse Prairie valley. Of course it had a creek called " Horse Prairie," and a valley named like the creek. We entered the valley at the lower end. The Indians had crossed it higher up. This was that wonderful country that Washington Irving described in his " Bonneville's Adventures," where is the first historic account of the Nez Perces. The Horse Prairie was the place where they made their toilet with care before they would see Captain Bonneville.

I do not know why it is that this valley appears to be such an exception to the lands of the interior in point of fertility. We encamped upon a grand farm, well fenced and well kept. Other farms stretched off in the broad valley, above and westward, as far as we could see. Good horses, good cattle, abundant grain and grass.

Our second camp was named for Captain Logan; this one for Lieutenant English. To me "Camp English" is memorable, for here I had two annoyances. First, from some volunteers, who thronged my tent, and severely called me to account for the way I did things in the military line. Second, from citizens, and volunteer messengers, who came from the next valley, situated to our right and across another spur of the mountains, where old Fort Lemhi is located. They declared, "The Indians are upon us; they are surely turning back; they will destroy Salmon City. Colonel Shoup, with sixty volunteers, and Ten-doy's Indians, have retired to Fort Lemhi. We are "forted up" at the cross-roads. Push straight for the fort, and you'll have them. Indians went west, passed us at the cross-road, and are camped between that and the old fort."

I finally decided to yield a little to the pressure. I feared to move off much to the right, for reasons before given, but I would take a trail to Lemhi Valley, ten miles east of the hostiles, and reluctantly began my preparations, when, to my great relief, a swift messenger reported, after midnight, "The Indians have broken camp, and rushed past the cross-road, and its 'forting up,' doing us no harm, and have gone eastward as fast as they could." The annoyance was over, then; so that, as first intended, we made a drive for the Corinne and Deer Lodge stage-road, hoping almost against hope to catch the Indians as they emerged from the mountains, and attempted to cross this road.

Browning and his men kept on with us; while Captain Norwood, one of those gentlemen who seem born to command, with his company of the Second Cavalry, was reported as not far behind; also, a few of the volunteers continued with us. With a renewal of strength and energy, we pressed down the Corinne road. Joseph was yet west of this line, and was running, as Indians only can, to get past Dry Creek Station before we could possibly reach there.

The evening of the 17th August brought us as far as Junction Station. Firewood three miles off; poor grazing, owing to the superabundance of alkali. Here fifty-five Montana volunteers, under Captain Calloway, came up, — good, sturdy-looking men, well mounted and well armed. This camp was a sort of a new place of departure, so we will defer an account till next chapter.

CHAPTER XXXII.

JOSEPH AND THE PURSUIT.—JUNCTION STATION.— AN ATTEMPT
AT REST, AND WHAT CAME OF IT. — LIEUTENANT BACON
SENT TO HEAD INDIANS OFF AT HENRY LAKE. — THE TOWN
MEETING. — PLEASANT VALLEY. — NO ESCORT. — INDIANS
AHEAD. — THE INDIANS GET PAST DRY CREEK. — BUFFALO
HORN OBSERVING. — A GENTLEMANLY OLD MAN. — CAVALRY
SLOW. — STAGES ROBBED AND MEN KILLED. — OFFICIAL RE-
MONSTRANCE. — ANOTHER CAMAS MEADOWS. — JOSEPH'S
NIGHT RAID.

TAKE a map of the United States, and look along the
Union Pacific Railway till you find Corinne. Then
follow a north line, past Fort Hall, up almost to Virginia
City, to a junction of stage roads, where we arrived on
the night of the 17th of August. The road from Corinne
to Virginia city is very direct. It supports a daily stage.

Junction Station, where we were encamped for a night
and forenoon, was a lively place indeed. The stages and
stage lines are institutions, *sui generis*. Passing through
a wild, uninhabited region, a station is planted about
every fifteen miles.

The hostler and his assistant live sometimes at their
stable, where horses enough for the daily changes are
kept, rested, and fed. In places where hay is convenient,
or where there is a promise of crops in the near future, as
a reward of labor, the population increases to a hamlet.
A fertile valley always stretches out with farm-houses,
and often, as at Pleasant Valley, some fifteen miles south,

has its village, stores, saloons, and shops. Thus, gradually, a newly established stage line, here in the interior
of the continent, is peopled by fully as many souls as
such a dry region will support. We must not forget
that much of this country is rough and mountainous, and
that many valuable mines of gold and silver have been
discovered, and are worked not far from the road.

The morning was fine. There was seldom a cloud in
that sky. The dust was lying a little closer to the earth,
and the air was clearer in the morning. O that we had
the ability to get more rapid motion from the tired animals! But when they wanted rest and food, they were
not like those mothers of ours, who are almost sure, at
such times, to move a little faster, and work a little
harder than usual. A horse will look reproachfully at
its rider, settle down into a solemn, hopeless gait, which
neither scolding, kicking with boot-heels, nor use of whip
will quicken for more than five paces at a time.

A mischievous lieutenant, who thought that the reduction of the army, which was, during Joseph's campaign,
under consideration at Washington, meant doubling his
present hard work, said, that he wished from his heart
that he could have the military committee of congress ride
a set of "played out" horses for one thousand miles.
Poor fellows! I fear they would not care whether they
had a country or not, and would, from sheer vexation,
abolish the army altogether, and all its horrid horses.

This clear, fresh morning I had arranged for part of
the animals to have a few hours' rest. This was the plan.
A line of mountains leads off to the left, meeting another
line at an angle, at the head of Madison River. At this

point is a charming lake, where an enterprising citizen, Mr. Sawtelle, fifty miles from other habitations, had a fishery. East of this lake, and close by, is the gap or pass in the ridge that forms the western gateway to the national park. It is called Tacher's Pass. It became evident to my mind that Joseph would attempt this pass. I hesitated, at first, owing to the stage-men. They thronged me. They declared that it was the nearest way to go by Dry Creek; plain road there; no trail in the straight line. I deliberated whether to take my main force by the straight line north of the mountain ridge to that key point, or send thither a smaller body. I yielded, finally, to the positive reiterated information; chose Lieutenant Bacon, with forty picked men, and Robbins, with his Indian scouts, and sent them direct to Henry Lake and Tacher's Pass, while I moved by the more circuitous road recommended. They had already been six hours on the march, when I sent for Calloway, who had been a volunteer colonel during the war of the rebellion.

"Colonel, my horses are so jaded that I wish to rest them a few hours. My white scouts are beyond Pleasant Valley, and I wish to be nearer them; will you escort me?"

"Oh, yes, general, I'll go and get the boys together. You know we have a little town-meeting. We can't do as you do; just give orders, and have done with it."

I said, "All right, colonel; I wish to leave very soon."

In about ten minutes, the volunteers, in a body, came to see me, and I told them my wishes, as I had already done to their commander. They delayed a little to talk it over, and then they said, "Come, boys, let us go and get our horses."

My team — for we were to ride to Pleasant Valley in a wagon — was ready. Lieutenant Fletcher, with his carbine in his hand, sat by me. Just as we were leaving, a fine-looking young citizen, fully armed and equipped, and riding a handsome fresh horse, rode on beside the wagon. This gentleman, Fletcher, and the driver, constituted the actual escort.

Joseph had reached the stage-road beyond Pleasant Valley. Shortly we met a half-breed scout, who had become frightened, lost his gun, and deserted. Next we met a citizen scout.

"What's the matter, my man?"

"My hoss is played," he replied.

"Well, come with us, and try to keep up."

In a few moments more another scout came with a note from the front.

"Indians are on us! We are skirmishing with them beyond Dry Creek."

I looked back to see if I could catch sight of the dust of the volunteers. The road was dangerous, and Pleasant Valley itself would soon be threatened; might be taken. No volunteers! At last I sent back for the entire command. Lieutenant Wood's record reads: "General Howard leaves word for volunteers under Captain Calloway to come on as escort. They held a council of war, and declined to do so until all their comrades had caught up, and rested their horses."

The result was that the dangerous journey of eighteen miles was made without escort. The command, i. e., the cavalry, increased by Norwood's company, overtook me at Pleasant Valley, and on we went to Dry Creek Station, to find that the Indians had already crossed the stage-road several miles below, and had gone on to Camas Meadows.

One of Robbins' scouts, the famous Buffalo Horn, who, a Bannock, has since fought against us and was killed, at this time, with two others, crept to the top of the mountain ridge, succeeded in getting upon a prominent point, whence he could see Joseph's camp in the Camas Meadows below; they were fifteen or eighteen miles from the Dry Creek Station. Buffalo Horn sent one of the Indians with a message: "Joseph, and all his Indians are here." How confident I then felt!

Bacon and Robbins ahead of Joseph, and my cavalry only eighteen miles behind, and on the direct trail! If it were possible, I would reinforce Bacon; but he is seventy miles off.

"He can annoy and stop them, if he cannot do more!" I exclaim.

It was late, after dark, when at the end of some twenty-eight miles we came to Dry Creek. A fine-appearing man, apparently over sixty years of age, saluted me. He used so good English in conversation that I was surprised. He did not curse and swear, or piece out every sentence with some crude provincialism. He had been a sea-captain; was a native of Maine, evidently well edu-cated, and well bred. "Uncle Mac" knew every path in that country. The quartermaster arranged with him for forage, wood, and for guiding me in the morning. He told us that the Indians had done great mischief along the stage-road. They had destroyed Shoup's train of wagons, killed several men, also broken up a station, and run off the stock.

The cavalry horses were indeed slow in their progress, and the command had been much reduced by Bacon's detachment. The volunteers were behind at Pleasant Valley, and the footmen at least a day's march farther in the rear; so that the general aspect of things affected our best officers quite unpleasantly. That night my bright hopes were greatly dampened in consequence of a formal remonstrance against further progress till the Infantry should join. But I decided that we must not let this opportunity slip; so, with the aged guide to lead us, at dawn the next day we broke from the stage-road to the left, and marched rapidly to Camas Prairie, to the very camp the Indians had occupied, where Buffalo Horn had looked down upon them. These are the famous Camas Meadows, where we gave most occasion for sport to our good friends in the east, who make and love caricatures. It is where " Howard was surprised by Joseph, and lost his mules ! " How the enterprising young chieftan made a fair march, established his encampment for women, children, and surplus animals beyond our reach, and then, with his freshly stolen horses and picked men, returned in the night, surprised and circumvented our pickets and sentinels, presents in the following pages a subject of special interest.

CHAPTER XXXIII.

JOSEPH AND THE BATTLE OF CAMAS MEADOWS. — THE CAMP
OF THE 19TH AUGUST, AND ITS SURROUNDINGS. — THE LAVA
KNOLLS. — POSITION OF THE VOLUNTEERS AND TROOPS. —
THE MULES GRAZING. — MASON PLANTED THE OUTPOSTS. —
A TENT SCENE. — A TERRIFIC NOISE. — THE VOLUNTEER
PANIC. — STAMPEDE OF THE ANIMALS. — HOW JOSEPH AP-
PROACHED. — THE BELL-MARE. — PROMPT PREPARATION. —
MULES OVERTAKEN. — INDIANS FLANKING OUR ADVANCE. —
NORWOOD'S FIGHT. — LIEUTENANT BENSON WOUNDED. —
BURIAL OF THE DEAD.

ALMOST the only English writers who, describing
battles, have succeeded in giving to my mind a clear
conception of the location of troops and of their actual
movements during the engagements, are Carlyle and
Thackeray. The former gives a careful description of
the ground, the streams, the thickets, the villages, and
the hills. He arranges the troops in a graphic way, so
that if you had your pencil and sketch-book you could
map out the field of conflict. Thackeray is less formal
and precise, but seizes upon prominent points, and gives
enough of minutia to help the imagination fill out the picture; and does not, as do most writers, leave you with a
confused impression. Perhaps, however, a confused impression is the true one to give concerning a surprise and
the terrible din of arms like that of Sunday night, the
19th and 20th of August, 1877.

But as there was no confusion in the arrangements, and

none in the operations, after the dawn began, we will proceed to lay out our field, and for observation drive down
a few prominent stakes.

Conceive a broad, grassy meadow. You enter it midway from its western edge. To your left is a chain of
hills, or "mountain spurs." On the nearest height, Buffalo Horn and his comrade scout had sat and watched the
meadow the day before; straight ahead of you, and a
half mile forward, were a few large stacks of meadow hay,
from fifty to a hundred yards asunder. Just beyond the
mown flats, from which the hay came, were two streams
of water, running quite swiftly; each stream was fringed
with bushes higher than the men's heads. The two streams
ran across our path, and were nearly parallel with each
other. Beyond, some two hundred yards, we touched the
higher ground. The meadow sweeping off to the left,
northward, becomes narrow near the mountain spur, and
extends eastward. Here on the higher ground, acres
upon acres, for ten miles or more, are thrown into curious
lava-knolls, each knoll so much like another, that you
cannot fix your whereabouts by the distinct and diverse
features around you. Should you drive to pasture five
horses over these wave-like knolls for a mile, and then
leave them for an hour to graze, it would be next to impossible to find them.

We took for the centre of our night camp one of these
knolls which was near to the meadow bottom. From my
tent I looked back to the parallel streams. Across the
first one, the Calloway volunteers encamped. Norwood's
Cavalry and the forty infantry occupied the west side.
The other companies of cavalry covered all approaches to

my own, the central position, which was upon a comparatively high lava pile, that, studded with bushes, constituted our castle-like defence. This position was strengthened by knolls and lava-rocks on three sides, north, east, and south. We took plenty of room, and Mason, as was his custom, located the outposts and pickets well in advance of each front. The Indians had gone, as we knew by their full trail, up the north sweep of the meadow, and were, when we arrived at the Camas, in their camp fifteen miles in advance. Ahead of them, forty miles or more, was Henry Lake and the Tacher's Pass, which leads into the National Park; and as I had hoped there, likewise, on the look out, with his command, was Lieutenant Bacon.

"Well," says Lieutenant Wood, as we were preparing for rest, "I'll take off my pants to-night, it is so safe a place."

Lieutenant Howard laughed, and said, "I've loaned my pistol to a scout for to-night, so think likely the Indians will come back."

We all ventured, in spite of the latter's humorous prediction, to get between the blankets without the pantaloons. How quiet was the night; starlight, but no moon. It is wonderful, that stillness of a sleeping camp, so like death. I remember to have slept beside some soldiers at Antietam. They, with their heads covered, appeared sleeping soundly. In the morning I was shocked to find that they were the dead whom their comrades had laid there, prepared for burial.

At Camas Meadows, after midnight, nothing could be heard but the tread of a sentinel, the occasional

15

neigh of a horse, bray of a mule, or bark of a startled
dog. But suddenly, while the darkness was yet intense,
there came a terrific noise, the rattling of musketry; a
sharp, quick, multitudinous roaring, followed by the
shrill Indian yell.

"Here they are!" we exclaim, as we all sit up in our
blankets.

"Lie close, or a stray bullet will hit you."

"Oh, no, I must be up for this. Nothing can be better, if they only will stay, and give us a battle."

Our clothes and equipments were resumed quickly
enough. Horses and men were ready by the time we
were beyond our tent fly.

Calloway and his volunteers, not so used to sudden
alarms, find it hard to get in order. One takes another's
gun, some get the wrong belts, others drop their percus-
sion caps; their horses get into a regular stampede, and
rush in the darkness toward the herd of mules, and all
the animals scamper off together, while the citizens plunge
into the water above their knees, and cross to the regular
troops at a double-quick.

The Indians, under Joseph's lead, sent a few of their
numbers, who had crept in slyly between the pickets.
These cut the hobbles of the bell-mares, and took off the
bells, and were ready at the signal to give the herd a direction the instant the firing began. The yell was so terrible, that mules tied to wagons tried to break loose, and
the horses at the picket-ropes did all they could to manifest their fear by pulling, pushing, and springing.

Joseph had so organized a few of his Indians, and
marched them toward camp, as to make the picket think

it was Bacon's party coming back. They, the Indians, came on by fours, steadily, and very like our troopers, till challenged. Not being able to reply correctly, the picket fired upon them. This was doubtless the first sound. Then came the big firing and yelling, and then, quickly enough, the reply from our camp.

When I had advanced to Norwood's wagons, I could just get glimpses of the herd of animals making off beyond the first stream, but whether westward or northward could not be determined till the sun should get nearer to the rising.

The cavalry was put in readiness. Norwood's, Carr's, Jackson's three companies, under the Major, Sandford.

With orders to pursue and recover the mules and horses that had been stampeded, away they went at a gallop, company after company, while we organized the camp for a possible attack from the knoll to the east of us. I had remaining, Wagner's and Bendire's Cavalry, and the fifty infantry, under Captain Wells, with a couple of pieces of artillery.

As we had to wait for results, our breakfast at the headquarters was prepared as usual, and we sat crosslegged upon the ground around our canvas table. I confess it was a little exciting to be aroused from sleep in this way, and so the bread and coffee had to be forced somewhat. The first messenger, a soldier, came galloping in, and quickly dismounted.

" The compliments, sir, of Major Sandford; the mules have been overtaken, and some fifty to seventy-five of them have been brought back."

" Tell the major, all right. I do hope that he may get them all."

Another messenger, before we had finished breakfast, galloped up in hot haste:

"The major says, sir, the Indians have come back to attack in large force, and are turning his left."

The remainder of the cavalry was soon brought out, with the infantry and the artillery, and moved on toward the threatened point.

Through the irregular ravines, over the rough lava-knolls, we crept along. A few volunteers, who still had their horses, followed the artillery from point to point till we came in sight of the line, — our line retiring.

"What is the matter, major?"

"We were rushing ahead, Carr in front, when we ran into a sort of ambush. The Indians began to get first around Norwood's left, and then around Jackson over on the right. I thought as there were so many of them that I would draw back a little."

"But where is Norwood?"

"That is what I am trying to find out."

"Why, you haven't left him?"

"No, I sent to him the order at the same time as to Carr, but it seems that he has stopped."

"Well, let us return to him at once."

So, stretching out our line, making it as long and formidable as possible, we kept on.

"Come here, Carleton," (the citizen scout,) "where are Norwood and his company?"

"I left him over yonder, fighting hard, over there by the bushes."

I asked two or three others; one pointed in one direction, and another two or more points to the right or left, so confusing were those lava-beds. But we continued marching northerly and easterly, ready to make a good fight if the enemy should turn back.

At last a little clump of thick cottonwood appeared, and to its left a pile of rocks, more sharp-edged and craggy than the rest. Here, to our joy, was Norwood's company, dismounted. He had fought quite a battle, and the Indians had been beaten back. Some of our crazy mules, which we had recovered, were stampeded again, and in the most senseless manner ran off in the wrong direction — to the Indian herd.

Here, among the trees, we found Norwood's wounded, including Lieutenant Benson, who, gallant fellow, had volunteered but two days before, his own company not being with us. It was now afternoon. The Indians were ahead eight or ten miles. They had stopped now and then to fight, but had made off again toward the Henry Lake.

Not being prepared to advance farther that day, much to Buffalo Horn's disgust, I ordered the troops to camp.

We returned slowly with our six wounded men, and one dead. "One dead!" It seemed strange to us, there at the edge of the meadow, in the middle of the continent, that but one should be taken, and that one the favorite orderly and bugler of Captain Jackson. He was tenderly prepared for burial. The grave was dug by his comrades; Mason read the touching Episcopal service beside it, while officers and men stood around with solemn, and, often, tear-moistened faces. The farewell volleys were given, and the remains of young Brooks were left, to rest there in loneliness till the resurrection.

CHAPTER XXXIV.

JOSEPH AND THE PURSUIT. — EXTRAORDINARY MARCH. — PIC-
TURESQUE SCOUTS. — CAPTAIN BAINBRIDGE. — CHEERING
WORDS. — MORAL EFFECT OF KINDLY EXPRESSIONS. — FISH-
ER. — CHIT-CHAT ON THE MARCH. — THOUGHTS OF HOME. —
HEAD-WATERS OF THE SNAKE. — INDIAN DANCE. — BUFFALO
HORN'S MODEST REQUEST. — CHARGE OF TREACHERY. — A
VERY EARLY START. — TACHER'S PASS. — DISCOURAGEMENT
OF TROOPS. — NAKED AND HUNGRY. — HOT DAYS AND FREEZ-
ING NIGHTS. — GENERL HOWARD'S VISIT TO VIRGINIA CITY.
— HORSES AT A PREMIUM. — RETURN TO CAMP. — GENERAL
SHERMAN'S TELEGRAM. — CAMP EBSTEIN. — A FRESH START.

WHEN Miller heard that the cavalry had struck the
Indians, his command instantly quickened with a
surprising energy, and seemed to move with the swiftness of fresh horses.   He came up some forty-eight miles
in less than twenty-four hours.   Cushing, who had, under
General McDowell's instructions, started with his company for San Francisco, joined us.   Captain Bonneville's
interview with wild Indians on Horse Prairie, and its
picturesque ceremonial, have been referred to.   We had
at Camp Benson, the second day after the battle of
Camas Meadows, a repetition of the effects, if not of
the ceremonies of that occasion.   First a gay cavalcade,
riding with the speed and easy grace of Indians, appeared
in the distance.   It proved to be the advance guard of a
company of scouts from Fort Hall, about one hundred
miles to the south-west.   Their feathers and fur strips

were flying in the breeze, and the bright colors and taste-
ful decorations of each man and horse added to the brilliant effect. They carried a white flag in the front rank,
and rode grandly into our camp.

They brought messages from Captain Bainbridge, who
himself, before midnight, joined us with the remainder of
the scouts and his small guard of soldiers. Bainbridge
brought the good wishes of General Crook, as well as an
increase of our scouting force. Everybody knows that
there are times when a little help, or even a word of
cheer, goes straight to the heart. A thrill of joy ran
through our weary and almost discouraged company at
this accession.

The leader of these scouts, or the " chief scout," as he
was called, deserves a special notice. He was a tall, pale
man, of fair proportions, being slightly deaf. A stranger
would see little that was remarkable in him. Yet of all
the scouts in our Indian campaign, none equalled this
chief, Fisher. Night and day, with guides and without,
with force and without, Fisher fearlessly hung upon the
skirts of the enemy. The accuracy, carefulness, and
fulness of his reports, to one attempting to chase Indians
across a vast wilderness, were a delight.

For the remainder of the march our record will be
swift and graphic. On the narrowest trails we were
obliged to ride or march in single file, but habitually
Mason, or one of my aides, rode by my side, and the
command came on by twos. What did we not talk of?
Science, art, literature, poetry, homes; yes, *homes* —
theirs and mine. Every soldier will understand me when
I say that in these conversations, whenever the word

home is spoken, moistened eyes, gentle tones, and tender hearts, are the rule, and not the exception.

August 23. We had just crossed one of the branches of the Snake. We were nearing its head-waters. A mile or two beyond was a charming glade in the forest. This glade occupied the angle between the Snake and a small tributary. The animals must have all the grass, so we put our rough shelter and wedge-tents around the glade, in the edge of the wood. The Bannocks, our scouts, had for their tepees a slight knoll near the water, not far from the general's bivouac. Buffalo Horn came to him, and asked if the Indians might have a dance.

"Oh, yes; let them dance."

The echo of the wild singing, the weird shapes passing the fire during the dance, and the actual sense of danger, after Joseph's late night attack, appeared to impress the whole command with a feeling of apprehension, almost a panic. Added to this, the general was intending to wake the command at two o'clock, so as, with one more trial, by a forced march to come upon Joseph's heels before he passed through the Tacher's Gap into the Yellowstone Park, and therefore an unusual stir of preparation was kept up. It was a night to be remembered. The neighing of the horses, and the braying of the mules, one occasionally giving a high and prolonged screech, sounded, during this still night, ten times louder than usual.

About midnight, after the war-dance and its council had subsided, Buffalo Horn and a thick-set, semi-savage half-breed, who was called Rainé, came to head-quarters, and asked for authority to kill our Nez Perce herders, "Captain John," "Old George," and one other Indian of the tribe. Rainé said George and the other Indians were traitors; that they had rejoiced openly at Joseph's success in surprising our mule herd, and that old John was a Nez Perce, and ought to die.

We had George brought forward, to face his accusers. He was so frank, and evidently so honest, that the story against him was not for a moment believed, and Buffalo Horn was denied the small favor of killing the three. He was very angry in consequence, and never quite forgave me for this refusal. The third Indian may have been guilty. He, at any rate, so much feared these suspicious and exacting Bannocks, that he escaped into the forest that night, and went back to Kamiah. But the jolly "Captain John," and the demure "George," herding and bringing up the "played-out" horses, from day to day, in a wonderful manner, remained with the command to the close of the campaign.

How vast appeared this opening, this immense prairie, into which the column emerged from the forest at peep of day! Miles of tall grass; yonder, straight ahead, the mountain ridge, rough and irregular; a beautiful lake off to the left and north.

"That must be the gap, Tacher's Pass," says Wood.

"Oh, yes; and sure enough there is an Indian camp where the smoke rises," Mason quickly replies.

Our scouts and advance guard are close on them. "Let us ride." So we did, as fast as the poor horses could get on. Finally, the command had mastered the stream, ditches, and unexpected gulches that turned us off wearily to the right and left, and we came to the mouth of the famous pass.

"Well, general," says Chief Robbins, "we found 'em gone. Fisher and his Indians have followed on through the gap." Being thus eluded again, the greatest discouragement seized upon officers and men, as they were put into camp that day. They appeared to themselves much like a poor dog watching the hole from which the badger had just escaped.

Bacon and his party, on his arrival, not seeing any Indians at or near Henry Lake, which was in plain sight of this Tacher's Pass, had turned back, and were obliged to complete a junction with us by a stern chase; and the proverb that "a stern chase is a long one," did not here fail. But what a disappointment! There, Bacon had come into full view of the beautiful lake, and the Pass, just beyond, two days before the Indians rushed through. If Bacon only could have known! If the cowardly messengers only had gone to him, instead of returning to me with a statement that they could not find him, our tedious work might have terminated at this point.

Fisher, with the Indian scouts, was still pursuing. "They are not far ahead," I said to myself, and issued orders to move. "We cannot, we cannot, general! Come, look at your soldiers; look at their clothing, ragged already, and tied with strings; look at their feet, some barefooted, and the most with shoes so badly worn that in one or two days they will be gone. The ice froze an inch in our basins last night, and we have no overcoats, nothing but thin blankets, now falling to pieces. There are no spare blankets for nights like these." "You can go no farther," says Doctor Alexander. The inspector, the aides, the quartermaster, and the other officers echo the sad response, "You can go no farther."

The general decided to telegraph, sending fifty miles, to the nearest station, for instructions, suspended his orders, and changed his plans; for, in view of these terrible facts, what else could be done? It will be remembered that this was almost the only halt for upwards of two months.

Virginia City was seventy miles away. "Take the best team you can find, Guy, and I will go and get clothing and supplies. Let Cushing and Norwood, with their companies, proceed to Fort Ellis, and take a re-supply by way of Crow Agency, and join us again two hundred miles on, while the main body rests here for four days, keeping its scouts close to the Indians, and well informed of their movements." The needs of the command were written out, and with such memoranda Captain Adams, as quartermaster, Lieut. Howard, and myself set out. We had a pretty good team, and a good driver. The stout wagon wasn't made for comfortable riding, but it could rumble over small and large bowlders, and across acres literally sowed with stones. We were so exhausted that it was a comfort to change, as Mason says, from the "clothes-pin method," to ride even in a springless lumber-wagon. Thus we were pulled on, all day and all night.

Before noon, the 24th, we crept out from under the seat, from fitful dreams, a sort of "make-believe" sleep, to catch a glimpse of a few houses. Soon we reached the town, a mining village, planted here in the midst of a wilderness of hills and mountains.

"Plenty of stores, such as they are," says Guy.

Imagine the delight of traders, Jew and Gentile, at this visitation; for shoes, and clothes, and blankets we must

have. We nearly bought them out. Our jaded cavalry-
horses were remembered, and a goodly supply of fresh
animals were ordered from the most accommodating of
ranchmen, and I fear also from the shrewdest of jockeys.

"Horses, is it?" asked a bystander. "Why, yes, I
have an abundance on my ranch, all in good order, and
well broken to the bridle and saddle."

You should have seen these same horses when Indians,
frontiersmen, and packers tried to put on the bridle and
the saddle. Refer to the description of a "Bucking Cayuse," and hold your breath. Such a pitching and plunging, hooting and yelling, running and falling, made one
think of danger ahead from something beside Indians!

After a few hours' work at Virginia City, we set out on
the return. The Madison and the Jefferson are two
mountain peaks near the grand dividing ridge, not far
from Henry Lake. They are also the names of two
mountain streams, tributaries of the Yellowstone. Our
wagon had to ascend to the mountain-divide along the
bank of another stream, the Galatin, crossing it several
times. Its water is very clear, tumbling and rustling
over its strong bed, hereabouts always wide, but shallow
enough to ford.

After crossing the divide, as we descended the clear
woodland slope, we soon caught a glimpse of Henry
Lake, and then of our camp, which had, during our ab-
sence, been moved around to the side of our approach.
What a grand view was before us! Nothing more picturesque! The mountain ridges, the broad meadows
between, and the lake at the foot of our glacis, with a
small city in the foreground, of tents and temporary

shelters, which were flanked on either side by the numerous horses and mules that were grazing peacefully along the shores.

After our one hundred and twenty miles ride, we find at camp telegrams like the following:

"Where Indians can subsist, the army can live. . . . The country and the government expect you to do your duty. No troops near enough to take your place. Continue the pursuit. If you are tired, general, put in a younger man, and return to Oregon; but the troops must go on."

How hard to bear some things are! The general wasn't tired, of course, nor did he mean to be tired. His business was to die in his tracks, if need be. But the chafing, stern order to the general worked like a charm upon the command. Officers and soldiers, now re-supplied, were ready, to a man. "We will go with you to the death." It was worth while to bear a little chagrin in order to awaken such a loyal spirit.

Behold us, then, setting forth, bright and early the Monday morning of the 27th of August. That beautiful camp by the lake, where, in weariness, poverty, and heart-sickness we had been halted for four days; where we renewed our supplies, and were finally inspirited by a gentle reprimand, we named for our quartermaster, "Camp Ebstein." Lieutenant Ebstein's equanimity had never failed him. He came speedily out of difficulties. This name headed the numerous letters and reports which left this neighborhood, and which, like water coursing from banks of snow in spring-time, always flow from a halted camp.

Our column looked well. Even the horses had picked up a little, and the movement was passably brisk, as we wound like a silvery serpent around the lake, and passed through the mountain gorge to new fields, and dangers still unknown.

CHAPTER XXXV.

JOSEPH AND THE PURSUIT. — THE NATIONAL PARK. — THE GEY-
SER PARTY. — CONTINUED INDIAN OUTRAGES. — THE LAW-
YER'S ACCOUNT. — THE HOT SPRINGS AND SULPHUR PLAINS.
— THE GEYSERS. — THE MUD SPRINGS. — JOSEPH'S HINDRANCES.
— THE TERRIBLE TRAIL. — THE YELLOWSTONE CROSSING.

OFFICERS and men were naturally enough on the *qui vive* as our little pursuing column made its way through the western gateway and rough avenue into the grand National Park.

The smallness and sparseness of the trees, like eastern maple-groves, thinned out and shorn of the older growth, were the first things noticeable. The level, lengthy openings, the beautiful mountain-streams, the dryish, grassy bottoms and occasional bubbles of land, named "buttes," partly dressed with trees, — these, for the first three days, afforded a pleasant change, at the end of which the extraordinary Geyser landscape, with its vast seas of almost barren sulphur-crust, burst upon our view.

Here we met that unfortunate Geyser party, which caused at the time so much public interest on account of having fallen, during a pleasure-trip, into the hands of the hostile Indians. The first man we encountered, breathless, hatless, almost starved, with his feet wrapped in rags, was so wild that he could give no intelligible account of himself. It was: "Three Indians fired on me, and I got

away. They are all killed. The rest all killed!" The
next one was Mr. Oldham, a tall, stout young man, with
very straight, black hair. He was shot through both
cheeks, and of course could hardly speak. The very next
day we encountered the third, a lawyer, Mr. Cowan, who
was twice wounded, and left on the ground for dead.
Cowan revived so much as to be able to explain the situation and give important information: "The Indians surprised us. Our camp was not far from here, — over there,
where the broken wagon is. At first they treated us
kindly; two of our number got away into the bushes
when the Indians fired at us for sport; then they took our
horses. Abandoning me while unconscious, they carried
off my wife and a young lady, her sister, and their brother."

It was not long before we found the dead body of the
missing one of this party. The women and their brother
were spared by Joseph, and were afterward rescued.

Mr. Cowan succeeded in getting home to find his wife
dressed in mourning for him: for had she not seen him
fall under the ruthless hand of the savage, and left him
for dead on the ground? Her sudden joy, however, was
but short-lived, for a relapse set in, and his death occurred
shortly after his return.*

It is very difficult for a frontier family thus outraged,
to believe much in "peace measures" with Indians.

We named this camp, of the 30th of August, for the
wounded lawyer, "Camp Cowan." Lieut. Wood, in his
notes, called it the "sulphurous camp."

A woody height, or butte, just to the south of us, furnished a picket-post with a good outlook. North of this

---

* An army officer from Montana says: the report of Mr. Cowan's death is an
error; he is still living.

butte were several hot springs; these springs were only a
few feet across the mouth, and appeared like wells of
water. They betrayed their presence by constantly sending up clouds of steam.

As I sat on the crest of the picket's butte, a barren
sulphur plain stretched off southward, presenting, here
and there, very regular mounds, or swells of ground, of
slight elevation. Here, for the first time, my eye was
delighted by the curious spectacle of those water-spouts
which we now call "geysers." I do not wonder that they
are named as if they had life, as Giant, Giantess. Some
of them, for fifteen minutes at a time, would throw jets of
water straight up into the air. The action was like that
of a steam fire-engine with its hose, the nozzle being held
erect; the important difference was that the geyser really
propelled a column larger than a hogshead. It was of
course the distance that gave these geysers the appearance
of smaller spoutings. During the short time before sunset, after our arrival in camp, officers and soldiers, except
the pickets, guard, and herders, were allowed to investi-
gate these strange phenomena. The most curious results
of this intense chemical action, so near the crust as to be
constantly breaking through and overflowing, were found
also in occasional deep chasms, at the bottom of which
there was a muddy fermentation like that in the plasterer's
lime-bin in active operation. The mud was of various
colors, from the clayey white, through varying shades of
red, purple, and brown, to the blackest muck.

In one corner, with a crater-like opening, the dark, hot
mud was in perpetual motion. It was thrown up, and
falling back, from ten to twenty feet, produced an effect,

16

that Doré could hardly excel, of a pit of sulphurous smoke and darkness and noise, not easily described.

There is no end of surprises in this wonderful park. Following the Indian's crooked trail, our scouts, after the march was resumed, led us of a sudden against a mountain which bristled with extensive forests of small trees. The trees had been killed and hardened by the forest fires, which had swept hither and thither through them. By a zigzag course everything in the command, except the wagons, after a moderate amount of cutting and of swinging to one side the fallen logs, managed to get to the mountain-top. But how were the wagons ever to be hauled up the height? If you conceive of a man so constituted, broad-shouldered and deep-chested, sufficiently tall, as to have a weight of two hundred and twenty-five pounds without corpulency, with a bearing such as to make the roughest frontiersman obey his slightest command, and so plucky as to regard obstacles as only made to be overcome, you have imaged Major Spurgin, of the Twenty-first Infantry, our chief of the pioneer battalion.

While we camped for the night, just beyond the beautiful Mary Lake, in the top of the mountain, a practical wagon-road was made by Spurgin's pioneers, and the wagons which had joined us in Montana were brought on, so as not to detain the march of the next day.

We were next in camp on the Yellowstone, near one of those noisy, dirty, heated smoke-holes, such as I have mentioned, bearing the descriptive name of "Muddy Springs." The Yellowstone bottom broadens out in this neighborhood, giving to us plenty of grass and a good encampment, notwithstanding the immense herds of Chief Joseph which had here just preceded us.

We received news at this point from Fisher, in the shape of a discharged soldier whom the Indians had captured, and whom, lagging behind, Fisher's scouts had recaptured and brought in. He pointed out the direction the Indians had taken. They crossed the Yellowstone, and went up the river toward the Yellowstone Lake, quite a distance, and then struck off along a tributary creek in the direction of that wonderful river with an odorous name — Stinking Water; and then, turning square to the left, endeavored, with much detention and loss of animals, to make their way through a dense, tangled forest.

They left the Stinking-Water trail, doubtless, because Joseph heard that the prairie ahead of him had been set on fire and was burning, and that some of General Crook's troops were coming up from that direction. By this information my command was saved nearly a hundred miles of the circuitous following, the toughest journey which this pursuit occasioned, for we traced the chord of the arc which the astute young chieftain was forced to describe.

Next there came to us here evidences of a Bannock treachery, which culminated a year later in the murders and outrages of the Bannock campaign.

At the foot of the mountain, near Mary Lake, where Spurgin made his zigzag road, forty horses belonging to citizen-teams, which were doing the transporting work for us, were turned out to graze. During the night these horses all mysteriously disappeared. The quartermaster's clerk, encountering some Bannock scouts, who had suspiciously lingered in the rear, was treated to very rough language by them. I sent at once a small detachment of mounted soldiers, who soon returned to camp with ten of the Indian scouts as prisoners.

Their leader, a half-breed, and brother to the Rainé who had desired to murder old George and Captain John, was cross and mutinous in his manner and language. I had them all disarmed, and their handsome horses and rifles taken from them. I found also, on inquiry, that all the Bannock scouts, except one or two, had deserted the brave Fisher, and had come back to the troops, and were planning to return to Fort Hall.

An old chief of the tribe soon begged of me to let the prisoners go free, assuring me of their innocence. I said, "What you say may be true, but Indians are good to hunt horses. They follow blind trails better than white men. Send out some of your young men and look up my lost horses. I will never set the prisoners free till the horses are brought back." The old man replied, "Yes, Indians good to hunt horses. I will send them." In a few hours twenty of the horses came galloping into camp, chased by his young Indians. Then, with the old man, they came to me, and declared that these twenty were all they could possibly find. I said, "All right: I shall never let the prisoners go till I see the other twenty horses." The old Indian gave a grunt and shrug of the shoulders, and left me. Soon I saw him mounted, and then, with his party, leave camp. That night the remaining twenty horses overtook us, and the prisoners were released, except the leader, Rainé, who was dispatched as a prisoner, under escort, to Fort Ellis.

Under our new guide, the discharged soldier brought in from Fisher, whose name was Irwin, we took our course across a mountain-range; we pursued a route that our guide believed would be a fair wagon-road. But, though the trail did lead in the right direction, it took us over such fearful steeps, and across such deep and rough ravines, with precipitous banks, that it seemed utterly hopeless for our train of supplies ever to get through.

One canyon, near the remarkable Yellowstone passes, called the "Devil's Canyon," proved so much worse than all the others, that my heart almost failed me as, with the greatest difficulty, my poor horse worried his way into the water-channel and up the crest to the opposite heights. I said to myself, "Impossible for wagons!"

These difficulties being in view, the troops gave up the wagon-train and took what provisions they could carry with the pack-train, and went on to cross the Yellowstone at Baronet's Bridge; the indomitable Spurgin was to get to that point if he could, and then, bearing to the left, go on to Fort Ellis, or, if that was impracticable, turn back and go to Ellis by another and much longer way. It was not till after the campaign was over that I found, to my gratification, that Spurgin had actually made a wagon-road, and brought his teams over the seemingly impassable chasms, including the Devil's Canyon, as far as Baronet's Bridge, and proceeded thence directly to Fort Ellis. So much for will, energy, and work!

At the river-crossing the hostile Indians were already abreast of us, on the other side of the Yellowstone, and our scouts found too abundant evidence of their usual murder and rapine for twenty miles down the river to the

Mammoth Falls, where a raiding party from Chief Joseph had met and robbed some wagons, and burned a store.

The Baronet's Bridge, a slight structure, stretched across the roaring torrent of the Yellowstone, had its further end so much burned by the raiders that it had fallen out of place, and was not passable; so that we were allowed to rest three hours, long enough to repair the broken bridge.

CHAPTER XXXVI.

JOSEPH AND HIS PURSUIT. — OUR WHEREABOUTS. — BARONET'S
BRIDGE. — ENGINEERING UNDER DIFFICULTIES. — THE MAM-
MOTH FALLS. — SWINGING ROUND THE CIRCLE. — SUPPLIES
FROM FORT ELLIS. — SODA-BUTTE CANYON. — SILVER MINES.
— A GENTLEMAN SCOUT. — LODGE-POLE TRAIL. — HEART-
RENDING OUTRAGES. — A WARRIOR CAUGHT AND SCALPED
BY OUR INDIANS.

IN order to show where we were on the morning of
September 6th, and where is Baronet's Bridge, we
will again invite the reader's attention to the map.
Find the south-eastern point of the grand National Park,
then run the eye up the Yellowstone about twenty miles,
and you have the location. Our bridge has just been
finished; the beams, shortened by the fire, were tied to
some heavy timber that was fortunately on hand. Mr.
Baronet's house, the only one we had seen since Henry
Lake, stood a few hundred yards away, on Joseph's side
of the river. It was appraised at three hundred dollars,
and much of its lumber was brought to the river, for re-
planking. The bridge, which was probably fifty feet above
the water, extended from bank to bank, had but one inter-
mediary support, and that fearfully near to demolition.
As the first animals were started across the patched-up
structure it trembled, and swung laterally very percep-
tibly, but by a little setting of teeth, and what a Chicago

orator called " clear grit," on the part of our improvised bridgemen, — standing as they did, on the shore, crouching and peeping under to watch the shaky pier and the ropes, and ever calling out, till they were hoarse, " Why don't you go on there ?   She is all right ; them men mustn't step together," — in the short space of half an hour the work was done ; led horses, loaded pack-mules, and marching men had crossed the flood.   I think we must have realized something of the feeling of the Israelites when they had reached the other shore of the Red Sea and looked back.   This joy at a great obstacle overcome, is, indeed, a living force in leading men on to success.

At the Mammoth Falls, twenty miles below, where the store was burned,—probably a small hut for Indian trading, — there were signs that Gilbert's Cavalry had been there, and suddenly departed.   Lieutenant-Colonel Gilbert, with two companies, came so near as that to forming junction with us; but the proximity of the Indian raiding-party, and want of knowledge of our whereabouts, swung him off, by a remarkable detour, a hundred miles to our rear, where, upon our trail, he pursued us for days, till his horses were exhausted, and his command worn out with the chase.   He finally, in weariness, turned back to Fort Ellis.

Cushing, whom I had sent with foot and horse, on arriving at Fort Ellis, had been shorn of his cavalry to reinforce Gilbert; yet he bravely took up his supplies, and pressed his remnant, now but two foot companies, down by the Crow Agency, in order to head off Joseph, when that Indian should emerge from the mountain gaps into the valley of Clark's Fork.   Cushing did not succeed in anticipating the Indians, but he brought up the supplies in time to prevent any delay of the pursuit by our main body. Clark's Fork cuts the Yellowstone after its big bend, and forms almost the only practicable crossing in that quarter.

As we wound along the sharply-marked tributary valleys, which here run at right angles to the yawning river, we found a bevy of mounted frontiersmen watching us from knolls and heights which were in plain view to our left. Cautiously the horsemen approached, and, at first, showed a singular reluctance to join us, or communicate. The partisan leader is apt to dislike the regulars, is probably jealous of his independence. At last I learned that the greater portion of the hostiles were thirty miles from us, trying to make their way among the mountains and forests to Clark's Fork. They were avoiding the Soda-Butte Canyon, which is a shorter cut across a mountain range that rises more and more grandly to the left of our pathway.

This Soda-Butte Canyon in itself afforded a magnificent picture. The little land bubble, which has some symptoms of soda about it, lifted itself at the entrance to the canyon.

Select grass, a variety of small trees, a mountain stream, clear, shallow, and stony, and then a gradual rising by slopes, steppes, and precipitous evergreen acclivities, to the right and left, and finally, old castellated formations, towering above you from two to three thousand feet in height, and with your avenue through them,— by comparison as narrow as Thermopylæ, — select these features, and arrange them with the artist's skill; thus you may give a faint picture of this wonderful region.

Judge of our joy to find at the famous Soda-Butte Silver-mine, near the back entrance to this canyon, some twenty miners, still hovering about their new crushing-mill, resolute and well-armed, ready to defend their treasure with their lives. George Houston, now one of the miners, was a favorite, and already celebrated guide. A man who, when we discussed him at our mess-table, drew out the cream of language, as, "He's a natural-born gentleman," "He is full of interesting anecdote," "I've never heard him use an oath," "I never knew a more genial companion," "What he don't know about this vast wilderness isn't worth knowing," "You cannot beat him in hunting game." In fact, our messmates along the subsequent marches took turns in studying this new volume of human nature; for Houston and all his companions were employed to scout the country, and, if possible, bring us upon Joseph before he could get past the point where we should debouche into the before-mentioned Clark's Fork Valley.

Indeed, we made a run for this point; but fortune, or Providence, was against us. The Indians' big trail, now in plain view, swept down the valley, and not a soul was in sight for ten miles and more.

George Houston knew a curious path just beyond the Indians course, and shorter, which had the significant name of "Lodge-pole trail." Away we went then to follow where the Crows fled from the victorious Sioux, and strewed their narrow forest road with lodge-poles, which,

nicely peeled and pierced, indicated their previous wealth.
The scouts, many of them who had fresh horses, followed
the hostiles directly for thirty miles around, while we
accomplished the twenty-five across.

The terrible work of our enemy was developed by the
scouts. Four miners were encamped in the valley. They
had horses, guns, mining implements, in brief, their all,
with them. Three, begging for their lives, were killed
outright, while one, a young German, a recent immi-
grant, dreadfully wounded, and losing everything he had
in the world, escaped. How my heart ached for him as
he tried, in broken English, to make me understand his
deplorable situation. A part of our white scouts, having
with them, I think, one or two Indians, coming suddenly
upon Joseph's last bivouac, at the foot of a broad mountain ascent, surprised and killed and scalped an old, ail-
ing warrior, who had been left behind by Joseph that
morning. Twice before had our scouts committed a similar savagery. It is hard to make them understand any
other war principle than "a scalp for a scalp."

Perhaps, as the Quakers allege, the inconsistencies are
all with us, who profess to be a Christian people. If we
do not believe in the savage operations of war, in taking
life for life, property for property, in giving deceit for
deceit, and in the inflictions of extreme injuries and pen-
alties, why do we set the example?

However we, who are the nations soldiers, may stum-
ble over troublesome queries such as these, still we certainly do like to keep pace with civilized nations in miti-
gating the horrors and evils of war as much as lies in our

power. The taking of life may be necessary, but the savage triumph, and the savage tokens of triumph, such as fingers cut off, and scalps severed from the heads of the dead and the dying, are certainly not. They fill our breasts with horror!

CHAPTER XXXVII.

JOSEPH AND THE PURSUIT. — STURGIS' SCOUTS. — GOOD NEWS. —
A PROBLEM FOR PHILANTHROPISTS. — HART'S MOUNTAIN. —
JOSEPH'S CONSUMMATE GENERALSHIP. — A SMALL HOLE. —
JUNCTION WITH STURGIS. — THE GAME IN SIGHT. — A GAL-
LANT CHARGE. — THE THIEVING CROWS. — COLONEL MER-
RILL. — "WE'VE STRUCK THE ENEMY." — STURGIS' BATTLE-
FIELD. — THE DARKNESS AND SWAMPS. — A SICKENING SIGHT.
— PURSUIT.

IT was during this march from the Soda-Butte mines to
the foot of Clark's Mountain that we were watched
by three unique, distinctive persons, — a jolly half-breed,
more French than Indian, an Indian of the Crow Nation,
and a veritable, though timorous, American. They were
couriers from General Sturgis, who had ensconced themselves near the summit of different sightly hills, till they
had obtained unmistakable signs that our moving men
were not Indians.

We were delighted to find that Sturgis, with six or
seven companies of the Seventh Cavalry, was within fifty
miles of us, and that the hostile Indians were surely between us and Sturgis. The latter, when the couriers left
him, was just about to move to " Hart's Mountain," with
a view to block the only practicable pathway which led
from us to the mouth of " Clark's Fork."

It would be gratifying, indeed, if Sturgis only could
know that our force was so near. His messengers had

come out, not to meet our column, but to warn the miners; for none of my later couriers had succeeded in reaching his camp.

It was the 10th of September, at dawn. Our small force scattering out, and leading up their horses a short distance at a time, near the fresh Indian-trail, began in earnest the ascent of the mountain.

"This is hard work," says Mason. "I don't know which is the worse, for me to walk, or for my poor trembling horse to carry me."

Fletcher, pretty well "blown," sits down with bridle in hand, and noticing the dead or half-alive ponies, with an occasional deceased mule, which the hostiles had killed and abandoned in their haste, exclaims:

"What a pity General Sturgis could not have known of this trail, and moved to yonder crest! The worn out rascals would have fallen an easy prey to his force and ours."

"True; but one must be behind the scenes to know everything."

This conversation indicates the situation. At the crest of the toilsome ridge an immense expanse of mountains, hills, valleys, and rivers broke upon our vision. An aide declared, "We're out of the woods, at last!"

Hart Mountain, ten or twelve miles straight before us, is a single elevated peak. There we supposed Sturgis, with his cavalry, was waiting; or that he had already, as Joseph, with his people and herds, was attempting to pass, broken out upon the hostile flank.

Fletcher, with Chapman and Roque, the little Frenchman who came from Sturgis, set out at once for Hart

Mountain, while our expert signal-men began to wave their flags furiously toward the mountain, and watched with strained eyes, with telescope and field-glass, for some return signal. But it was all in vain. General Sturgis, we afterwards found, getting information that the Indians were going toward the "Stinking Water," and probably misled by some treacherous Crows, had made a forced march off to our right in that direction, just at the opportune moment, i. e., opportune for Joseph and his followers. With consummate generalship the latter made a regular feint towards the odorous water, while he plunged into a forest which, to us, was apparently thick and impassable, and, under its cover, kept around the base of an immense ledge, and then passed into a narrow and slippery canyon, without exposing a man to the view of General Sturgis. My command, discovering Joseph's ruse, kept the trail which Sturgis had been so near, but had not seen, and, finally, slid down the canyon, many a horse, in his weakness, falling and blocking the way. The mouth of this canyon, which debouches into Clark's Valley, was not more than twenty feet across from high wall to high wall. And one may imagine the scene of cavalry, infantry, and pack-mules crowding through it, and admire the quick wit of an Indian who had the hardihood to try the experiment, and break the almost impassable roadway.

Near our second encampment from this point, Sturgis, who had at last turned back, and beholding our force in the distance, had been wondering who we were, soon, by a rapid movement, overtook us. Though Sturgis and I were disappointed, we formed at once a close combina-

tion. I was delighted to observe the elastic tread of his
horses, which could in a very few minutes walk away
from ours. Noticing the general's feeling of disappointment at Joseph's adroit escape, and also believing that
this feeling would be a spur to extraordinary exertion, he
was given a slight addition to his force, — some scouts,
artillery, and cavalry, picking the horses, — and placed
in command of the swift advance; while I confess with
considerable reluctance, and much protest by Wood and
Guy against it, I myself remained behind to form junction with Cushing, who was coming from our left, and to
bring up the reserve and supplies. But my personal
chagrin at Joseph's success was soon relieved. After
Sturgis had crossed the Yellowstone by the South-Fork
road, and reached the heights beyond, the Indians, near
the mouth of a rocky canyon-head, five or six miles off,
it is true, were before him in full view. The sight of the
game, we know, is inspiriting. I need not say that he
charged the foe and fought a gallant battle, and had a
running squabble with them through the canyons and
rocky barrens, even to the Musselshell. He captured
hundreds of ponies, and delighted not a few of his Crow
allies with the opportunity afforded them to steal. It
seemed to matter little to them whether they took from
Indians or white men. They were made happy just to
steal!

It was in this Clark's Valley where was drawn up and
sent to General Miles, who was then located far below our
front, at Tongue River, the letter which was to apprise
him of the situation. Colonel Merrill, of Sturgis' command, seeing me about to send a messenger, said:

"Why not use a boat down the Yellowstone?"

"Sure enough," I replied, "if we can find one."

The boat was found, and the despatches were sent, in duplicate, by boat and by a horseman. Some twelve or fifteen miles from the ford — I had just come into camp the evening of the 13th of September — I received a brief note from Fletcher, who had gone with Sturgis:

"We have struck the enemy," he said, "and are fighting."

I rested from six to nine at night, and then, with fifty cavalrymen, set out. It was a bitter-cold night. In the darkness and swamps our guide soon lost his head, and we were obliged to pick our own difficult way without his help. Chilled through and shivering, at last the tired escort wore out the night. At sunrise we crossed the Yellowstone, and reached the battle-field by half-past ten in the morning.

It was the most horrible of places, — sage-brush and dirt, and only alkaline-water, and very little of that! Dead horses were strewn about, and other relics of the battle-field! A few wounded men and the dead were there. To all this admixture of disagreeable things was added a cold, raw wind, that, unobstructed, swept over the country. Surely if anything was needed to make us hate war such after-battle scenes come well in play.

Sturgis and Sandford, already twenty miles further on, were declared to be in hot pursuit. But as the Indians, who were running night and day, and still had remounts, had managed to outstrip Sturgis and get away beyond hope from his movement, my only remaining chance of ultimate success lay in my confidence that General Miles,

17

now notified, with his fresh command, would strike diagonally across our front, and reach the Missouri before the hostiles. Should they succeed in crossing that river, the British line was too near to afford much prospect of thereafter dealing a successful blow. So Sturgis was requested to rest for a while at the Musselshell, till I had gathered the remainder of my somewhat scattered troops upon the left bank of the Yellowstone. Then we would move forward together.

CHAPTER XXXVIII.

JOSEPH AND THE PURSUIT.—BAKER'S BATTLE-GROUND.—WEL-
COME SUPPLIES.—NEWS FROM GILBERT.—INTERCHANGE OF
VIEWS.—CAPTURE OF THE MAIL-COACH.—JOSEPH'S PEOPLE
IN A NEW ROLE.—OUR CAMP LIBRARY.—MAJOR EARNEST'S
QUICK JOURNEY.—A BEAUTIFUL CAMP.—NEWS FROM MILES.
—FEAR LEST WE "FLUSH THE GAME."—JUDITH BASIN.—
ON TOWARD THE BRITISH LINE.—HOPING AGAINST HOPE.—
THE INDIANS ACROSS THE MISSOURI.—MILES' COURTESY.
—STEAMER "BENTON."—SAND-BARS.—A TOUGH, COLD RIDE.
—SUTHERLAND'S COAT.—WOOD'S BUFFALO.—BEAR-PAW
MOUNTAINS.

IT was a charming place, on the bank of the Yellowstone, some ten miles below the Clark's Fork crossing, where the escort, Mason, Cushing, Sandford, and
Lieutenant Otis, with the Battery, came together. We
were to push down the Yellowstone to the old Baker's
Battlefield,—a ground already known as the place of a
fierce engagement, several years before, with the wild
Sioux. We were to meet some of our supplies of clothing and food, coming thither from Colonel Buell's post,
which was forty miles to the south, and turning square
to the left rejoin Sturgis at the Musselshell, and then
follow to the Missouri. We trusted to General Miles to
deliver one more blow to the swift-footed hostiles.

Our Yellowstone camp, at which a part of us remained
a whole day, the 16th of September, became a lively
one.

Here a note from Colonel Gilbert, explaining his futile chase of us, was received. Here, as we sat on the ground, around our square canvas, each contributed something to the news.

Fletcher described Sturgis' battle and pursuit. I asked:

" Why didn't the artillery do something? "

" Oh, General, horses so played out that one piece never got up, and the other only succeeded in putting in one shot ! "

" Why didn't the General head them off in the canyon? "

" Why, the rocks were too precipitous; but the trial was made. The Indians were off before we could get in there and hinder them."

" What has Mason to say? "

" Not much. I found Cushing all right. He was vexed enough because Norwood (commanding the cavalry company) was taken away from him at Fort Ellis, and all sorts of hindrances were thrown in his way."

" Did any couriers come up? "

" Yes, sir; that fellow whom you sent to Sturgis did not go to him at all, but went to the Crow Agency, and he is now back. He doubtless saw those messengers and scouts who were lying dead along the Indian trail near Hart's Mountain, became frightened, and so made off."

" What have Wood and Howard to say about the people who ran from us so rapidly this morning? "

" I think, General," says Wood, " the scouts have overtaken them, and they have come back. At first they took us for Indians. Another party was hidden in the brush, one of them being a woman. These, some of them, are ranchmen, and some were passengers on the coach that Joseph captured. The Indians were at this very place when Sturgis' scouts first discovered them. The sight of him made them leave.

My son said : " I went as far as the second house below. The buildings were burned to the ground. The remnants of the old stage-coach were lying around. The Indians, I learned, in wild sport, took an active drive in the coach before they dismantled it and destroyed the mails."

Such are specimens of the table-chat. Of course there was fun as well as serious talk ; but, habitually the songs, the stories, and the jokes had their place after the dinner.

It is said of President Lincoln, that his enjoyment of humor was his safety-valve, hence his desire to attend comedies and joyous entertainments. Under the pressure of heavy care and constant bodily fatigue, our officers found their relief in a social way ; but more especially in occasionally reading books of an exciting character. We had but few ; but by borrowing and lending, our camp library sufficed us for some time.

This was a prairie-like country, much of it very dry and dusty, but vast in appearance. Low mountain-ranges afforded here and there landmarks in the distance. In order to show what energy can do, I may tell how Major Earnest left the Yellowstone camp the 16th, rode fifty-seven miles, obtained teams with supplies, and drove them back thirty-seven miles to a junction with us before ten P. M. of the next day ; and how Fletcher and Otis, by remarkable forced marches, brought up further necessaries to the moving column.

The 20th found us in camp a few miles below General Sturgis, on the Musselshell. It was a beautiful camp, on a fine plateau, like an oasis in the vast treeless desert, adorned with handsome shrubbery, abundant grass, clear running water, with fish plentiful enough for every soldier's mess.

Here it was that we received the return messenger from General Miles, who was stationed at Tongue River. Merril, one of Sturgis' battalion-commanders, a lively officer, inclined to be prophetic, was looking over the maps of this country before Miles' messenger arrived. He said, "Miles is ambitious. He will start at once and head Joseph off before he gets to the Missouri. I know the country." Then, pointing out a diagonal course, which extended from Tongue river to near Carroll on the Missouri, he said, "He will go across there! He will never allow such an opportunity for a brigadiership to escape him." I said, "Yes, if he gets his message in time." A few hours later, glad, hearty tidings from Miles did come. He promised to move at once, and indicated how long it would take him to accomplish the march.

I know of no period of my life when I needed sympathy and encouragement more. These dispatches, from a brave officer and a tried friend, were full of cheer, and I shall never forget the lift they gave me, nor grudge to him a grateful acknowledgment for them.

Our movement was much enlivened, not only by this news, but by the presence of the Seventh Cavalry, under the command of Sturgis. It spurred up our way-worn command, and helped it to keep in sight of our new friends; but, as Sturgis declared in one of his notes to me, "We must not move too fast, lest we flush the game." So I recognized the necessity, and for a time moderated the rate of marching.

We knew from a long experience, that the Indians watched well to the rear, and moved very much as we did, keeping one and two and sometimes three marches ahead. When we stopped to rest they did so, when we moved short distances they shortened their journeys; therefore we planned for the same operation to continue. Meanwhile I endeavored, through our numerous scouts, to keep informed where the Indians actually were.

On the Twenty-seventh Sandford's weary cavalry, now being replaced by Sturgis', bade us good-bye just as we were entering the famous Judith basin.

Robbins, and nearly all of our old scouts went back. George Houston, the National-park guide, with his companions, continued with us, and followed the Indians, as he believed, very closely. Then, in this broad and open country, trails began to diverge, multiply, and grow dim. Between Houston and the mouth of Judith River, where it flows into the Missouri, thousands of acres of the prairie were on fire, and so, on reaching it, the new trails were annihilated. Great uncertainty, for the want of information, began to press upon me, but I had resolved to go at least as far as the Missouri, and carry out my orders "To chase the Indians to the British lines."

One day Colonel Mason and Doctor Alexander were riding near me. I had in my heart earnestly petitioned for God's help, expressing a sentiment that I hope was sincere : "If thou wilt grant my request, do so, I beseech Thee, even at the expense of another's receiving the credit of the expedition."

I said to Mason, as my spirits grew lighter : "Colonel, I believe that we shall capture these Indians yet."

Alexander asked, with a hearty laugh, "What is more hopeless? There isn't one chance in a million for Miles. I cannot see, General, where you found your hope." "All right," I answered, "mark my words, and see if I am not right!"

Mason hoped, with a slight despondency of tone, that my prediction might prove true. It was not long after this conversation before some message-bearers hove in sight. We had not met horse or man for several days ; a manifest excitement quickened the motion of the entire command as two horsemen were discerned coming on at a steady gallop, and every moment approaching nearer.

"Well ! what news?"

"A dispatch from Fort Benton for General Howard or Colonel Gibbon." The courier dismounted, and handed me a note. It informed me that the Indians had crossed the Missouri at Cow Island, had a fight with some of Gibbon's men, burnt a freight-train of wagons, but had all moved over and gone. Miles reached the mouth of the Musselshell, twenty miles or more below, crossed the Missouri there, and is still in pursuit. Such in substance was the startling information brought.

It did not take us long to pass the next fifty or sixty miles to Carroll. Here, leaving headquarters and part of my command with Sturgis and Mason, I took passage on the little steamer "Benton", which, doubtless by General

Miles' kind provision, was tied to the shore, and made subject to my orders.

The Artillery battalion under Miller, also my two aides and a few scouts, sprang on board.

We steamed up the river as rapidly as possible. The Missouri is shallow at the season when we were there, and our vessel often ran aground. I was curious to see how the river could be navigated with so little water. Soon I noticed that when the steamer struck a sand-bar, as she often did, that she put out her immense wooden arms, which are vitalized by a steam windlass, and lifted herself, little by little, over into deep water.

Cow Island was reached early the next day. With a small escort of seventeen mounted men, including the aides, I made a push along the large Indian trail, with the hope of reaching Miles, or communicating with him. Dispatches which I had received at Carroll on the Missouri were confirmed at Cow Island by a messenger from him. The tidings were to the effect that his movement had not yet been discovered by the hostiles, and that he hoped still to be able to strike them in flank; the messenger had left him near a line of abrupt hills, which were called "the Little Rockies," and he was moving then northwesterly towards the upper extremity of the Bear-Paw mountain range. With this man for a guide, and the Nez Perce herders "Captain John" and "George" for interpreters and keen-scented scouts, we, for a time, followed the Indian trail, but finally deviated from it, hoping to intersect Miles' course. The weather was fearfully cold and the ground covered with a fresh coating of snow. Fortunately for me, Sutherland, the correspondent, had wrapped me at starting, in his own enormous great-coat. It had a warm hood secured to the collar; this attachment, occasionally thrown over the head, kept me very comfortable.

We found plenty of wood the first night, but the water was alkaline, and made every man who drank it, sick, so that the second day was attended with great delay, as well as discomfort.

Just as we passed the bluff at the north end of the Bear-Paw, and had been some time following Miles' plain trail, and while Lieut. Wood was amusing himself in taking the skin and nice cuts from a young buffalo which he had killed, two very handsome, well-mounted scouts were met. They had descended from a neighboring height, where they had been watching a party of Indians who were hunting antelope between Miles' position and theirs; so they told us. They declared that these Indians were hostiles. They said, also, "we have carried the news of a battle, going on when we left, from Gen. Miles to your troops with Sturgis and Mason, and have got back this far." Lieut. Howard declared to them that he didn't believe that the hunters were hostile, and laughed at their fears. One of the scouts at this became angry, and said, "We are going back to your troops. We know as much about Indians as you do."

This colloquy had proceeded thus far, before I had come close enough to hear. The excitement was soon quieted, and the scouts invited to join us and ascertain whether the Indians were hostile or not.

This they did, though their horses, doubtless partaking of their riders' feelings, during the next ten miles appeared very nervously inclined. It was difficult to keep them in the column. The distance from the head of Bear-Paw to Miles' camp was not more than twelve or fourteen miles, still it became quite dark before we had approached near enough to catch a glimpse of it.

CHAPTER XXXIX.

JOSEPH. — HIS PURSUIT AND CAPTURE. — A LONG CHASE, AND
A LONG STORY COMING TO AN END. — SLIPPERY DICK AND
SITTING BULL. — ARRIVAL AT MILES' CAMP. — INDIANS IN-
TRENCHED AND PREPARING FOR A SIEGE. — A FLAG OF
TRUCE. — PROPOSAL TO SURRENDER. — JOSEPH AGREES. —
ESCAPE OF WHITE BIRD. — GATHERING IN PROVISIONS AND
WOUNDED. — DESCRIPTION OF MILES' FIGHT. — HOMEWARD
BOUND.

OCTOBER 4, 1877, we not only encountered the messengers, who knew of Miles' engagement, but also
another curious and solitary courier by the name of "Slippery Dick." He was approaching us to rejoin General
Miles, on his tall, black horse, at a rapid gait, having returned from Sitting Bull's camp by the way of Tongue
River. He described the position of the famous Sitting
Bull. He believed that this chieftan had about twelve
hundred warriors, and stated that he was in British territory, not more than forty or fifty miles from us toward
the northeast. It appeared evident, that when he encountered our troops, Joseph was attempting to cross the line
and form a junction with Sitting Bull. Our several parties were now consolidated, and we rode rapidly toward
the point where the messengers had last seen Miles.

Suddenly, as we neared the brow of a hill, numerous
small fires, scattered over the breadth of a mile, made
their appearance. Continuous musketry firing was heard.
At first we feared that in the darkness the outposts had

mistaken our party for hostile Indians, and were therefore firing at us; but soon we found that it was not so. It was the Indians in the ravine, who, from their holes and trenches, were firing at Miles' investing forces.

When Miles heard that I had come forward and was approaching his camp, with his staff, and mounted, he came out to meet me. We were guided to his tent, where, before much-needed refreshment and sleep were allowed to ourselves, he explained to me the situation.

The journal of my aide-de-camp for the next day, says:

"October 5th. Firing is continued by our troops, with an occasional reply from the enemy. They are evidently saving their ammunition for a siege.

"About eleven o'clock, 'Captain John' and 'George' were sent into Joseph's camp with a flag of truce. General Howard and Colonel Miles were awaiting their return, near the advance rifle-pits. After much communication, Joseph, at 2 P. M., agreed to surrender on condition of good treatment, and 'White Bird' said: 'What Joseph agrees to is all right.' . . . Joseph, first offering it to General Howard, delivered his rifle to Colonel Miles. The coming-in was prolonged till long after dark. The lame, maimed, halt and blind, came crawling up the hill. Meanwhile, White Bird and two wounded squaws, with a party of fourteen, under cover of the darkness, escaped between the pickets."

October 6th. Miles received information, at 2 P. M., from the Red River half-breeds, of thirty Indians, twenty of them wounded in Miles' fight, who had escaped across the boundary. Also, from scouts, of six killed by the Assinniboines, of two or three killed by the Gros Ventres, and a squaw and two children captives in the Assin-niboine camp. We sent for these prisoners.

These notes sufficiently indicate the situation, which may be briefly described, as follows:

When Miles, with his active column, had passed Bear-Paw Mountain, he had struck the flank of Joseph's march; surprised him while resting in camp. Joseph was well posted in a ravine. His immense herd of ponies and captured mules were permitted to feed along the slopes. Miles' force was immediately deployed, and hurled upon the Indians and upon the herd in such a way as to defeat the former, driving all but the killed and wounded and the few that escaped, into the narrow, crooked ravines, and capturing the most of the herd. The work was bravely done, though the gallant charge cost the lives of several officers and many men, and disabled many more. The Indians, quickly putting themselves under the cover of the uneven ground, dug holes and rifle-pits, and were thus able to stand on the defensive.

Finally, after a series of interesting and exciting negotiations, the surrender of Joseph and his Indians took place.

My force proper was stopped twenty-five miles back, at a point which was more nearly opposite Sitting Bull's position than the battle-field. After the surrender had been completed, all our forces slowly returned to the Missouri. With my staff and escort, I separated from Miles at the battle-ground, the 7th of October, and we came together again the 13th, on the Missouri. The force was now divided into three parties. Sturgis' command remained to watch the Sioux. Miles, taking the Indians with him, crossed the Missouri, and returned to Tongue River by the same route that he had come. While with my infantry, artillery, and staff I again embarked on the Steamer Benton, and set out for home. A part of us made our way *via* Chicago, and the remainder *via* Omaha, the Pacific Railroad, and the Pacific steamers, to our several stations in the Department of the Columbia.

After Miles' march and engagement, there arose all sorts of heart-burnings, reports filled with claims and counter-claims for credit. There were necessarily diversities of statement, rivalries, criminations, and controversies, such as we read of in Europe after an important battle or campaign.

Such jealous disputations, like the smoke on the field, often obscure for a time the results of the conflict, but have a way of correcting themselves by the lapse of time. Accomplished results are the things that, in the main, concern a general, an army, a historian, a man.

I was sent to conduct a war without regard to department and division lines. This was done with all the energy, ability, and help at my command, and the campaign was brought to a successful issue. As soon as the Indians reached General Terry's department, Gibbon was dispatched to strike his blow; then Sturgis, in close alliance, and, finally, Miles in the last terrible battle. These troops participated in the struggle with exposure, battle, and loss, as we have seen. They enjoyed the appreciation and thanks of their seniors in command, and of their countrymen. But when, with the fulness of an honest and generous recognition of the work, gallantry, losses, and success of all co-operating forces, I turn my attention to the troops that fought the first battles, and then pursued the swift-footed fugitives with unparalleled vigor and perseverance, amid the severest privations, for more than a thousand miles, would it be wonderful if I magnified their doings, and gave them, were it possible, even an overplus of praise for the part they bore in this campaign?

Personally, according to the covenant which I have recorded, I shall be satisfied to let another bear the crown of triumph, while my heart is deeply moved with thankfulness that the work itself was brought to a successful conclusion.

It is a difficult matter to ascertain the doings and sayings of Indians, after they have gone on the "war-path." As soon as Joseph's Indians had passed Kamiah to traverse the Lo-lo trail, I had but a few opportunities to gain knowledge from the inside of their lodges.

At the obstructing barricades in Montana, which were dangerous to pass, Looking-glass appeared as the diplomat. He succeeded by his ability in deceiving the commander of the defences, and brought past the hindering works Joseph's whole people in complete safety. He was killed, and buried under the river-bank at Gibbon's battle-field in Montana.

After Gibbon's battle, Joseph showed his influence over the Indians by rallying them on a height, just beyond the reach of the long-range rifles. He gathered the warriors, recovered lost ground, and recaptured his numerous herd of ponies, which had already been cut off by Gibbon's men, buried the most of his dead, and made good his retreat before the force with me was near enough to harm him. Few military commanders, with good troops, could better have recovered after so fearful a surprise.

At the Camas Meadows, not far from Henry Lake, Joseph's night march, his surprise of my camp and capture of over a hundred animals, and, after a slight battle, making a successful escape, showed an ability to plan and execute equal to that of many a partisan leader whose deeds have entered into classic story.

Again : his quick penetration into my plan of delaying my march between the Musselshell and the Missouri, so as to make all speed, cross the broad river at Cow Island, defeat the guard, and then destroy an immense freight-wagon train, replenish his supplies, and make off beyond danger from the direct pursuit, is not often equalled in warfare.

And even at the last, the natural resources of his mind did not fail him. Broken in pieces by Miles' furious and unexpected assault, burdened with his women, children, and plunder, suffering from the loss of his still numerous, though badly crippled herd of ponies, yet he was able to intrench, and hold out for several days against twice his numbers, and succeeded in pushing out beyond the white man's pickets a part of his remnant to join his allies in Canada.

The cheery brother, Ollicutt, and old Too-hul-hul-sote, were among the slain on Miles' field.

From the beginning of the Indian pursuit across the Lolo trail, until the embarkation on the Missouri River for the homeward journey, including all halts and stoppages, from July 27th to October 10th, my command marched one thousand three hundred and twenty-one miles in seventy-five days. Joseph, the Indian, taking with him his men, women, and children, traversed even greater distances, for he had to make many a loop in his skein, many a deviation into a tangled thicket, to avoid or deceive his enemy.

So that whichever side of the picture we examine we find there evidence of wonderful energy, and prolonged endurance. It will be indeed fortunate for mankind, if these same qualities which we cannot help commending, can hereafter be turned into a common channel, and used for the promotion of the arts of peace. What glorious results would have been effected, could these non-treaties have received the same direction that the worthy missionaries were, in early days, able to give to the remainder of their tribe, and have shown the same ability and persistence in peace that they did during this fearful Indian war. Certainly it would be gratifying to me, at any time, to see the remnant turn from savagery to civilization. They are a people, even in their wildness, picturesque and replete with interest. May not these, in the far-off Indian Territory where they have been sent, — the Esaus of the world — as well as the crafty Jacobs, have a portion in the labor and the comforts of the world's progress?

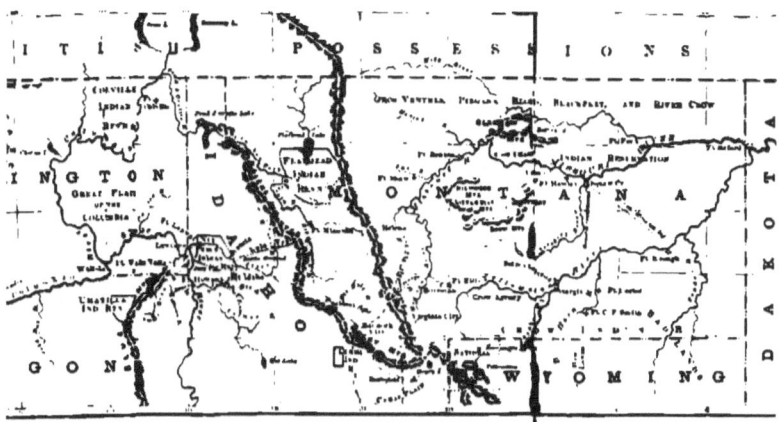

Map to illustrate Gen'l Howard's Nez-Percé Campaign in 77.

www.ingramcontent.com/pod-product-compliance
Lightning Source LLC
Chambersburg PA
CBHW031343070726
47496CB00017B/1639